PRAISE FOR *HOUSTON*

"Zepeda…presents a debut about the everyday struggle to find one's way
namely the vibr
emphasis on Tex-

"Jessica's evoluti
empowerment is
on the popular fascination with good luck charms, horoscopes, psychics, and unreliable predictions is laced with rueful zeal."
                                        —*Publishers Weekly*

"Reading Gwen's book was like going to a family BBQ— full of drama, juicy gossip, and lots of laughs."
                                        —Mary Castillo, author of *Switchcraft*

"An entertaining lighthearted Latina chick lit romp focusing on the metamorphosis of a young woman…Fans will enjoy this fascinating coming of age tale."
                                        —*Midwest Book Review*

"The premise is quite cute and flows nicely, casually integrating Latin culture into the fold. Madame Hortensia, the entrepreneurial psychic, is a great comedic stand-out character."
                                        —*RT BOOKreviews*

"Zepeda is great at both voice and dialogue; the dialogue is clever and powers the story forward."
                                        —SadieMagazine.com

"[A] funny and heartwarming tale that follows the life of Jessica Luna through love, tears, and plenty of laughs."
                                        —Bookpleasures.com

ALSO BY GWENDOLYN ZEPEDA

Houston, We Have a Problema

LONE STAR
LEGEND

GWENDOLYN ZEPEDA

GCP

GRAND CENTRAL
PUBLISHING

New York Boston

Copyright © 2010 by Gwendolyn Zepeda

Grand Central Publishing
Hachette Book Group
237 Park Avenue
New York, NY 10017

Visit our Web site at www.HachetteBookGroup.com.

Printed in the United States of America

First Edition: January 2010
10 9 8 7 6 5 4 3 2 1

Grand Central Publishing is a division of Hachette Book Group, Inc.
The Grand Central Publishing name and logo is a trademark of Hachette Book Group, Inc.

Library of Congress Cataloging-in-Publication Data
Zepeda, Gwendolyn.
  Lone Star legend / Gwendolyn Zepeda.—1st ed.
    p. cm.
  Summary: "An aspiring young journalist stuck blogging for a gossip site stumbles across a story that gives new meaning to the word legendary"—Provided by publisher.
  ISBN 978-0-446-53960-9
  1. Journalists—Fiction.   2. Blogs—Fiction.   I. Title.
PS3626.E46L66 2010
813'.6—dc22
                                          2009011213

Book Design by Renato Stanisic

FOR ALICE VALDEZ

LONE STAR
LEGEND

1

Blog entry from *My Modern TragiComedy*, Wednesday, March 8

Here's a little story that's also a metaphor, or maybe a pattern in my life?

It was a sunny September afternoon, the first day of school at Lorenzo de Zavala Senior High School, East Austin, 1997, and I was on top of the world. It was my sophomore year, and yet I'd already been made Assistant Editor of The Monthly Bugle, our school paper. I was sitting at my new desk—which was actually just a table, but closer to the teacher's desk than the table where I'd sat the day before—licking my teeth. Not only was I Assistant Editor, but I'd had my braces removed the week before, so I was literally sitting pretty. Prettier, I guess. Well—at least less nerdy-looking than before.

Aaron Lieberstat, our best boy reporter, walked up and asked me how my summer had been. I'd always thought Aaron was kind of cute, but had never spoken to him outside of academic discussions on student council elections or the merits of various brands of glue sticks.

"You got rid of your braces," he told me, a nervous smile lighting his freckle-rimmed lips. "It's nice. Your face is very symmetrical now."

How romantic, I remember thinking, to be complimented by a boy who knew such big words.

From there we segued into a conversation about our plans for the paper. I was looking forward to trying some new features and formatting that would finally bring our publication into the (very late) twentieth century. Aaron was excited about a photo essay he wanted to do on the Chess Club's annual tournament. We were in Nerd Heaven.

Ten minutes after the tardy bell rang, Mr. Jenkins, our beloved editor-slash-teacher, still hadn't put in an appearance. My classmates and I set to work without him. Whereas other students, given that opportunity, would've cut class or set about destroying school property, we newspaper staff students were single-minded in our scholastic dedication.

I'd fired up my trusty IBM Selectric Word Processor and was already typing up the first draft of a story when the Assistant Principal showed up with Coach Taylor, a woman for whom a broken tibia had long ago ended the dream of a professional cheerleading career.

"Kids, I'm sorry to have to tell you that Mr. Jenkins won't be back this year. He had some family issues and went to teach at a school in North Carolina. Coach Taylor here will be your new editor. Coach Taylor, here you go."

His words rang in my ears, for those few moments and for the entire school year that followed. For they signaled the end of my budding success as an editrix. Coach Taylor ushered in a new era at our paper, an era filled with sports scores, jock profiles, and cheer, cheer, cheerleaders.

We entered Nerd Hell, and in junior year I switched my Newspaper elective for its distant, genetically inferior cousin, Yearbook.

It wasn't until college that I'd attain journalistic nirvana again. As you all know, I've been working at a very respectable online publication since my second senior year at the University. (And no, I'm still not going to tell you which one.) But that, I fear, is about to end. We've just had a visit from our own Coach Taylor, and it looks like the writing's on the wall.

Love,
Miss TragiComic Texas

2

Thursday morning, Sandy Saavedra sat in front of her former editor's desk, in his Longhorn-orange tweed visitor's chair. Two faces faced her. Frida Kahlo with her monkey and her iconic bad eyebrows, from the yellowing print in its cheap frame on the yellowing wall. Below that, Angelica Villanueva O'Sullivan—the face of Levy Media, owners of the hippest, the hottest, and the *meanest* news sites online.

Sandy couldn't look at Angelica, whose blond hair, cream suit, and gold jewelry shone too bright in the room full of plywood. So she looked at Frida instead, or else down at the desk, where Angelica's corporate-length French-manicured claws rested on a piece of Sandy's work. Sandy's own bitten nails clutched a brand-new contract.

"The key is page views. Keep it short, keep it sharp, keep it *clickable*," Angelica was saying. It sounded like an ad, like a woman reading lines about a smart, cute, and very expensive car. That's how the new editor talked, Sandy realized. Everything she said was like a sales pitch to someone much richer.

Over to their right, through the window, a parking garage gleamed in the already-starting spring heat. It wasn't the very best view for an editor's office, but above the garage's top level, only a few blocks away, you could see floating the dome of the Texas State Capitol building, another iconic ugly woman standing right on top. Sandy felt this stone goddess watching as Angelica sat there and said those ad words. Words that meant the end of the best writing job Sandy had ever scored. Well, the only *real* writing job she'd ever scored, not counting all those tech writing contracts.

"This is good," Angelica said, flipping through a file with Sandy's byline—her real name, Dominga Saavedra—neatly stickered to the tab. She pulled out the piece that Sandy recognized as the last article she'd turned in to Oscar. It was about suspected kickbacks between politicians and prominent local Latinos, the one that Sandy had researched and rewritten for months, and she could see that it'd been edited all over, all in purple ink.

"This is good," Angelica said again, "but it *could* be even better. You could make six whole posts from these two pages. For example..." She indicated a paragraph about restaurant inspector bribes. It was circled and someone had written a new subheader in the margin: WHO'S UP FOR MARGARITAS AND RAT TOSTADAS?

"You know, something like that. But sharper and wittier, hopefully." Angelica handed the pages over the desk. Sandy took them with reluctance, and read.

The paragraph of accusations that she'd worked so hard to make subtle and ethical? Now blared WHAT PAID FOR HENRY LOPEZ JR'S TRIP TO THAILAND? YOUR TAXES! Then several paragraphs of crossed-out lines. Then her most prized story detail, the leaked e-mail between Congressman Jimmy Diaz and his secretary, was captioned WHAT'S NEXT? JIMMY D SEX TAPE ON FACESPACE?

As she read over Angelica's bubbly cursive, dismay

bloomed inside Sandy like a small toy capsule that becomes a spongy monster in water. She couldn't say anything. But she kept thinking, *This is how they do it. This is the way they make excuses before they lay you off.*

"You're very talented, Sandy," Angelica said. "I've read a lot about you, and I know you've worked hard to get here. Your writing is good, well researched, and you have a subtle, sophisticated wit."

Angelica's flattery stood in stark contrast to the purple words she'd splattered on Sandy's pages. If the writing was good, Sandy wondered, why did this woman want her to change it so drastically?

Angelica leaned back in Oscar's chair and struck a thoughtful pose. "I think, with just a few changes, you can give me what we need for the new site. You can look at our sister sites for inspiration and mimic their style. And I think you'll find it easier than what Oscar had you doing."

Sandy didn't see how that was possible. Writing articles for Oscar had been the most natural thing in the world for her, just like writing book reports at school had been. She couldn't think of an easier job, or a job that she'd ever enjoyed more. And now here was this Angelica woman, taking it away from her.

Angelica went on. "If you can deliver the kinds of posts we need, you'll be one of our staff writers. As such, you'll turn in twelve posts, minimum, per day. They don't have to be long. The shorter the better, in fact. This"—she indicated the poor butchered article in Sandy's hands— "would already be half a day's work for you. You're ahead of the game. Use these as part of your audition samples. Write a few more—shorter, sharper, and edgier—and e-mail them to me by Sunday at six. We'll go from there." Her smile, pageant-y and full of well-crafted veneer, wasn't as comforting as she probably imagined it was. Angelica stood suddenly and, just like that, was herding Sandy to the door.

"Remember, Sandy: Nacho Papi is 'Not Yo' Papi's Web Site.' It's new, it's savvy, and it's *readable*. And it's going to make its staff famous. Do your best so you can be a part of it."

Sandy cringed. Just the *name* of it—Nacho Papi's Web Site Dot Com—made her nervous. She was a reporter, not a pun-writing entertainment blogger. She couldn't even begin to write what Angelica was asking for. Nor could she imagine how it would make her famous. In fact, she didn't even know if she wanted to *be* famous. She wasn't the fame-seeking type. She didn't even have her photo on LatinoNow's virtual masthead.

She was going to get fired, she suddenly knew. Laid off. Have all future submissions rejected in one fell swoop.

Angelica gave Sandy's arm a brief, sharp squeeze, and then Sandy was ejected to LatinoNow's—no, Nacho Papi's shared office space. She stumbled toward her desk like a reality-show contestant emerging from a dignity-draining obstacle course.

Behind Sandy, Angelica called out George's name, presumably planning to disillusion him next. George gave Sandy a smarmy smile as he sauntered into their new boss's office.

Sandy stood silently, clutching her mangled prose and feeling just as scribbled on. She looked around the old LatinoNow offices for what was most likely the last time. The nervous, sad, or unreadable faces of her part-time co-workers looked back at her.

Sandy looked at Lori, Francisco, Carolina, and the others with a lump forming in her throat. She was going to miss them.

3

Blog entry from *My Modern TragiComedy*, Thursday, March 9

I'm starting to have doubts about my relationship with HeartThrob GeekBoy.

Is that horrible? Am I stupid for even thinking it?

Yes, I know there are hundreds of girls who'd kill to take him off my hands—and that's at the University alone. He's the hottest TA on campus. So hot that, as you know, I sometimes wonder how the hell I landed him.

Not only is he hot, but he's smart. And gainfully employed. And the man writes poetry, you guys. *Poetry*. About *me*.

So what's not to like?

I wish I could tell you. Maybe I'll meditate on it and get back to you.

Love,
Miss TragiComic Texas

4

Sandy and Daniel were at Samurai Noodles again because Daniel was trying to go vegan, again, and Samurai had tofu in all shapes and sizes. But then he'd ordered the pepper ahi instead, and now Sandy watched him scrape all the pepper off each raw tuna slice while she told him what'd happened with Angelica that afternoon.

It was too late for lunch and too early for dinner, but this was the only time she could catch Daniel that day, between his freshman comp English classes. Nonetheless, a steady stream of hipsters, tourists, and homeless people walked down South Congress, providing constantly shifting scenery for Sandy to focus on as she told her tale. Her tofu noodles sat cold on her plate.

"So you turned in your resignation?" Daniel said when she was done.

"No, I didn't resign. I told Lori I was leaving to investigate another story, and then I called you. Why, do you think I *should* resign? Before even trying to pass the audition?"

Daniel snorted. It would have been an unattractive sound, but he made it while flinging his long black bangs back from his forehead, like a smug but beautiful horse, and Sandy could never be annoyed when he flung his head like that.

"I can't even believe she's making you audition," he said. "You, with your credentials? You were an honors journalism student. You shouldn't have to beg for that kind of job."

He took a bite of his scraped red tuna and made a face before going on. "If you want my honest opinion, you never should've taken that job to begin with. You belong at a real newspaper, not some 'online journalism' racket. I keep telling you, Sandy, you're better than that. You should take a year off, actually, and finish your novel."

Sandy cleared her throat in order to remind Daniel, not for the first time, that she couldn't afford to stop working for a year. He should have known that. It'd taken her six years to work her way through a B.A., while he went on to graduate school and her friends went on to full-time jobs in the real world. And now she had student loans to repay. There was no such thing as "taking a year off" in Sandy's world.

But Daniel went on. "So, now this pseudo–news organization is formally turning into a gossip blog. And you're worried that you aren't good enough to write for a gossip blog? Seriously, Sandy, ask yourself: Why would you even want to ruin your reputation by writing for this site, anyway?"

Sandy picked at the sticky ramen on her plate. "It isn't a gossip blog. It's a news and entertainment site."

He snorted again. "That's an oxymoron."

She knew what he expected her to say: "You're right, Daniel. I'm too good for that job. I'm quitting right now." That's what she would have done in the past—agreed with him immediately. But she couldn't say with a straight face that she was too good for this job. She was fresh out of college, practically, with only a year and a half of experience under her belt. And that experience was at Latino-

Now, a site that had gone under despite all her hard work. Nacho Papi and its sister sites may not have been "real" journalism, but they were making real money.

Somehow, Daniel telling her she was too good didn't convince her. And the way he described her situation made her not want to give the answer he expected.

In her mind, she was framing the argument "What if this turns out to be a big opportunity for me?" But the door chimes tinkled behind her, and his attention wavered.

"Mr. Thomas! Daniel!" cooed a whole flock of female freshmen who'd obviously wandered over between classes. Sandy watched her boyfriend flip his long bangs off his glasses in response and sit up a little straighter against the red vinyl of their booth. She felt herself become temporarily invisible. Like the super-powered girlfriend of the much more super guy.

It should have annoyed Sandy, the way this always happened. Daniel's female students—or any of his students, actually—showed up and then she ceased to exist. But what could she expect? He was their hero. Their demi-god, almost. He was handsome and smart, and he was a published author. He was, in short, everything they aspired to be. And Sandy was his girlfriend, the role that so many of his female students, and probably some of the male ones, too, would have killed to play. So she sat still and let them have their moment in the sun, basking in Daniel's company.

This little group—the chubby girl, the gawky girl, the kind-of-cute-but-very-annoying girl—posed questions about essays and readings. Daniel answered them with dry jokes and they giggled like middle-schoolers. They may as well have had big pink hearts flashing above their heads. Sandy couldn't blame them, could she? She'd fallen for Daniel in just the same way, two years before, in the poetry class they'd taken together.

While he graced the young women with his attention, Sandy took the opportunity to gather her thoughts. Her arguments, really. For some reason she felt a need to argue. To play devil's advocate, as it were.

Daniel dismissed the young women with a benevolent air, and she popped back into existence. By then she'd come up with a few points to make about Nacho Papi's Web Site and the possibility that she might end up writing material that was edgy and entertaining but still literary. Before she could get into it, though, Daniel pulled out his tattered briefcase.

"Listen, Sandy—sorry, but I have to get back to my office soon. Can you... Would you mind looking at something for me really quickly?"

Sandy bit back her words, momentarily annoyed. But then Daniel flipped his hair back again and she nodded. He wanted to show her a new poem, she knew. And she was one of the very few people Daniel trusted to read his new poetry. He was working on a book-length collection for his thesis, and she'd read everything he'd written for it so far.

Pushing his barely touched plastic plate aside, he removed a worn Moleskine from his briefcase, opened it to the designated place, and turned it to face Sandy. The inky, scratchy piece on the page was titled "She Walks into Obscurity." Sandy eagerly pulled the book closer while Daniel, unable to stand watching anyone read his work, went to the cashier and paid for their lunch-slash-dinner.

Marching, obstinate, she fades from me and
I, disconsolate, am touched/not touched
By she who is maybe nothing more

Than a mask? shell? a shade of what
Once seemed indispensable, now just
Indistinguishable, a thousand pretty faces
Marching onward.
And I am touched/not touched by
Myself, I walk alone, into aching hills of
Inscrutable lonely horizons

Daniel returned from the register and fell into his seat heavily. "So? What do you think? I mean, not your opinion of the piece, itself, because it isn't ready for that, yet. But any, you know, anything you notice that's worth further development…"

"I know," she said. He meant that he wanted only positive feedback. That was all he ever wanted. Like all the other writers she knew, Daniel was sensitive to criticism. He was more sensitive than most, in fact. Which was strange, considering that he was also the most successful writer she knew, and the most literary. But Sandy always worded her critiques very carefully. She didn't want him to stop trusting her with his work.

"It's good," she said. "Very…" She searched for a comment she hadn't already recently used. "…lyrical." She paused, then went ahead and asked what she couldn't help but wonder. "This isn't about us, is it? About me?"

"Sandy." His sigh was obviously exasperated, even though he tried to hide it. He took the notebook from her, packed it away, and made motions as if he might run out the door at any moment. "Come on. You know I don't write about any specific person or situation. You know I work in metaphor, in allegory…."

"Right, right," she said. "Well, then I only have one other comment. I'm not sure it's the kind of feedback you want yet, but it seems kind of important."

He waved impatiently for Sandy to go on.

"There's a line in there about touching yourself."

"What? No, there isn't." He stood up, then, and made as if to help her out of the booth with abrupt, unnecessary chivalry.

Sandy grabbed her bag, but kept talking. "I think there is. Something like 'I am touched or not touched, by myself'? You want to be careful with that. You don't want it to sound like—"

"Okay," he said, cutting Sandy off, turning his back on her and heading for the exit. "Thanks, sweetie. I appreciate it. Come on. I have to get going."

As he walked Sandy to her car, she asked if she'd see him later. It was Friday night, after all. Date night, as she'd heard it called.

"I don't know. Can I get back to you on that? I have a late department meeting and then two classes' worth of essays to slog through. Maybe you can come over and help me grade? Or we could have a beer with the gang at the Fat Man, if you really want to go out."

"Hmm. Maybe." She left it at that and, with a quick, bumpy kiss, they parted.

She was almost relieved, to tell the truth. She wasn't in the mood to grade Daniel's papers or listen to his friends wax poetic about their own poetry. Plus, she had a lot to think about. So maybe it was just as well that she did her own thing that night.

5

Reader comment on My Modern TragiComedy, Wednesday, March 8

Hey, Miss TragiComic TX!

Yes, I know *exactly* how you feel. Seems like those popular kids follow you everywhere, doesn't it? I've been working in engineering for seven years now. I thought I'd be safe from them there but, wouldn't you know it, we had to get a *marketing* team and it was nothing but those cheerleader and jock types.

So I feel you. Keep your chin up, girl! I'm sure they can't run that business without you, no matter how it seems.

Comment left by: **Sunny B**

6

Sandy read the comment from the stranger on her laptop, on her coffee table, in her garage apartment. It was a stranger she kind of knew, actually, one who read her blog—her online journal—every week. Each week strangers like Sunny B and Moan-a Lisa commented on Sandy's virtual messages-in-a-bottle, and reading their comments made her smile. It was comforting to know that someone understood you and empathized, even if you'd never met that someone in real life.

When Sandy had first told Daniel she was considering starting a blog, a year ago now, his immediate response was "Why? Only untalented, attention-starved teenagers write blogs." By that time she'd already posted a few entries under her pseudonym that she'd been prepared to show him if he took an interest. But obviously he didn't, so she said nothing more about it.

Sandy had told her best friends Veronica and Jane about it, too, of course. But she'd sworn them to secrecy, so the blog was practically anonymous. Sandy was pretty sure her friends had forgotten about it, or had lost the link. They never left comments on it or said anything about its contents to Sandy on the phone. So it was, for all intents and purposes, completely safe. It was nothing more than a way for Sandy to get stuff off her chest and to keep her writing skills sharp in the process.

Having read the only blog comment she'd gotten so far that day, Sandy stood and walked over to her closet to change into something more comfortable. Spring had just started, which meant that the mornings were still cool but the afternoons were boiling hot.

Sandy felt a little guilty because she'd been home for an hour already and hadn't done any work on the procedure manual she was writing for QBS Systems or on her audition samples for Nacho Papi's Web Site. But she couldn't help it—the QBS stuff was too boring, and just thinking about doing her Nacho Papi samples was freezing her into major writer's block. She needed to quit thinking about it for a while, if possible.

As she crossed the tiny main room of the garage apartment, she stole a glance at the front windows, making sure that hers was still the only car in the driveway. If Sandy was lucky, she could change her clothes, call and find someone to hang out with, and then leave before her landlady got home.

In the bathroom-slash-dressing room, she switched out her work jeans for evening jeans and her short-sleeved maroon knit work top for a slightly darker maroon T-shirt. Pulling it over her head, Sandy readjusted her glasses and checked her reflection. Her dark hair had stayed in its ponytail okay. Her makeup wasn't smudged because she hadn't put any on that day. Therefore, she looked fine.

Making the three steps back to her living room, Sandy was sighted from the front windows before she could even think to hide.

"Sandy! What are you doing home so soon, m'ija? Come in the kitchen, baby—I'm gonna make quesadillas!"

Her landlady was home. Obviously. The woman had seen Sandy's silhouette and had no qualms about simply yelling up invitations from the backyard.

Sandy stood still in the middle of her room and considered declining the offer. In the end, however, she turned and headed for the stairs. It wasn't a good idea to hurt your landlady's feelings, she decided. Especially not when your landlady was also your mother.

Sandy sighed as she took her little staircase down to inevitability. It'd been sixteen months since she'd moved out of her mother's house, into the garage apartment, and she'd paid rent every month on time. But her rent money hadn't bought her the independence—the *privacy*—she'd been hoping for.

It was true that she wasn't yet independent enough to afford a real apartment—not at Austin prices, anyway, unless she wanted to live with a roommate or three. But she'd hoped that establishing a formal business relationship with her mother would also put in place a sort of professional buffer zone.

She'd been mistaken, though. At best, she was merely helping her mother with expenses on the two-bedroom yellow house Sandy's father had left them. At worst, she'd become a fellow working woman in her mother's eyes, and therefore someone her mom would try to commiserate with more often.

As Sandy crossed the backyard to the door that led to her mother's kitchen, she told herself that she'd just eat one quesadilla and let Mom probe her life a little. The woman worked hard and got lonely. She needed Sandy to humor her once in a while.

IN HER MOTHER's kitchen, which was about eighty percent yellow Formica, Sandy sat and ate the quesadillas, the generic sandwich cookies, and the fruit-flavored drink that were set out for her. It was the same snack her mother had been serving since Sandy was in elementary school, except that Sandy had finally, mercifully, convinced her mother to switch from Kool-Aid to sugar-free Fruit-Ade.

"So how's my Danny doing?" her mother asked first thing. She meant Daniel. She called him Danny after John Travolta's character in *Grease*. She called Sandy Sandy for the same reason. Sandy's real name was Dominga, after her paternal grandmother. Domingo meant Sunday in Spanish and, as her mom reasoned, Sunday *kind of* sounded like Sandy, which is what she would've named their baby if Sandy's father had let her. Thus, the nickname had been born.

Mrs. Saavedra, as she liked to be known, had been feverishly excited when Sandy started dating Daniel two years ago. She was convinced that Daniel was Sandy's soulmate, just like Danny was the other Sandy's, in the movie. Never mind that her mom's favorite movie seemed to be all about this Sandy person getting a slutty makeover in order to keep Danny from cheating on her. Every time the real Sandy pointed that out, or pointed out that no one called Daniel Danny, her mom just blew her off and started singing "Summer Nights."

So Mrs. Saavedra wanted to know how "her Danny" was doing, and Sandy told her that she didn't know, that she hadn't seen much of him lately.

"Uh-oh," her mother immediately said. "That's not good. He's not hooking up with one of those little hussy students of his, is he?"

Sandy saw her mother's eyes gleam as she licked the filling off her chocolate cookie. It was as if the possibility of Daniel cheating was fascinating enough to warrant any hurt feelings Sandy might have over it. Her mother always loved stories about adultery, for some reason.

"No, Mom," Sandy said firmly, wishing she'd never confided in her mother about Daniel's flirty students to begin with. She'd learned her lesson since then and now gave her mom as little information as possible.

"You know, Sandy, maybe it's time for a change."

Sandy already knew where her mother was going with this, but there was no stopping the woman, so she didn't even try.

"A change with your hair, m'ija. Maybe it's time for some highlights." Her mom patted her own brassy curls. "Or you could go red. This Elvira thing you have....Men like to see a little color, you know?"

The Elvira thing to which she referred was another old movie reference, this time to Sandy's natural dark hair and to the fact that she preferred dark clothing. Sandy wore a lot of dark colors, in general, because it was easier that way. She was petite, so pastels had the tendency to make her look too girly. And she needed to be taken seriously if she was going to give this writing thing a serious shot. When she wasn't at LatinoNow—Nacho Papi now, she reminded herself—she was at software and engineering companies interviewing serious men about serious products, then turning their scientific explanations into words that normal people could understand. Serious as a heart attack, at triple minimum wage per hour.

"And when are you going to get rid of those glasses, m'ija? Jesus Mother Mary, those glasses!"

Her mom made a move as if to reach for said glasses, and Sandy shielded them protectively. She needed her glasses—not only to see, but to look professional. No matter how many times she'd explained it, her mother had refused to understand.

Mrs. Saavedra had the same naturally dark hair and the same nearsighted eyes, and the same petite frame, plus about twenty pounds that she swore Sandy was responsible for, since Sandy had come out of her via C-section. But their personal style philosophies couldn't have been more different.

Sandy's mother always wore bright pink or purple or orange, preferably all at once, along with some kind of animal print. And she'd been covering her gray with golden blond and sporting long, razored-to-hell layers for years and years, before Sandy had begged her to cut off all her split ends and assume a blunt bob like a normal mother.

"Mom. Please. I've already told you. I'm not going to change my hair, my clothes, or my anything. Daniel's just fine with the way I look."

She pouted a little, but Sandy could tell her mom had gotten the message and wasn't going to risk driving Sandy out of the house by saying anything more on the subject. Instead she switched to mining info on Sandy's job.

"So, how was work today, m'ija? Your new boss is there now, right? The fancy lady from New York?"

"Yes. I met with her yesterday." Sandy left it at that. There was no use telling her mom that the fancy lady from New York hadn't even decided to keep Sandy on as a staff writer yet. Sandy had until Sunday night to get her audition samples done, and she needed to concentrate on that without any maternal distractions. She'd had a hard enough time convincing her mother that writing for a Web Site was a real job, in the same way that sitting in her apartment typing software manuals for faceless employers was also a real job that paid Sandy real money. Her mom knew what a freelance writer did, in theory, but Sandy suspected that she preferred to imagine her daughter crafting paperback romances under a pen name.

"So, your old boss, what happened to him again? Did he get fired?"

Sandy reflected, not for the first time, that her mother should have been a journalist herself. She was always trying to sniff out a scandal.

"No, he didn't get fired. He got transferred to another media entity. He moved to San Antonio."

"And so they brought this lady in from New York? Sounds like a demotion for her. I wonder what she did."

"I don't think it's a demotion," Sandy said, hurrying to explain before her mother got carried away and started up rumors. "She was in charge of putting *Mujer* magazine online, and she was really successful at it. So, LatinoNow's new owners hired her away from them."

"Oh-h-h!" breathed her mother. "You didn't tell me she ran *Mujer*! That's my favorite! I always look at their Web page at work."

Sandy nodded. She'd seen the *Mujer* site, of course. She'd looked it up the moment she and her co-workers had first discovered Angelica was taking over. And she'd learned that Angelica had taken the glossy, gossipy magazine with its endless features on Latina stars and their boob jobs and made it into the most successfully interactive Web site Sandy had ever seen. Readers were invited to comment and vote on every photo on the site, and it was chock-full of contests and promotions by advertisers. Even though *Mujer* had gone out of print, it was apparently making all kinds of money in its new incarnation as a Web site, and Angelica was the one responsible. Sandy had to admit that it was exactly the kind of entertainment that would appeal to her mother, and to thousands or maybe millions of other women like her.

"Is your new Web site going to be for Latinas?" her mother asked.

"Sort of," Sandy answered, keeping her tone vague. Nacho Papi would be like Levy Media's other new sites, Don't Call Me Sassy and Banana Nation. Sandy hadn't examined those sites in depth yet, but she could already tell that they'd follow the lead of Levy Media's flagship "news" site, Hate-O-Rama.com, where celebrities, politicians, and media professionals got the "hater" treatment on a daily basis. She didn't feel like trying to explain the ironic, irreverent, mean-spirited-but-funny tone to her mother, for whom *Mujer* magazine and the occasional romance novel were the highest-level reading.

Having finished the last bite of her quesadilla and washed it down with the pink saccharine juice, Sandy stood. "All right, Mom. I'd better go upstairs. I have a lot of work to finish."

"Work? Baby, it's Friday. You're young. Why aren't you going out tonight?"

Enough of the third degree, Sandy thought. It was time to resort to a dirty trick to get her mother off her back. "Speaking of going out, who was that I heard at your door last night?" she asked.

Immediately, like magic, her mother clammed up. "Never mind," she said primly.

Sandy smiled. She may have been secretive, but she came by the trait honestly. Her mother could be quite the secret keeper herself when she wanted to be. Sandy knew Mrs. Saavedra was probably dating someone, but that was all she knew, because that was all her mom would let her find out.

They cleaned up the snack debris in relative silence and then Sandy turned to go.

"Wait, Sandy, I forgot to ask you: Can you still go with me to Aunt Linda's house tomorrow? Remember, I told you last week?"

Sandy hadn't remembered, actually. She'd completely forgotten until that moment that she'd half promised to help her mother clean her recently deceased aunt's house and finish putting the old woman's affairs in order. That meant a long drive out to the dusty, hilly middle of nowhere. Not exactly how she wanted to spend half her weekend.

She wanted to make up an excuse. She *had* the perfect excuse—she had her Nacho Papi audition posts to write. But her mother was looking at her so hopefully that Sandy decided to give in. She could write the posts after, she told herself.

"Yeah, I'll go," Sandy said, feeling relieved at having something else to do, all of a sudden.

She ignored the fact that the relief only barely covered an underlying, slow-simmering sense of panic about her career.

7

Blog entry from *My Modern TragiComedy*, Saturday, March 11

I love my mother, but

sometimes she drives me crazy. I'm sure you're familiar with the feeling.

In my particular case, it's like my mother and I are complete opposites. The way we act, the way we dress, the things we watch, listen to, and read (or don't read) . . . Everything about us is different.

I take after my dad. Which is strange, when you think about it, because that means he married someone completely different from him. I wonder, sometimes, if those differences are why they divorced.

And I wonder, sometimes, if he's ever realized how much he and I are alike.

Maybe that's why he left me to deal with my mother—as a sort of substitute for himself, when he couldn't handle it anymore?

Okay, sorry to get so deep there. . . . I've already written tons of angsty stuff here about their divorce and all the trauma it caused me. Thanks again, guys, for reading this site and saving me the therapist fees.

I'm overanalyzing, I guess, because I'm about to take a road trip with my mom to deal with some somber family issues. And what better time than a road trip to hash out your differences with someone, right?

Wrong. I intend to keep the conversation light and the radio on, all the way. ☺

Love,
Miss TragiComic Texas

8

With her right hand, Sandy steered her mother's Lincoln Town Car south, down a quiet two-lane highway. With her left, she drank an iced chai latte, as quickly as possible, in order to infuse her brain with the caffeine it needed in order to cope with Mrs. Saavedra's constant chatter.

"I told Aunt Ruby we'd go over there and see what needed doing. Put away the last of Linda's things, clean out the cupboards, make sure there aren't any important papers still lying around. It's the least we can do, you know, since we didn't even go to the funeral." Her mother heaved a guilty-sounding sigh.

"Mom, it was in California. They didn't expect us to fly over. We barely knew Aunt Linda, anyway. It's not like if you or I died, we'd get mad at *them* for not showing up at *our* funerals."

"Jesus Mother Mary, Sandy. Bite your tongue!"

Despite the macabre theme of the day, a fresh breeze blew through the window and perked Sandy up a bit. The drive would take an hour and fifteen minutes, assuming they didn't get lost. Sandy had been to her great-aunt's ranch house only a few times before, as a girl, and her mother wasn't good with directions. She'd mapped the location online and printed the results, but that gave her a piece of paper with much more white space than ink.

Her mother narrated the trip to one of her friends via cell phone. "We're on a little road trip, just like Thelma and Louise. Sandy took me to one of her coffee places. I thought we were going to Starbucks but no, she took me somewhere special. I'll have to show it to you, if I can remember how to get there on my own. Sandy knows the neatest little places. Uh-huh, closer to San Antonio. I know, it's so sad. No, we never did. We didn't even know she was sick until she went to stay with my aunt Ruby. No, that's how it always goes. Yes, I-35 South, until we get to some exit. I forget which one. Sandy knows. No, not yet. I don't know. She won't let me ask her anything. You know how they get. Hmm? Two years now. No, they don't live together. He still lives at the university. His family? I think they're from Atlanta. Is that right, Sandy? Are Daniel's parents in Atlanta?"

"Mom," Sandy said, putting the warning note into her voice.

"Oh, okay. Sorry. See, she won't say. You know how kids are. Right. Oh, really? Okay, then. Bye, Tina. I'll call you later."

Well outside Austin's city limits, the landscape changed completely and had a sort of hypnotic effect on Sandy's mother. She stopped fishing for information and simply stared out the window at the hills and twisty trees and the occasional slivers of slow-flowing brown river. When she did speak, it was only exclamations about their surroundings, or else one-sentence regrets about the funeral.

Sandy concentrated on the road, on finding signs and the few landmarks she'd been able to glean from the online satellite map. She'd brought her camera along, but there was nothing worth photographing so far. Just endless cedar and mesquite trees and low hills cut by the highway. The sky seemed bigger down here somehow. But Sandy knew from experience that you couldn't photograph the bigness of the Texas sky. It simply wouldn't translate into pixels. Every few miles, wooden crosses and fake flowers left on the roadside would mark the site of someone's misfortune. Sandy hugged each curve and kept her eyes on the road.

It took less time than Sandy had calculated to reach the neighborhood, but much longer than she'd expected to find the actual house. They were on a numbered ranch road, in the middle of a mostly rural county. Not even in a town, technically. Aunt Linda's "neighborhood" was actually a string of goat pastures and newly plowed fields, separated at intervals by long gravel driveways that led to small, colorless houses. There was no way of knowing the street address of any of them. Sandy finally picked the most inhabited-looking one, nearest the star on her map, and drove up its rocky drive to ask for directions.

As they neared the grayish wooden house, an old man walked out from behind it to meet them. He wore a plaid shirt, jeans so faded they were almost white, and a tan straw hat.

"Oh, I think that's her neighbor. I forget his name. I didn't know he still lived here.... You'd better let me do the talking, Sandy." Her mother sounded apprehensive, and Sandy knew it was because she was about to speak Spanish, something she wasn't very good at. But she was better at it than her daughter, so Sandy let her take the lead.

They emerged from the Town Car as the old man waited and watched. Sandy's mother, in her usual weekend wear—bright top, tight capri pants, metallic sandals, full makeup, and big gold earrings—stumbled a little on the gravel. "Hola," she called to the old man as she hobbled her way toward him. "Como estás? Buscamos la casa que éra de mi tía Linda Hernández."

"Linda's house, sure. It's next door." The old man pointed in the direction they'd just driven from. "You're her nieces? I remember you. Did y'all drive here from Austin?"

"Yes." Sandy's mother lifted her chin a little and stopped where she stood, seemingly indignant at having displayed her rusty Spanish for nothing.

"It's easier to walk over," the old man said. He moved toward the steps as if to enter his own house. "Do you have the keys? If not, we can use mine."

"No, we have a key." Sandy's mother was taken off guard. So was Sandy. Aunt Ruby had given them the impression that Aunt Linda's house was completely abandoned, exposed to vandals, raccoons, and maybe even evil spirits.

The old man led them across gravel and grass to a group of trees that must have been hiding Aunt Linda's house from view. "I'm Jaime Escobar, but you can call me Tío Jaime. Everybody does."

"I remember you now. I'm Connie Saavedra, and this is my daughter, Sandy."

"Oh, Connie and Sandy. Right. Linda talked about you." The man everyone called Tío Jaime turned to Sandy. "You're the writer, aren't you?"

Now Sandy was even more surprised. "Yes, I am." She wouldn't have guessed that her writing career had made it that far down the family grapevine.

There was a bark in the distance and then, almost before the bark had finished echoing in Sandy's head, a scraggly, patchy dog ran up to the old man's side and stopped on a dime, panting, before falling in step between them. Sandy's mother inhaled audibly and tensed up. She didn't like dogs.

"Cano," the old man said, snapping his fingers on the left, causing the dog to immediately jump to his other side and away from Mrs. Saavedra. "Don't worry about him. He won't bother you."

"Oh," was all Sandy's mother could say.

The party slipped through two short, bushy trees and, sure enough, just on the other side was a house that looked exactly like the old man's. It was another little gray cube of wooden planks with no paint left to peel. Although it was obviously uninhabited now, it didn't look as bleak as Sandy had expected. There was a pot of begonias on the porch and a striped cat sauntered through the yard. The cat and Tío Jaime's dog gazed at each other for a moment, then went back to their own doings.

The dog waited at the door while Sandy, her mother, and their escort entered the little house. Inside, everything was incredibly clean and smelled like pine and lemons. In the front room there was a dark wood desk, a dinette set, a TV stand, and several chairs, all of which seemed three-quarters the size of modern furniture, and all of which had been polished. The sofa, a camel-backed affair, was covered with a bleached white sheet. Pink calico curtains hung from the windows and had been pulled back to let the sun shine onto gleaming white walls and dark molding.

Tío Jaime led them past the small kitchen, all flowered white tile, which also gleamed, and into the house's only other major room, Aunt Linda's bedroom. Again, everything was immaculate. The full-sized bed was the biggest thing in the room, its mattress wrapped tightly in a pink and lilac quilt. There was a dresser and another little chair. The closet door stood open and emitted the scents of ammonia and lavender. There was nothing hanging from the rod, but Sandy could see several neatly taped boxes on its floor. There were smaller boxes and bundles on the bed.

"Those are all her clothes, in the closet," said Tío Jaime. "Here are her papers." He indicated a black box on the bed. "And this one is her jewelry and things...hair clips and the things that were still good. All the kitchen things are over there."

"Who did all this?" Sandy's mother asked.

"Linda did, most of it. Right before she went to her sister's in California. After she left, I just picked up a few loose ends and kept an eye on the place for her."

"Oh," said Mrs. Saavedra. Sandy waited for her to ask something else. She could tell by the way her mother looked around with narrowed eyes that she wanted to ask more questions, such as how much time Tío Jaime spent in this house and just how friendly he and Aunt Linda had been. But some miracle of unexpected tact had settled on her and, instead, Mrs. Saavedra simply let out a relieved-sounding sigh. "Thank you. We were going to...Thank you so much, Mr. Esco—Mr....Jaime."

Tío Jaime nodded and waved her thanks away. "I'm thinking you want to take the box of papers, at least, and maybe whatever else will fit in your Town Car?"

Mrs. Saavedra looked around helplessly. Obviously she'd expected to do much more to the house before reaching the stage of deciding what to take back with them. Now, with all the work done, she was at a loss. "What do you think, Sandy? The papers, for sure..."

"Let's just take the papers and then call Aunt Ruby and see what we're supposed to do with the rest."

Without a word, Tío Jaime went to the bed and picked

up the black box, stacking a smaller box on top of it. "Take her jewelry, too. I know she would have wanted you to. I'll carry these back to your car for you. Come get me if you need help carrying anything else." With that, he left them alone in the house.

Her mother was already fidgeting, either from discomfort or boredom or both. Sandy didn't blame her. Obviously this Tío Jaime had everything here under control, unbeknownst to Aunt Ruby. There was nothing more for Sandy and her mother to do, and there was nothing more for them to see.

Sandy looked around the house again and tried to imagine her great-aunt, whom she remembered only as a petite, gray-haired woman who liked to crochet dishtowels, living there alone. It was unthinkable. There was nothing here—no computer, no satellite dish, no shopping for miles around. Unless Aunt Linda had been having a torrid affair with Tío Jaime, there was absolutely no way Sandy could imagine her filling her days here. And even if they had been dating, or whatever elderly people did together, it couldn't have been enough to fill years on end out in the middle of nowhere.

After deciding to leave everything else as it was, Sandy and her mother walked back to Tío Jaime's yard and accepted his offer to have a drink.

Inside his house, which was even more sparsely furnished than Aunt Linda's, they sat at a tall square table in the kitchen and drank strong, sweet lemonade. Tío Jaime put out a plate of assorted Mexican cookies, and Mrs. Saavedra politely accepted a chocolate one.

"Did you know my aunt well?" she finally asked, as casually as she could.

Tío Jaime took a strawberry wafer off the plate and said, "We've been neighbors all our lives."

"Oh, really?" Mrs. Saavedra looked wary then, as if it had just occurred to her that this man might be untrustworthy, or senile.

"First in Del Rio, then here," Tío Jaime added.

"Oh!" my mother said. "So you grew up together?"

"Yes."

"Were you...were you at the funeral?"

"No," he said. "Was it nice?"

"Oh, we don't know. We couldn't make it."

"Me neither. Wish I had." And that was all Tío Jaime said. He didn't seem rude or secretive. He was just a man who didn't waste words. Sandy had gotten that sense right off the bat, and found herself admiring him for it.

Her mother finally realized it, too. She visibly shook off her moment of discomfort and filled the silence with her own chatter. "Well, Sandy, I don't know what's left for us to do. Mr.—Tío Jaime—already did everything for us. Thank you again, Tío Jaime. You took a load off my mind. I didn't even know where we were going to start. Well, I guess we'll just take Aunt Linda's papers, then, and come back later for..." She paused there and looked to Sandy, as if she had a piece of a puzzle. "Everything else? Or..." She turned back to Tío Jaime. "Did you want any of the—I mean, is there something I can give you for...I mean..."

Tío Jaime shook his head. "She gave me a few things before she left. The rest, she said, was for whoever in the family came to pick it up."

He fell silent again. Through the open window the breeze picked up a little. On a rug nearby the dog sighed in his sleep. Sandy got the sense that it might have been sort of insulting for her mother to offer this man payment or a keepsake for his services. It was almost, she started to realize, inappropriate for Sandy and her mother to be here. They'd hardly known Aunt Linda, after all. They obviously hadn't known her as well as Tío Jaime had.

Sandy peered at him over her lemonade glass. His face was politely expressionless. But who knew? Maybe he was hiding extreme grief.

"Mom, we need to head back now." Sandy stood and put out her hand. "Tío Jaime, thanks for everything you've done. I know Aunt Linda's family in California will be grateful to you, too."

Her mother followed Sandy's lead, getting up and shaking Tío Jaime's hand in turn. "Yes, thank you, Tío Jaime."

"It was nothing," he said. "Y'all come back just as soon as you're ready and I'll be here to help."

"Do you…" Sandy struggled to think up the protocol for this situation. "Do you want us to call ahead before we come back?"

"No. Just come on over when you're ready. I'll be here," he said.

With that, there was nothing else for Sandy and her mother to do but take their leave. Mrs. Saavedra hobbled her way back to the Lincoln, her gold sandals completely caked in dust now. But she waved gaily to Tío Jaime, who watched from the porch as the two women got into the car and backed all the way down the gravel drive.

"Well," Sandy's mother said as they pulled back onto the ranch road, "that was weird."

Sandy nodded her agreement. It *was* weird, and she was glad to be driving them back to real life.

9

Post from Don't Call Me Sassy site, Saturday, March 11

This Week's "Negro, Please" Goes to Tyrone Marshall
by Cleo J.

You all know Tyrone Marshall as the daddy from that tired '80s sitcom *We Are the Washingtons*.

Last week, Don't Call Me Sassy reported on Mr. Marshall's instantly infamous "Black children, put down those beat boxes and get you a voice coach" speech. This week, we have a little investigative reporting to share with you all.

1. Tyrone Marshall's production company just green-lighted a new straight-to-DVD series called Yo Mama: Backstreet Brawlin'.
2. Mr. Marshall was recently seen having lunch down in DC with conservative-as-hell Senator Tom McElveigh. Wonder what they're cooking up?

Now, Tyrone, don't be talking out one side of your mouth while taking money from both sides of the street. In other words: Negro, puh-*lease*.

10

Sandy gasped aloud at Don't Call Me Sassy's inaugural posts as she scrolled through them in her twilit living room. This was nothing like what she'd learned in journalism school. It was nothing like she'd ever seen, in any publication.

Again Sandy felt a quiet panic creep into her guts. How could she write pieces like this? She never had. Sure, she'd sometimes gotten angry over details of the stories she investigated, but she'd never imagined pouring that anger into print, or openly criticizing a politician in such a way.

She clicked over to Banana Nation, the tagline of which was "We're here, we've assimilated, get used to it." The first post was a video of a reporter, a young Asian woman, stopping Asian people on the street and asking how they felt about China's latest Internet restrictions. The answers ranged from funny to political to completely uninformed. Some of the funnier responses, Sandy thought, looked rehearsed.

Under that post was a pie chart breaking down Asian actresses' recent movie roles into categories: Dragon Lady, Exotic Sex Object, Kung Fu Chick, and White Dude's Girlfriend with No Speaking Part.

Under that was a piece about actress Mai Lee, wherein the author, Cuoc X., insinuated that she was acting as a beard for director Derrick Rogers, who was purported to be gay.

If Sandy felt uncomfortable about the idea of lambasting politicians online, she was just as unsure of her ability to report on Latinos in Hollywood. She wasn't big on celebrity gossip sites, much less on digging up the celebrity gossip herself.

Although Nacho Papi wasn't a "real" journalistic entity, Sandy realized, writing for it would require just as much research as writing for LatinoNow had.

She sighed and picked up her phone. She'd start the research by calling Lori, the LatinoNow junior staffer who used to be Oscar's assistant.

"Sandy," Lori said immediately into the phone, "I'm completely freaking out. Angelica said I have to write three audition posts, or else come up with some story ideas, if I want to remain on staff. What am I going to do?" Her voice became a whine at the end. Sandy pictured Lori in the corner of the bar where she worked nights, pulling at the ends of her black-and-white-dyed pigtails, chewing gum a mile a minute, full-arm tattoo on display.

"Calm down," Sandy told her. "She said you have to write *three* audition pieces?" Sandy didn't want to be insensitive, but she had assumed everyone would be asked to write six, like she had, and wanted to make sure she hadn't misheard.

"Yeah, three pieces. Sandy, you know I'm not a writer. I can't do that. She said if I didn't want to write, I needed to come up with ideas for videos or something. She said maybe I could tape myself doing interviews. I don't know. I was so nervous I was completely freaking out. I guess I'll have to find another day job or something."

"No, you won't. Don't worry. I'll help you." Sandy thought she could intuit Angelica's line of reasoning. She wanted to see if Lori could do the man-on-the-street interviews they were doing on Banana Nation. So Lori could easily make a few digital videos of herself talking with friends in front of her bar. In the meantime, Sandy needed to find out what she herself was up against. "Lori, did Angelica tell George he needed to write three posts, too?"

"I have no idea. He came out of her office and took off, just like you did. He didn't even speak to the rest of us."

Sandy felt her glasses slipping down and adjusted them. Then she took a deep breath. She could understand Angelica giving Lori less to do, since Lori wasn't an experienced staffer and had no real journalism credentials. But if Sandy found out that Angelica had gone easy on George, too, she was going to be really annoyed.

"Have you talked to any of the others?" she asked.

"Yeah. Carolina's completely freaking out, Monica's totally freaking out, Jesse told me he was quitting, and Francisco said he was going to make some videos or some graphics or something."

"Okay," said Sandy. "Stop freaking out. Everything's going to be okay. What time do you get off work?"

"Not until two," Lori said.

"I'll come down there at two, then, with my camera," Sandy said. "In the meantime, talk to your regulars and see if any of them want to be interviewed. Think of stuff you can ask them, and I'll be thinking, too."

"Oh, God, Sandy, thank you *so much*. I owe you big time," Lori said, and kept repeating it until Sandy hung up.

She looked down at her phone to check the time. It was 7 P.M. That gave her several hours to work on her own audition posts, and then a few more hours the next day, Sunday, before Angelica's deadline.

Sandy felt a rush of adrenaline flood her bloodstream. It was her right-before-deadline power surge, just like the rush she used to get when she crammed for finals in college. Ideas were coming to her a mile a minute now, and her nervousness was gradually being replaced by excitement.

She was going to show Angelica that she could do this. Dominga Saavedra was not going to fold. At least not without a good try.

11

Time: Sunday, March 12, 8:37 PM
To: Dominga Saavedra, George Cantu, Lori Gomez, Francisco
Tamez, Philippe Montemayor
From: Angelica Villanueva O'Sullivan
Subject: Meeting tomorrow 9 AM

Our first staff meeting will be held tomorrow at 9 AM CST sharp.
Bring the material you submitted to me earlier today, your signed
contracts, and your new ideas for upcoming posts.

    If you will not be able to attend this meeting, please let me
know immediately.

Cordially yours,
AVO

The meeting didn't actually start until 9:15. Sandy had
been in the office since 8:52, waiting and trying not to
sweat. It wasn't lost on her that Angelica had sent the
meeting invite to only a few of LatinoNow's original
staff, plus to a man named Philippe whom she had never
heard of.

    Sandy could probably assume, therefore, that the writers attending this meeting were the ones who'd been chosen to stay. But she was afraid to assume even that much.

The office had been completely changed. All their old desks had been pushed to the edges of the main room. In the center of the room, there was now a huge conference table, loaded with laptops and power strips. The wall that had formerly held a huge map of Austin now boasted a sparkling white projection screen instead.

Lori and Francisco were standing near the table, quietly fretting over their displaced possessions. George, Sandy's least favorite staff member, stood there with his usual cocky smile, as if he wasn't surprised by the changes at all.

Maybe he wasn't, Sandy reflected. Maybe he'd already brownnosed their new editor into being his buddy and she'd told him all her plans. Sandy wouldn't have put such a scheme past George.

Before she could ask what was going on, the Lady herself strutted into the room. Angelica, all glammed out in chic white linen and carrying a matching white laptop that must have cost more than all the computers Sandy had ever owned, combined, took the seat at the head of the table. The head corner, actually, in a leather chair turned on the diagonal to face her staff and the screen simultaneously. Francisco scurried to help their new bosslady plug her laptop into the projector.

"Seats, everyone," Angelica said. "Let's get started."

In a dazed rush, all the writers of the former Latino-Now plugged their laptops into outlets and their bodies into chairs. Something about the woman's voice commanded immediate obedience. She was nothing like their old editor, Oscar, who used to camp out in his office all day and have his writers come in, one by one, like students visiting a friendly old guidance counselor. For the first time since working in this office, Sandy suddenly felt like she was at a real *job*.

Angelica clicked an image onto the screen. Sandy recognized it as the front page of Hate-O-Rama.com. Mouse-clicking away, Angelica launched into an introduction of each of their new sister sites. While listening intently, Sandy managed to aim covert glances at her co-workers and gauge their reactions to this very business-like meeting.

There was George: smirking, smirking. He may have been annoying, but he wasn't dumb. Sandy was sure he'd already done his research, just like she had. She narrowed her eyes at the writer who'd been a thorn in her side and her biggest competition for the past year. For the hundredth time, she took in the "trendy" short crop that didn't quite disguise George's ever-receding hairline and the facial hair that didn't disguise the chubbiness under his chin. His faded concert shirt was topped with a faded black blazer, an ensemble meant to make him look hip and edgy. He claimed he was twenty-eight but looked more like thirty-eight to Sandy. Everything Angelica said made him shoot her a crap-eating grin, just like the ones he used to shoot at Oscar. Oscar had always ignored George's brownnosing.

Sandy glanced over to see how Angelica was taking it. Professionally, of course. Her expression remained pleasantly, robotically professional no matter which of the remaining staff members she faced.

Across the table from George, Francisco peered at Angelica's screen like it was a technological glitch that needed solving. Every time Angelica pointed out a video or graphical feature on one of the sister sites she gestured at Francisco, and he gave a slight nod. He appeared completely unfazed now by the changes going on and ready to work on whatever was put in front of him.

Next to Francisco, Lori tugged at the ends of her multi-colored braids while taking furious notes in a notebook covered in rainbows and unicorns. There was no one else in the room with them. Caroline, Monica, and Jesse were missing, but no one seemed to be missing them.

The projector light sent floating dust specks over Francisco's head like a cloudy halo. Sandy sat up straighter in her chair and focused like a laser on what Angelica was saying. She wouldn't be the next one to get laid off, she told herself. The only thing worse than going from journalist to blogger, she realized, would be having someone tell you that you weren't even good enough to do that.

After her presentation, Angelica shut down the projector and had Lori turn on the lights. Everyone blinked and stared. Sandy knew something was coming, though. She opened the file she had already prepared on her laptop.

"So," Angelica said, "who has ideas?"

Sandy raised her hand, calm and confident as she could pretend to be. But before Angelica could call on her George blurted, "How about Top Ten lists of Latino celebrities? Hottest chulas, biggest mama's boys? Credits to our Raza and biggest sell-outs?"

Angelica smiled wryly. "A little crass, but it'll generate page views. Good."

Sandy cleared her throat. "Angelica, I have a post about Amber Chavez in mainstream media and how many times they've described her using the word 'spicy.' I made a chart depicting how often food words describe Latina stars versus white stars. I'm thinking Francisco can create a graphic with Amber Chavez being barbecued."

Angelica flashed a quick robot smile. "Okay. What else?"

Sandy referred to her laptop. "I did another statistical analysis showing that celebrities who declare themselves

Latino get more stereotypical roles, and Latinas who go blond and don't mention their ethnicity get more varied roles."

A spark of interest showed on Angelica's face now. But she said, "It has to be funny. What's funny about it?"

"Uh...The title is 'Guess Who's in the Closet. No, Not *That* Closet.'"

That scored a dry chuckle. "Okay," said Angelica. "What else?"

Sandy wondered, then, why she was being asked for multiple ideas while George had only pitched one so far and everyone else was sitting there with their thumbs up their butts. But she plowed onward. "I did an introductory-level piece about gerrymandering called 'Who's Disrespecting Your Hoods?'"

Angelica nodded. "Good. I like this angry, fight-the-power angle you're taking." George snickered at that, but Angelica didn't seem to notice. "Keep going with it. But keep it funny." She turned back to George. "And, George, you continue with the lowbrow thing you're doing. It's a good counterpoint."

Sandy didn't just snicker at that, she let out a full laugh, which she tried to turn into a cough. But Angelica ignored that, too, and turned to the others. "What else? What other ideas do we have?"

Francisco piped up. "As Sandy said, I'll be making graphics for her posts. And for whoever else needs them. Then I was thinking we could do a piece on Latino presence on FaceSpace and the Spanglish version of Leetspeak. And one on Latinos playing online video games and forming their own guilds. And, um...Latino porn sites?" His voice cracked on that last phrase. George guffawed outright.

But Angelica nodded. "Good. Highlight the most popular Latino users on FaceSpace and the other social networking sites. That'll get them to visit Nacho Papi and bring their friends. Then, Francisco, you get us screenshots of all the Latino porn sites, with the raciest parts blackboxed, of course. George will rate the sites and Sandy will discuss how exploitive and disgusting they are. People will eat that up."

George agreed enthusiastically and Francisco seemed relieved to have come up with ideas that met approval. Sandy looked over at Lori, who seemed to be sweating bricks and fighting the urge to chew her black-painted nails. She knew she was next, and Sandy knew she had nothing. *Oh, Lori*, she thought. *Come on. Try.* Sandy had helped her make a few videos at the bar. It was bizarre to Sandy, the way Lori could be so lively and funny entertaining customers but then fell completely apart talking about real work. Sandy felt that she herself was just the opposite. Work stuff was easy—it was the social butterfly routine that was difficult in her mind.

"I, uh. I, uh," Lori said to Angelica's expectant smile. "I normally just helped Oscar...I mean, I help Sandy and George and the others with fact-checking and research. And, um...formatting and stuff."

"This is your chance to do more than that," said Angelica. "I reviewed your videos over the weekend. They were good—the camera really likes you. Do you enjoy doing the man-on-the-street interviews?"

Lori nodded.

"Would you feel comfortable doing video pieces exclusively, maybe in other cities?" Angelica asked.

Lori nodded again.

"Would you be willing to change your look?" When Lori didn't immediately nod, Angelica quickly said, "Nothing drastic. I like what you have going on now, but I'd like to polish it up just a bit."

Lori nodded for a third time. Sandy had the funny impression that she'd just nodded away her soul. She couldn't tell if Lori was genuinely enthused about Angelica's ideas or just relieved that someone else had made all the decisions for her.

"All right." Angelica stood, indicating that the meeting was over. "Good job. George and Sandy, e-mail your finished posts to me, then get to work on more. Francisco, get with George and Sandy to find out what graphics they need, then start on the pieces we've discussed. Lori, you'll work on formatting approved posts for now. Use the branding guidelines I gave you last week."

"Oh, uh..." That was Lori.

"Yes?"

"What about Carolina and Monica? Are they going to be doing anything?"

There was a deep pause, as if everyone around the table were collectively holding their breath. Angelica let the silence hang for a moment, then gave Lori her brightest smile of the morning and replied, "Carolina and Monica e-mailed me their resignations last night."

If they'd been in high school, Sandy thought, that would have been the moment for everyone to chorus, "Ooooh!"

But they weren't in high school. And they all wanted to keep their jobs. So Sandy and the others minded their own business and set to work.

12

Posts from Nacho Papi's Web Site, Monday, March 20

ATTENTION: This is not yo' Papi's Web site!
by Sandy S.

Welcome to Nacho Papi. I'm one of your hosts and I'm here to give you the latest news about Latinos in politics and popular culture. Our goal is to make sure our people get represented. We intend to keep it real and to force mainstream media to do the same.

Don't listen to Sandy S. up there
by PapiChulo

We're not here to give you news, we're here to entertain you! We'll be pondering the great questions of our time, like whether Kelly Morales got butt implants and whether Simon Bolivarez could kick Chuck Norris's ass. Also, I'll be representing Cubanos so it doesn't get too Mexican up in here. Consider me your man's man and your ladies' man, and call me your PapiChulo.

Keeping la Raza Plugged In
by Hi Tech Aztec

Using FaceSpace to interface with your peeps in Chiapas, San Salvador, or Bogotá? I can help you out. Need to know where to download the latest reggaetón? Hit me up. Whether you want to translate abuelita's RSS feed or upload videos of your lowrider, I'm your man.

On a Whirlwind Tour to Find Signs of Life Worth Living...
by Philippe

I'm writing to you from Luna de Miel in Beverly Hills, where they have the best tapas and the second best mojitos. I'll be dissecting the local scene all week, and then the local scene will switch to Austin, where I'll join my brothers and sisters at Nacho Papi HQ. I'm looking for the best in fashion, shopping, and society from San Antonio to San Francisco, from New York to New Mexico. Maybe your town next, if you write and let me know what's worth seeing there.

Hi, everybody. This is Lori G.
by Lori G.

I'm not too big on words, but I hope to see you soon. ;)

13

Blog entry from *My Modern TragiComedy*, Thursday, March 23

My work, it is a-changin'.

I feel safe telling you guys this, since, as I've explained before, HeartThrob GeekBoy doesn't read this site. Technically, he knows I thought about starting a blog a while back. But since blogs are too low-brow for his MFA-having self, he forgot about it almost immediately after I first mentioned it. As far as I'm concerned, that gives me poetic license, so to speak, to say whatever I want about him. It's not my fault if he isn't interested in my hobbies. :)

Besides him, my only readers are my two best friends (Are you reading this, you two? Probably not, huh? :)) and then all of you. Wonderful, anonymous You.

So, as I said, I feel perfectly safe mentioning here that, despite HTGB's reservations, I'm taking a new opportunity. That's right—the Cheerleader talked me into joining her squad. I'm going to be writing a genre that's completely new to me, and I hope you guys will read my work on the new site. Even if you won't know it's me writing it. I have to stay anonymous here, you know.

But here's a hint: If you hear about a hot new site coming out of Austin with hilarious and insightful cultural and entertainment commentary, think of me.

If, on the other hand, you hear about a crappy new site with boring, fluffy hack work...then forget I said anything, okay? :)

Love,
Miss TragiComic Texas

14

The Friday after the site's soft launch, Sandy stood outside the Fat Man waiting for Daniel. He was late, as usual.

The coffee-shop-slash-bar was on the edge of Austin's low-lying downtown. Although she was more than a mile from it, Sandy could easily see the top of the Capitol from where she stood waiting. There were only parking lots and one- or two-story buildings between Sandy and the famous stone lady, plus one shiny new skyscraper off to the side—the city's first-ever skyscraper downtown. As she always did when standing downtown, comparing her hometown to Dallas's or Houston's glittery skylines, Sandy thought about the endangered owls and salamanders that were supposed to be benefitting from Austin's lack of urban sprawl. She'd never seen any of these mythical beings, but she wished them well.

Students and grad students and everyone else streamed through the Fat Man's weathered wooden doorway, and Sandy began to feel self-conscious about standing there alone. She wished she'd brought her laptop so she could take a table by herself without feeling even more awkward.

Instead, she pulled out her phone and called her friend

Veronica, who answered from an art supply store in Dallas. They talked about Sandy's first week of posts on Nacho Papi, all of which Veronica, a longtime devotee of Hate-O-Rama.com, had loved. They talked about Veronica's upcoming exhibit, for which Sandy would drive to Dallas the next day.

Then they discussed their mutual friend Jane, their respective parents, and Veronica's dog. Veronica had begun giving Sandy a long list of suggestions for future Nacho Papi posts when Daniel finally showed up.

Sandy finished her phone call and followed him into the Fat Man without a word, letting her silence do the talking. He knew she hated to be kept waiting, but he always had an excuse.

"Am I really late? I'm sorry, but I had a student ambush me in my office to tell me some sob story about why she missed the last exam. I got out of there as fast as I could, believe me."

"Don't worry about it," Sandy said tersely. What else could she say? There was always a reason.

Someone called to Daniel—one of his fellow TAs—and, before she knew it, they were forging a path through the crowd to join his friends at a dark, crowded corner table under the shelf of replicated antique beer steins. Just like they always did.

Everyone at the table—Mike, Kerry, Donovan, Michelle, and their assorted girlfriends, boyfriends, or friends—greeted Daniel and Sandy as they took the offered seats. Daniel ordered Shiners from a waitress in shorts and long striped socks. He gave Sandy a quick kiss and asked her how her day had been. She opened her mouth to give him a standard answer, and someone said, "So, Daniel, what about Whitfield's new syllabus requirements? Total bitch, huh?" And then he was off and running with his buddies, down the endless road of university politics.

Sandy listened for as long as she could with an interested smile plastered onto her face. For what felt like the hundredth time she studied the oddities and antique signs nailed to the walls around them. She watched the other patrons, other groups of grad students and TAs winding down after a long week. International students laughing around a dart board. Girls clustered around the jukebox, punching in the latest indie songs that only got played on the college stations. The inevitable creepy old guy in an unseasonable jacket, sipping his lager and staring at the coeds.

She held a brief, strange side conversation about eighteenth-century literature with one of the other TAs' girlfriends. But then that ended and, before long, Sandy's thoughts drifted to her own work.

"Bored?" Daniel whispered into her ear. It was the first thing he'd said to her since they'd taken their seats, and he'd just ordered the third round. "Do you want to leave?"

Sandy realized that she must have been spacing out in an obvious way. "No, not at all. I'm good."

Assured by her smile, he went right back to his conversation with his friends. She went back to planning her posts for Nacho Papi next week. Gazing at her beer bottle, she was reminded of a billboard in her mother's neighborhood for new Limonveza lime-flavored beer. The billboard was in Spanish.

What, she wondered, was with the proliferation of lime-flavored products being marketed to Latinos? And what were the ramifications of targeted liquor ads? She'd have to research. If she could strike the right tone between humorous and skeptical, she'd have herself a winner.

Her mind wheeled idly through different possibilities, and then it occurred to Sandy that sitting in a bar, surrounded by incoherent noises, being ignored and ignoring the conversations of others, was actually a pretty productive way to brainstorm.

"We're leaving in a little while," Daniel whispered into her ear. He sounded irritated. Sandy wondered what was bothering him this time.

SHE FOUND OUT during the ride back to his place.

"You know," he started, "if you didn't want to go to the Fat Man tonight, you could have just said so."

"What do you mean? I didn't *not* want to go," Sandy answered. She turned to look at him, to see if he was serious. Behind his head, the lights of the university buildings and then those of Guadalupe Boulevard flowed by.

"Right. That's why you were sitting there ignoring everyone, then," he said. His tone was light, but he stared straight ahead at the road and wouldn't even glance at her.

"I wasn't ignoring everyone. At least, I wasn't *trying* to. Sometimes you guys get started with your UT stuff, and you talk about things that have nothing to do with me, so what am I supposed to do? I can't help spacing out a little."

"You could try *listening*. I would think you'd want to take an interest in my work and the things that affect my life." He'd reached Hyde Park now and turned onto the street that led to his house.

"I *am* interested," Sandy returned. "But somehow I didn't think Mike's theories about which adjuncts Kerry's slept with were something that affected your career."

Daniel sighed. "I'm not saying that. Mike's a jerk. I'm just saying…It's really important that I get along with these people, and you sitting there with an annoyed look on your face doesn't help."

"I had an annoyed look on my face?"

Daniel didn't answer until after he'd pulled into his driveway. Then, finally turning to look her in the eye, he said, "Not exactly. You just looked like you wished you were somewhere else."

It was Sandy's turn to sigh. "Daniel, if I hadn't wanted to be there, I would have said so the first two times you asked me."

He didn't reply to that. So she said nothing. But the air between them was crammed with unspoken thoughts.

Sandy wanted to ask if he expected her to kiss up to his co-workers, or if it'd be easier for him if he was dating another TA. But she wasn't brave enough to ask. She could tell he had things he wanted to say, too, but she couldn't imagine what those things were, and he obviously wasn't brave enough either.

They climbed out of his car and started up the sloped walk to his lopsided little house, which, run-down as it was, was worth three houses in any other neighborhood.

"Look," she said, finally, "let's not get into it, okay? I haven't seen you all week and I was really looking forward to it."

"Yeah. Me, too. Okay." He gave her a quick half-smile of truce and then unlocked the door. Pausing in the low-ceilinged living room only long enough to drop his brief-case on the coffee table, he went straight to the kitchen to get them more Shiner.

Sandy kicked off her shoes and sat on the squishy plaid sofa, facing the television set that was already running on mute. Daniel's housemate wasn't home, but they always left the TV on. She focused on the screen and didn't bother to take stock of the surroundings. One, because she already knew what was there, in Daniel's living room. There wasn't much, and it never changed. Two, she didn't like any of his furniture or decorations. His parents had chosen them, from among apparent cast-offs in their own collection. The resulting effect was that of a shabby 1990s hotel room, everything done up in slate blue, hunter green, and glossy burgundy chintz. Her garage apartment may not have been a wonder of modern design, but everything in it she'd picked out herself from the Swedish discount warehouse.

It was time for a change of subject, Sandy decided. "So, did you see the posts I sent you?"

"What's that?" he called from the refrigerator.

"Nacho Papi's first week of posts. Did you read mine?"

"Um…" He emerged with two beer bottles and joined her on the sofa. "Yeah."

"You read them? What'd you think?"

"They were good," he said. "Better than I expected."

A thrill ran through her. "Really? Which ones did you like? Which was the best?"

"Um. The first one. The intro." He took a sip of his beer and gazed at the television set.

"The intro? Really? I thought that was kind of stiff." Sandy leaned forward, eager to get his professional feedback. "I didn't really start hitting my stride until the end of the second day, I thought. What'd you like about the intro?"

"Um…I liked what you said about holding the media accountable. And representing Hispanics in politics. That was good. It was a strong mission statement."

Suspicion filled Sandy like a gust of hot air. "You didn't read the other posts, did you?"

Daniel's reaction was a mixture of indignation, impatience, and guilt. "Yes, I did."

Sandy said nothing. But her arms crossed against her chest as she waited for further explanation.

"I scrolled through them. Through yours. But I didn't have time to read in depth, no, because I've been so busy this week. I *told* you that." His voice became plaintive. He flipped back his bangs and appealed to her with his eyes. "Sandy, I bookmarked them all for later. I'm going to read them as soon as I can. I wanted to wait to give you my opinion until I'd had time to read them all in-depth. I was planning to take notes and e-mail them to you."

If Sandy had had feathers, she would have felt them ruffle and then un-ruffle and then re-ruffle again, back and forth, over and over. So he hadn't had time to read her work. On the one hand it stung a little, especially knowing as she did that he hadn't been impressed by her new gig to begin with.

Then again, how could she complain? He *had* told her all week how busy he was. Maybe she should have printed her posts and pushed them in front of him at the Fat Man tonight, the same way he always forced his work on her.

In the next moment, she conceived of a new suspicion. What if he *had* read all her posts but hadn't thought they were any good at all? What if he was just stalling for time until he could think of something constructive to say?

Sandy squeezed herself hard with her folded arms and then let herself go. "Okay. Well, hurry and take your notes, then. I really was looking forward to hearing your opinion."

"I will. I promise." He extended an arm over her for a quick half-hug. "Come on. Let's go to my room. Matt's going to be here any minute now."

Matt was Daniel's housemate. Although the house

technically belonged to Daniel, it had belonged to his parents first. It had been their rental property and Daniel had agreed to allow them to continue renting out one of the rooms.

Daniel stood and turned up the sound on the TV, then led Sandy to his bedroom, where he turned up the radio on his nightstand just as loud.

"You want to...?" He turned off the ceiling light and lit his nightstand lamp, then picked up a T-shirt from the floor and carefully adjusted it over the plain white shade to dim the bulb. Then he pulled his two burgundy-encased pillows from beneath the lumpy blue-and-green-plaid comforter, plumping them a little before putting them back against the pine headboard carved with scrolls that matched those on the nightstand and the dresser.

He looked back at her with a questioning smile.

"I guess," she said.

She watched as he began to remove his clothing, starting with his shoes and then moving from head to toe, shirt to socks, laying each piece carefully across the chair near the foot of the bed.

Sandy stifled a smile or a sigh, she didn't know which. She had already removed her glasses and set them on his dresser. Next she would remove her own clothing and lay it alongside his.

She might have wanted to laugh at his predictability, or to feel embarrassed at her own. But there he was, and there she was. She figured she may as well go through the motions.

15

Blog entry from My Modern TragiComedy, Saturday, March 25

Open Letter to a HeartThrob GeekBoy
Dear GeekBoy,

You're doing it again. Once again, you're taking me for granted.

I remember when I first met you. I thought that you were beautiful. Not just the best-looking TA I'd ever seen, but just as much a work of art as the poetry you loved. That was back before I knew just how long you spent working at those long, lean muscles you pretend not to work at . . . searching for those vintage shirts and close-cut trousers that make you so casually anti-establishment . . . sitting in the chair while Rolando dishevels your shiny black hair so it'll fall into your green eyes just perfectly, for $55 a session.

I used to feel so incredibly lucky that you wanted someone like me. Wanted to talk to me and to listen to me, or at least to my opinion of your work. Back then, it didn't matter to me that I was the one doing all the listening. I was happy to do it. You had so much to teach me, and I was more than willing to learn.

Now that I'm starting to find my own success, you don't seem as interested in me. Why? Because nothing I ever do will be good enough for you to notice? Or is it maybe because you're not interested in being with an equal? Maybe you can only be happy with someone who looks up to you. Looks way, way up to you, I mean.

How long do you expect this to last, HeartThrob GeekBoy? How long do you give it before I get tired of being one of your admiring fans? Maybe you're tired of it, too, but you can only say so in your poetry. You show it to me and don't think I'm clever enough to read between the lines. But I am, and I do.

Here's a poem for *you*, Mr. Poet, in response to the last one you showed me, written in your very own style:

He Walks on My Nerves
Call it metaphor, simile, grad-school-grade allegory
Your shady language can't/can not change the fact
That the other night, long after you went to sleep.
I rolled over to finish the job
You can't ever seem to complete.

That was fun. Maybe *I* should be the one getting a Ph.D. in poetry. Look out, HeartThrob GeekBoy. I'm catching up to you with my own career. Before you know it, I may have fans of my own.

Love,
Miss TragiComic Texas

16

"Sandy Saavedra? Never heard of you."

The hulking monster of a security guard handed Sandy and George their newly minted press passes and pointed to the sign above the convention center door. It said AUSTIN LOWRIDER SHOW: $15 ADMISSION.

"This is so embarrassing," Sandy muttered after they'd paid and made their way through the throng at the door.

"No biggie," said George. "Just save your receipt and Angelica will reimburse us."

"It's not that." Sandy removed her camera from her work bag and surveyed the scene. As far as the eye could see, there were cars. Bright, glittery, bouncy cars, flanked by the men who loved them. And by adoring fans with cameras and fried foods in paper bags. And by women in bikinis and high heels. "Why are we even here? And on a Sunday?" She'd hurried back from Dallas early that morning, skipping breakfast with her friend Veronica, to drive her hungover self back to this.

"I know why *I'm* here." George made a beeline for the nearest bikini model. "Come on," he called over his shoulder. "I'm interviewing her first!"

*　　*　　*

BACK AT THE office on Monday, Angelica reviewed their footage with a critical eye. Sandy watched, too. It was her first time seeing herself on video. She wondered if she looked as nervous as she'd felt while interviewing her subjects. It was hard to tell because George had done so many close-ups on the models and the cars that there wasn't much of Sandy in the frames.

She knew, at any rate, that she'd done a better job than George. Not only was her camera work better, but she'd come up with better questions for their subjects. All George had done, basically, was hit on the models. He'd even offered to make a couple of them famous.

"Good job, you two," said Angelica, causing George to preen. "Next time, though, I'll send Francisco along with you to run the camera. Also, next time, George, try getting a little more information from your subjects. Instead of just asking if the girls are single, ask if they slept with anyone to get the job. And don't promise them anything on camera, got it?"

George nodded dutifully and Angelica dismissed him. Then she turned to Sandy. "Have a moment? In my office?"

Sandy swallowed hard and followed her boss.

The office most certainly was Angelica's now. She'd removed every trace of evidence that Oscar had ever worked there. The walls had been painted pale taupe and matted watercolor abstracts took the place of Oscar's old maps and prints. The old plywood desk had disappeared and been replaced by a wide ebony wood table that now cradled Angelica's pearly white notebook computer and python bag.

Instead of going around the table to the sueded swivel chair, Angelica took one of the plum-colored visitor's seats and indicated that Sandy should take the other.

Sandy waited for Angelica to speak. She couldn't imagine what was on her boss's mind, but was certain she wasn't about to get fired. *Pretty* certain, at any rate.

"Sandy, you did a really good job with the interviews. You were poised, you improvised good questions, and your subjects trusted you. I especially liked the bit where the young man told you about getting his degree in jail. Really good work."

"Thank you." Sandy flashed a polite smile but felt nervous. She felt a "but" coming up.

"How did you feel about it?" Angelica asked. "Did you enjoy it? Were you comfortable?"

"Um...Yeah. I guess so." Sandy gave the question some thought. "At first I was nervous, but then I kind of got into it."

"That's the way it often happens." Angelica smiled. "Now, I'm about to give you my one critique, but I want you to understand that it's meant professionally, to help you be more successful, and not as a personal criticism."

Sandy felt even more nervous now, but also very curious. "Okay."

"I noticed that you looked most uncomfortable when you were on camera with the models in bikinis. And I can't blame you for that. However, your understandable discomfort, combined with your outfit, your hairstyle, and your general image made those segments read a little bitter. Do you know what I mean?"

Sandy's hand went up to her ponytail—the same type of ponytail she'd been wearing in the video. She willed herself to pull her hand down again, and to refrain from looking down at herself to see what Angelica was seeing at that moment. She forced herself to look the older woman in the eye with as much dignity as she could fake. "I'm not sure I do know what you mean, no."

Angelica smiled again. "You're an attractive young woman, Sandy. Anyone can see that, even with you in those clothes, wearing those glasses, and without any makeup."

Sandy's hand flew up to her rimless, glare-blocking, nearsighted-correction lenses.

Angelica went on. "When you appear in public like this, you're sending a message. That message is, 'Judge me by my brains, not by my looks.' And that's completely valid, but when you interview women who get paid to be judged on looks, it can give the impression that you're standing in opposition to them, so to speak. To some of our less enlightened audience members, it could read as 'angry feminist' or 'bitter, jealous frump,' or some other ridiculous thing. Even though you and I know that nothing is further from the truth. I don't think it's fair that you and I, as women, have to worry about our image in this way, but the reality is—"

Sandy got the message. She decided to cut to the chase and save Angelica more explanation. "What you're saying is, you want me to be prettier. Like Lori."

"Not at all." Angelica shook her head. "How pretty you are makes no difference to me. What I want you to be"—here she leaned forward conspiratorially, and Sandy couldn't help but lean forward too—"is more polished, and more *confident*. I want you to look like a woman who can hold her own with anyone. You already are that woman, and I want to make that fact more obvious to our audience."

Sandy frowned. She wasn't sure she *was* that woman, actually, but she figured it'd be unwise to contradict her new boss on that point. What she did argue was "I just don't see how makeup or a new hairstyle can convey that kind of message."

Angelica sat up straighter and smiled in a way that Sandy couldn't help thinking was triumphant. "I'll show you. Do you have a couple of free hours this afternoon?"

IN THE SAME amount of time that it'd taken Cinderella to ride her pumpkin to the castle, probably, Sandy found herself at her optometrist's office, picking up a copy of her prescription, and then at Angelica's optometrist's office, picking out new frames.

"These," said Angelica, holding up the same dark-rimmed pair that the blond in one of the display posters was wearing.

Sandy modeled them in front of the mirror but was unable to gauge the effect without her own glasses on. She took them off and read the price tag. "There's no way I could afford these."

"Don't worry," said Angelica, brandishing a silvery credit card. "Corporate expense."

Next stop was a salon all the way down in Brody Oaks, where the receptionist knew Angelica by name and a stylist in a white lab coat immediately ran over to kiss her on the cheek. "What have we here?" he said, eyeing Sandy like a golden cat standing over a dazed mouse.

Angelica touched Sandy's shoulder and said, "Make-over."

The stylist spun Sandy like a dancer, pulling the elastic band from her head and running his fingers through her hair all in one graceful move.

"Mm," was all he said. Then, "What are we thinking?"

Angelica leaned forward and spoke quietly, but not quietly enough to keep Sandy from hearing. "I'm thinking sexy librarian, but not *too sexy* librarian."

"Tina Fey, but sleeker? Eva Peron, but alive?"

"Exactly. I *knew* you'd understand, Rod."

Rod took Sandy's hand and started to lead her to the back of the salon. But Sandy dug in her heels. She pulled her hand away and protectively touched her glasses, her hair, her glasses again.

Something in the pit of her stomach was telling her this was wrong. Whatever they wanted her to be, she wasn't sure she could pull it off. She was already stretching her limits by writing things she'd never learned to write in J school. But now Angelica was asking her to be someone else.

Sandy knew she could write anything, learn anything, understand anything that anyone put before her. But she wasn't at all sure that she could be what Angelica was asking, or even fake it. Sandy was afraid she couldn't deliver. She was afraid she would fail.

"Sandy," Angelica said, putting her hand on the younger woman's shoulder again. "Trust me. I promise you're going to like it. And, if you don't, I promise that you can go right back to the way you were."

"It's not that I don't think it'll look good," Sandy said. "It's just that…I'm not sure I can *change*."

What would Daniel say? she suddenly wondered. He'd say he'd told her so, that this job wasn't about her writing or her intellect, but something crass and shallow.

She imagined him reacting to a more polished—no, a *sexier* Sandy. Would he think she looked shallow? Or would he be more upset that she no longer looked like one of his adoring students?

Again Sandy felt the impulse to rebel against Daniel's ideas of what she should be.

What would her mother say? Sandy grimaced. Probably that Angelica wasn't going far *enough*. If her mom were there, she'd consider this a dream come true. A free makeover, by the editor of *Mujer*? Her mom would be crying out for tacky blond highlights and rhinestoned, two-tone nails.

Thinking of it that way, Sandy felt her impulse reverse. There was nothing wrong with the way she was now. Why should she change?

"I'm not asking you to change," Angelica murmured into her ear, as if she could read Sandy's mind. "I just want to bring out what's already there. Show everyone who Sandy Saavedra really is."

With that the balance was finally tipped. Sandy let them lead her to the inner room of the salon, to find her new, real self.

17

Reader comments on *My Modern TragiComedy*, Tuesday, March 28

I found your blog by searching for information on divorced parents. What you said, I totally agree with. I feel the same way about my mom and dad sometimes. Thank you for writing it. It's good to know I'm not alone.

Comment left by: **Anonymous**

OMG, you go girl! I've been thinking for a while now that HTG Boy doesn't appreciate you enough! He'd better watch his step or else he won't have you around to take for granted anymore!

Comment left by: **Pilot Girl**

Hi, TragiComic Girl. Keep your chin up. Hopefully HTGB will come around soon. :)

Comment left by: **Sunny B**

18

The latest blog comments were very touching. Plus Sandy had apparently gained a new reader. But, for a split second, she regretted saying what she had about Daniel. She'd been angry at the time and had been overcome by the desire to vent.

Now that she *had* vented, now that she sat on her sofa, re-reading her words from the other night, they sounded pretty harsh. Daniel was annoying sometimes, but he wasn't *that* bad. Was he?

Sandy wondered if she should delete that blog entry now that it no longer expressed her current feelings.

But then, she realized, she'd have leftover comments from readers relating to that entry. So she'd have to delete those, too. And, somehow, it seemed wrong to delete readers' comments once they'd been posted. It seemed unethical. She was sure, in fact, that there was an applicable rule somewhere in one of her old journalism textbooks.

The thing to do, she decided, was to print a retraction. She would post another entry, explaining that she'd been angry and had overreacted, and that HeartThrob Geek-Boy was actually a pretty good guy. She'd write that for her very next entry.

But not right now. First she needed to finish some work for QBS Systems and e-mail it to her supervisor there. Then she needed to go to QBS physically and renew her contract. Then she needed to hurry back downtown for a noon meeting at Nacho Papi.

But before she did any of that, she needed to e-mail Veronica and Jane a picture of her new hair. And, after scrolling through all the pictures she'd uploaded the night before and picking the best one, she did just that.

Jane was at work at the Capitol already, which meant she was already goofing off online. She replied immediately: OMG, is that you? You look fabulous!

Sandy was pleased, to say the least. They volleyed a few e-mails back and forth, catching up, and then Sandy got back to work in earnest.

"JESUS MOTHER MARY, Sandy, is that you? You look beautiful!"

Whereas Jane's comment had looked moderately enthusiastic on the screen, Sandy's mother sounded, in the driveway, like she was about to burst into tears. She ran up to her daughter as if they'd just won the lottery and gave her a big, disproportionately emotional hug. "Oh my gosh, oh my Jesus! Baby, I'm so happy for you! I'm so glad!"

"Mom! Quit. You're freaking me out."

Her mother made a visible effort to get hold of herself. "When did you do it? Last night? Where'd you go? Oh my gosh, you got new glasses, too! Sandy, what happened? Did you get a raise? Wait—did Danny break up with you?" Within this one paragraph, her mother's voice had gotten loud again.

"What? No. Why would we have broken up? Why would *he* have broken up with *me*?"

"You know. I just meant, how sometimes, when women break up with someone, they suddenly start caring about how they look again. Or for the first time. Or—you know. Whatever. So what happened?"

Sandy decided to overlook her mother's verbal blunders. "Nothing. Angelica, my new boss, is having me do some interviews on camera for the site, and we wanted to change my look a little. That's all."

"Oh, Sandy. You mean you got a *Mujer* makeover? For free?"

"For free, yes. Related to the magazine Angelica used to edit, no." Sandy would have laughed at her mother responding exactly as she'd predicted if that reaction weren't so exasperating.

"Let me see." Mrs. Saavedra gently touched the new shoulder-length inverted bob, which Sandy hadn't even had to blow out that morning, thanks to her naturally stick-straight locks. "You always had your daddy's hair. Indio hair," her mother said, shaking her head. "But it looks good like this. Let me see your eyes."

Sandy dutifully closed her eyes so that her mother could see that slightest dusting of taupe powder and the thinnest line of black liner on her eyelids.

"Pretty!" her mother breathed. Next she examined Sandy's silk blouse, pencil skirt, and high-heeled mary janes. Angelica's two-hour makeover had led to a full evening of shopping. Sandy had let her boss pay for a few items of clothing, pretending it was a sort of required uniform, but then ended up picking out many more things to buy for herself. It was strange, she'd never really enjoyed shopping with her mother or even with her friend Jane. But with Angelica it was different. Her boss knew boutiques Sandy had never visited, and her shopping technique involved getting in, grabbing the good stuff, and getting back out in one streamlined process. It had been a whole new experience for Sandy—one she hoped wouldn't become an expensive habit.

"Why didn't you get a new bag, too, though?" Mrs. Saavedra touched the olive green corduroy work bag that hung on Sandy's shoulder from its black canvas strap.

"Because I like this one. I'm used to it. It has the perfect number of pockets and the strap is the perfect length." Sandy had carried that bag for so long it felt like part of her body, sometimes.

Her mother blinked but said nothing. She herself preferred snakeskin. Kind of like the purses Angelica carried, but in patent vinyl instead of real leather. Apparently realizing there was no accounting for taste in the end, she went on. "I'm so proud of you, m'ija. You look so beautiful. Like a real lady."

Sandy was a little disconcerted. This was the first time in a long while that her mother had expressed pride in her. The last time must have been at Sandy's college graduation. But even then her mother hadn't sounded this sincere.

Here she was, proud of Sandy because she was wearing makeup and nice clothes. It was more than a little unsettling—it was downright annoying. But Sandy shrugged it off, not wanting to ruin the moment. Instead, she returned her mother's hug. Then she disentangled herself and drove away to work.

"WHOA! WHO ARE you and what did you do with Sandy?" George practically bellowed as she walked into the office, ensuring that all their co-workers would turn and stare. "I mean, I know it's almost April Fool's Day, but this is some joke." He laughed at his own wit but no one joined him.

"You look good, Sandy," Lori said, throwing George a scornful look.

"Yeah," Francisco chimed in, sounding somewhat in awe. "You look great."

"Thank you." Sandy used her most gracious tone and majestically took her place at the staff table, where she got to work unpacking her laptop.

"Hey, that's what I meant, too. I was just kidding. You know that, right?" George asked, more to the room at large than to Sandy herself.

Everyone fell silent when Angelica emerged from her office to start their meeting. Sandy braced herself, in case their editor was about to make an announcement about her makeover or otherwise call more attention to Sandy's new look. Instead, however, Angelica smiled and greeted everyone as normal. Right before launching into her agenda, however, she gave Sandy an almost undetectable wink.

Sandy smiled and looked down at her laptop screen. This makeover, she decided, had turned out to be a good thing.

19

Time: Wednesday, April 5, 8:12 AM
To: Nacho Papi Team
From: Angelica Villanueva O'Sullivan
Subject: MEMORANDUM

Per our last meeting and one-on-ones, here are items that require follow-up:

1. **New banner ads: Francisco**, please run our new Limonveza banners on test site to make sure they work. **Sandy**, please revise your lime-flavored product post to reference Limonveza in a more positive way, now that they are a sponsor.
2. **New "in-line" sponsor: George** and **Lori**: As we discussed, you are each to mention Thuggin' jeans once within the next week. Keep it natural-sounding.
3. **New writer:** Philippe Montemayor is flying in this weekend and will join us on Monday.
4. **New assignments: Lori** and **Francisco**, you are going to San Antonio tomorrow to cover Iguana Cantina. **George**, you are covering the leaked Minute Men memo. **Philippe**, you are turning in the expose on Heather Santiago's wedding freebies. **Sandy**, you are researching the Chupacabra story for angles.

Please notify me if you are unable to complete your assignments. Thank you all. You're doing a great job and I know you'll do even better in the coming weeks.

One more thing: Everyone, please do not mention local bars and restaurants more than once per month, regardless of how many free drinks they're giving you, unless they have purchased sponsor packages from the site.

Cordially yours,
AVO

20

Blog entry from *My Modern TragiComedy*, Thursday, April 6

My look, it is a-changin'

So I had to get a makeover for my new job. Don't hate me because I'm shallow, but I really like it. I had my doubts when my boss first suggested it. But I have to say that it feels pretty good to look pretty. Prett*ier*. Instead of just witty and bright, you know? I'm no bombshell, but the drag worms are actually complimenting me when they panhandle now. Instead of just saying "Hey, brainy girl, got a dollar?" like they used to.

HTGB seems to like it, too. Well, if his stunned silence was any indication. I told him I'd felt like making a change. He said "Looks like change agrees with you."

Hey, speaking of—disregard all that stuff I said about him last week, would you? I was just talking crazy talk. Just venting. You know how it goes. Everything's back to normal now and we're as happy as we can be, two lovebirds in a tree, K-I-S-S-I-N-G, et cetera.

Crazy Mom Report

Not only did my mom like my makeover, but she managed to completely traumatize me while telling me so, too. She's so good at that: turning random moments into events that make you question all your life decisions up to that point and probe at the illusion of your own freaking sanity.

I remember that day I graduated, two years ago now. It was a bittersweet day. On the one hand, I was proud as hell of myself for having busted butt towards my bachelor's, through a hellish Copy Center job and with minimal help from loans and my dad. All my friends were there, ready to help me celebrate.

On the other hand, my parents were there, fresh from their divorce. My dad—smart as hell but clueless when it comes to relationships—had brought along his new girlfriend, who was much younger than my mom and who happened to work at the university. So, even if she felt awkward showing up at her boyfriend's daughter's graduation, at least she was in her element.

Unlike my mom, who'd shown up alone. And way overdressed, of course.

Maybe it was only because she was nervous, but I remember that she picked at me the whole time. "You should have worn more makeup!" and ""You should have worn higher heels!" and "Why is he with her? She isn't even pretty!"

And then, on the way home, she said the words that have been burned into my brain ever since: "I hope you're not going to have a big head now, like your daddy."

It was supposed to be a joke, but I didn't feel like laughing. Basically, that's what my six years of hard work boiled down to for my mother—an excuse for me to feel superior, and a point for my dad's side in their everlasting battle.

Why am I bringing all this up now? I don't know. It's just been on my mind, I guess. Almost two years later, my dad's still with the same girlfriend, and my mom's still annoyed by it. I wonder if that's why I haven't heard from him lately—he doesn't want to stir up any more drama.

Almost two years later, and my mom's still picking at me. Are my heels high enough? Is my hair done enough? Is that all she cares about? Is that still what she thinks is going to make me succeed in life?

I love my mom, but sometimes I wish I had a slightly better female role model. Someone who knows how the real world works, you know? Someone who can understand what I'm trying to get out of life, and isn't only concerned with lip gloss and nail polish and he-said-she-said.

Well, there I go again, getting all deep. But you don't mind, do you? This is a message in a bottle, landing on your shore. You don't have to open it. And you can always throw it back to me.

Love,
Miss TragiComic Texas

Reader comments:

Miss TragiComic,

Oh my God, I feel like you spied on my life and then turned around and wrote about it like it was your own.

My mom does the exact same thing to me, and I haven't even graduated yet. In front of her friends and our family, she says she's proud of me. But when we're alone, she's always making these little comments like "I guess you think you're smarter than the rest of us, little miss college girl."

I don't know what to do about it. Like you said, she pretends she's kidding. But it still hurts.

Thank you so much for writing this. At least I know I'm not the only one feeling it.

***Comment left by:* Anonymous**

Hey, Miss TCTX! Any chance we can get some before and after pictures of the makeover? :) :) :)

***Comment left by:* Peaches**

21

I t's not fair," Sandy said into the phone as she drove down I-35 toward the middle of nowhere. "I should be the one covering the Minute Men leak, but Angelica gave it to that idiot. I know it's because he's always in her office, sucking up to her."

"But I thought she liked you, too," said the disembodied voice of her friend Jane, through the cell phone.

"She does. At least, I *thought* she did. She told me all that stuff, when we were shopping, about how I reminded her of herself when she was young. But who knows? Maybe she gives that speech to everyone." Sandy felt glum at the thought. She took her exit on mental autopilot, eyes on the road and head full of worry. Cacti flecked the road on either side of her, almost like bread crumbs leading the way.

"So what are you going to do?"

"I'm driving out to where they allegedly found the chupacabra tracks. Check this out—it's right by my Aunt Linda's house. The one who died, whose house me and my mom just went to? I can't find anything good online yet, so I'm going out to see what I can see. And—I don't know, talk to the neighbors or something." Saying her plan aloud made Sandy realize just how little she had to go on with this story.

"Wow, that sucks," said Jane. "Well, good luck. Here's hoping you find a chupacabra. Hey, why don't you look for Bigfoot out there, while you're at it?" She stifled a laugh.

"Why, you looking for a new man?" Sandy returned in the same tone.

"No, but I am looking for more free stuff from my famous friend. When are you going to get us VIP at Red Top again?" Jane was talking about last weekend, when Sandy had covered a show at a new club downtown and was able to invite Jane and her boyfriend along.

"I *told* you," Sandy said, rolling her eyes. "That was a one-time deal. Believe me, the next time something like that comes up, I'll let you know. Don't tell me you're going to start planning your social life around my job perks."

"I'm trying to," rejoined Jane. "I can keep giving you Capitol gossip, but only if you keep scoring us more free booze."

THE SITE OF the alleged chupacabra sighting was practically in Tío Jaime's backyard, just as Sandy had suspected. She passed two news vans on the way to his house, across the road from each other, both taping their Latino anchors standing in front of mesquite trees. Sandy slowed to get a look and the crews spared her nothing more than weary glances. There was no chupacabra in sight.

Sandy drove directly to Tío Jaime's house, figuring she might as well. The old man was standing on his porch with his hat in his hand and his dog at his side, looking hot and tired, as if they'd just arrived there after a morning of hard work. There was a clump of goats in the distance, milling around slowly and peacefully. No monsters among them. Although Sandy was in her Malibu and not her mom's Town Car, Tío Jaime recognized her and waved for her to proceed up his driveway.

"How are you, m'ija? Where's your mama?" he asked as she emerged from the car, her trusty olive corduroy hanging from her shoulder.

"She's at home. I came by myself."

"Did you need to get into your aunt's house? Do you need the key?" he asked. Before she could answer, he said, "Do you want something to drink? I was about to get some lemonade."

"Thank you." Sandy was obliged to follow him into the house. "Actually, Tío Jaime, I came out here for another reason."

He led the way into his kitchen. His dog waited outside the screen door like a sentry. "I'll get you some water, too, Cano."

Sandy stood quietly for a moment, wondering how to explain what she was doing. Tío Jaime didn't seem overly curious. He filled a glass with tap water and carried it out to the dog's water bowl. When he came back into the kitchen, he washed his hands methodically before taking two glasses from a cupboard and setting them on the table. Then, still silent, as if waiting for her answer but not in a big hurry to hear it, he went to the old, yellowed Frigidaire in the corner of the kitchen and removed a glass pitcher that had been draped with a piece of plastic wrap. It was filled with pale yellow lemonade and slices of lemon. It looked tantalizingly cold. Sandy realized she was thirsty and sat down gratefully, setting her bag on the chair beside her.

The old man poured them lemonade and then went back to the refrigerator for another glass, this one full of plant stems and water. "It's mint," he explained as he pulled leaves from the stems and put them in Sandy's glass. "It makes it taste better. Linda taught me that."

"Thank you." Sandy took her glass and sipped. Her great-aunt had been right—it did taste good with the mint. "Do you..." She glanced at Tío Jaime, who was now seated and sipping his own drink, looking out the front door at his dog or maybe just looking into the distance at nothing. "Do you miss her?" she ventured.

"Every day," he said with a smile. And that was all.

Sandy absorbed the gravity of his words. He had loved her great-aunt. It was obvious. And the way he'd said it, it sounded like the most natural thing and not subject to prying questions. She reminded herself that she was supposed to be on assignment. "The reason I came out here was that I work for a news Web site. I'm sort of a reporter."

"You're a writer," he said.

"Right. And there's been a report about a chupacabra in this neighborhood." Tío Jaime snorted at that. Sandy went on, feeling foolish. "And I have to do a story about it. That's my job. And I thought I'd ask you, since you live out here. Maybe you've seen...maybe you knew something about—"

The old man laughed aloud then. "Maybe I've seen a chupacabra? M'ija, I've seen a lot of things out here, but a chupacabra ain't one of them. I'm more likely to have seen a rabid dog eating one of my goats. Or some drunk running off the road and hitting one of them. Or a bunch of fraternity boys coming out here in the middle of the night and doing God knows what with each other in their underwear, and one of my poor goats getting caught up in the crossfire."

Sandy set down her glass and opened her bag, scrambling for her notebook. She knew good quotes when she heard them. But her hand landed on her camera first, giving her a better idea. "Really? *Have* you seen those things?" His answer almost didn't matter. His words created good visuals.

"I've seen that and worse in my years. All kinds of crazy things."

Sandy pulled her camera out of her bag. "Tío Jaime, would you mind if I interviewed you, and recorded it? With this?" She held up her tiny digital camera, wondering if he'd ever seen one.

He glanced at it, bemused. "Sure, m'ija. Do whatever you need to do."

Sandy set up as quickly as she could, not wanting to lose the mood. She decided against holding the camera and, instead, quickly propped it on her bag on the kitchen table, using the view finder to make sure that it kept Tío Jaime's face in frame. Once it was recording, she returned to their subject.

"So you're saying that it probably isn't really a chupacabra killing goats around here—that it's more likely a rabid dog or a drunken frat boy?"

Tío Jaime laughed again. He didn't look at the camera at all, but he did seem aware of it as he looked at Sandy. His voice picked up and there was an extra sparkle in his eye. "Hell, there's no chupacabras around here. If there's any chupacabra in this town, it might as well be *me.*" When he said this, his dog barked. Sandy quickly turned the camera to capture Cano watching them through the screen door, tail wagging and a dog smile on his face as if he were listening and enjoying his master's remarks. She panned back to Tío Jaime's face as he expounded, "No one pays me any mind out here. I could work all day, or I could keel over and die, for all anybody cared. I don't ask anyone for anything and nobody offers. But if I were to skip paying my property taxes *one time*, then the government would scream bloody murder, as if I was a monster stealing their goats in the middle of the night." He laughed grimly at his own idea and paused to take a sip of his lemonade. "They found a goat half eaten, half a mile away. Nobody knew whose it was or where it came from. Then someone said it must have been a chupacabra, and now we have the news out here. Well, I'll tell you…last time a goat came up missing, it belonged to one of the white ranchers out here, and the first person he suspected was me. I was the damned chupacabra that time, and the news came out here looking to do stories about illegal aliens hiding out in the sticks. I was the big monster—the evil mojado."

"Did they do a story about you? *Are* you an illegal alien?" Sandy asked.

"Nope. I got amnesty way back, twenty, thirty years ago. I took it when they offered it and became a U.S. citizen. I figured it was the least they could do for me, after all the years I worked here for less than minimum wage. I thought of it as a bonus, you know? A Christmas bonus for thirty years of faithful service. They came out here to find the evil goat-stealing chupacabra, but I had shifted my shape, and all they found was a harmless old man with his papers all in order."

Cano barked again and Sandy turned the camera again, wishing she could catch him in the act. Tío Jaime sipped his drink and fell into silence. Sandy prompted him, "Was it worth it, then?"

He took a moment to consider. "I guess so. In the end, it was. I have my land. I have my place here, whether people think I deserve it or not. I have a couple of spoiled nephews and nieces who live in the suburbs and play video games all day and wouldn't know hard work if it bit them on their soft behinds. I guess it's worth it, then, huh? That's the American dream they keep telling us about, right?" He looked right at the camera then, as if remembering it was there, and laughed. Sandy had to laugh along with him.

AN HOUR LATER, after Sandy had turned off her camera, she remembered her duty and pulled a fresh, blank release form from her bag.

"Tío Jaime, would you mind signing this?"

He took the piece of paper from her and held it at arm's length, squinting as if farsighted. "What is it?"

"A release form," Sandy said. "It's a document that you sign, showing that you give permission for me to use this film of you on our Web site." She reached into her bag again for a pen. The old man peered at the form and Sandy wondered if she should go over its clauses with him one by one. She didn't want to insult him by assuming that he couldn't read and understand them for himself. But before she could risk doing that, he handed the paper back to her.

"It's okay. You have my permission."

Sandy smiled. "Thank you. But, if you could just sign..."

Tío Jaime shook his head. "I don't need to sign. I trust you. You're going to put this stuff on your Web site. I don't know who'd want to look at it, but you can go ahead."

"But Tío Jaime, it's a little more than that. The form has a few details about you granting us the rights to use your image, and I need you to sign it before I can turn in my footage." Sandy handed it back to him hopefully.

The old man took it but, instead of signing, folded it in half and tucked it under his lemonade glass. "Well, I'll look at it, then. It's kind of hard for me to read it right now. If I decide to sign it, I can give it to you next time you visit."

Sandy sat back, deciding not to push it. She didn't blame him for wanting to read it carefully—a lot of people did—but got the impression that he was too proud to admit to her that his eyesight was poor. Maybe he preferred to wait for her to leave before pulling out his reading glasses, she thought. "Okay. I'll get it from you next time. If it's all right with you, though, I'd like to go ahead and turn in this interview to my editor when I get back to town. Is that okay?"

"Sure, m'ija, sure," he said. "I already told you—I trust you."

Relieved, Sandy smiled and took a sip of her lemonade. Now she could enjoy herself for a few moments before driving back to the office.

And, when she did drive back, she would turn in what she'd discovered about the chupacabra. And, she hoped, Angelica would love it.

22

Reader comments on Nacho Papi's Web Site, Friday, April 7

Who is this Chupacabra guy? He cracks me up!
JB

Word up, Chupacabra. Nobody gives a shit about Latinos until it's time to find somebody to do some hard work, or somebody to blame. Tell it like it is, hombre!
The Wild Juan

Who is this old man whining about getting free citizenship? He should be greatful. This is exactly the kind of crap post I've come to expect from politically ignorant Sandy S.
Boston Mike

Shut up, Boston Mike. More from the Chupacabra, please! He kicks it!
La Sirena

Yeah, more Chupacabra...and more Sandy S., too. Show us
your cute glasses again. I'd pay to see you in those glasses and
nothing else. ;)
Donny the Man

You'd better be careful, Donny. I'm pretty sure Sandy's spoken
for.
Michelle

23

Sandy scrolled through the comments on her Chupacabra interview and felt a little sick.

"It's great, isn't it?" Angelica had sneaked up behind her like a cat. She was even wearing a leopard-print top. "We've received nearly a thousand page views on that Chupacabra piece, and it's only been up for six hours."

"Where are they all coming from?" Sandy wondered aloud.

"Some followed links from our sister sites, and some followed links that we seeded elsewhere."

"Oh." Sandy hesitated, then ventured to say, "Somehow, I didn't think the comments would be about *me*." She was used to negative opinions from readers, of course; she'd gotten her share of crank e-mails while writing for LatinoNow. But this anonymous commenting on Nacho Papi was a whole new ball game for her. Especially now that the readers could see her online, in digital video.

Angelica leaned over Sandy's shoulder for a closer look at the computer screen. "Oh, that. Yes, that happens. Just ignore it. Don't take it personally. Listen, can you interview this Chupacabra character again? Make him a regular feature?"

Sandy nodded and Angelica sailed off to another corner of the office, leaving her alone with the comments of twenty-odd strangers. It was difficult *not* to take it personally, she thought. At least, she reminded herself, she wasn't using her legal name on the site. It was small comfort, but it helped to know that potential future employers wouldn't be able to search for Dominga Saavedra and find out that Boston Mike thought she was politically ignorant, or that Donny the Man wanted to see her naked.

LATER THAT DAY the mysterious Philippe finally put in his appearance. He walked in with Angelica, having come directly from the airport. He was explaining to her about a cancelled event and an issue with his living situation that had allowed him to leave California and fly into Austin early.

The first thing Sandy noticed about him was his extreme physical attractiveness. He was model handsome, practically. Tall, slim, and impeccably dressed. His hair was cropped very short, but, unlike George's, it wasn't only because he was starting to go bald. It looked like Philippe's curly hair was purposely cut short to show every inch of his face and the perfect shape of his head.

Sandy couldn't help wondering what kind of Latino he was. He was either a very light-skinned Dominican or a somewhat island-looking South American. Or, no, he was probably mixed, she decided. Filipino with Puerto Rican? Salvadoran with Samoan? Whatever the combination was, it had blended beautifully.

She and George were the only staff members in the office at the moment. Angelica introduced them, and Philippe shook their hands and expressed admiration for their work. "George, I really enjoyed your piece about the Minute Men taking on Chuck Norris. It was hilarious. Sandy, I admire your political commentary. And I *loved* your interview with the Chupacabra."

Sandy felt herself flush with pleasure as she took Philippe's hand. She liked this guy already.

"Yeah, it's nice meeting you, man," said George. "Can't wait to work with you. Angelica, I'm out of here. I'll talk to you guys later."

With that he made good on his word and left the office. Sandy looked at the clock. It was already six. Where had the time gone?

"Well." Philippe rubbed his hands together. "Which of you ladies wants to show me the best place around here to have a drink?"

Two HOURS LATER, Sandy was sitting next to Philippe on a velvet sofa at the Grenadine Lounge, in as deep a conversation as she would have had with Jane or Veronica, or with Daniel, if they ever had deep conversations anymore.

Angelica had joined them for one cocktail, and then left to fulfill a prior engagement. Sandy had enjoyed socializing with her boss, but she was enjoying herself even more now that Angelica was gone and Philippe could tell his stories about her.

"So Angelica told her, 'Leave your contact at the door, then. Because I can train you for the job, but not if you're going to spend all your time under my boss's desk.'"

"What? No *way!*" Sandy squealed.

"Oh, yes, she did." Philippe took a sip of his dirty martini and nodded. "You haven't seen yet how she can be. But wait until someone acts up."

"Oh, I believe it. We're all kind of scared of her already."

Philippe laughed. "You don't have to be *scared*. Just do your job well and you won't have to worry. You take care of business, and Angelica will take care of you."

"She gave me a makeover," Sandy quietly admitted.

He nodded again. "I could tell. Your look has her signature all over it. Plus she said you were born here in Austin, but you don't look like it now."

"Really?" Sandy laughed. It was true. All around them women wore flip-flops with their shorts or jeans, or, at the most formal, cotton sundresses. Sandy almost felt overdressed in her trousers and red patent flats. No, actually, she felt professional, like she had a career that encompassed more than the local scene. "You know, I was scared to death when she made me do it. I was afraid..."

"That you'd end up looking like her? With the big blond hair and long sharp nails?"

Sandy laughed again but lifted her cosmopolitan to her mouth so she wouldn't have to agree or disagree.

"That's her own personal style, and everyone who knows her expects her to rock it to the limits. But Angelica keeps up with the rest of the world, and if there's anything she knows how to do, it's build somebody's image. You should feel lucky she's taking an interest in you. You gave her good material to work with."

"Thanks." Sandy felt herself blush again, but completely innocently. Over the course of the evening

Philippe had dropped hints that he had at least one man waiting for him in the wings and, therefore, it'd be a waste of time for Sandy to get too revved up by his compliments. She'd had gay friends before, of course, and knew better than to fall for men who were so completely unavailable.

Nevertheless, she was having a really good time with him. Philippe was witty and chivalrous and full of good stories. She had the feeling, already, that they'd be friends.

"Are you getting tired of this place? It's kind of quiet here, isn't it?" he asked. "Let's go somewhere else, maybe get a bite to eat. Do you have to be up early tomorrow? Do you like to dance? Let me treat you— we'll call it research for my upcoming posts on Austin's nightlife."

"Sure." Sandy reached for her purse just in time to hear her phone ring. It was Daniel calling. She flipped her phone open and, after a second's hesitation, hit the Ignore button and let him roll to voice mail.

"Do you need to take that?" Philippe asked politely.

"No." Sandy put her phone back into her purse. "No, I can call him back later." She stood and smiled at Philippe brightly. "Come on. Let's ditch this dump and go have some fun."

They did have fun then. Sandy was embarrassed, at first, that she didn't know any place to go other than college hangouts. But they called Lori for suggestions and ended up at a much swankier lounge than Sandy would've ventured into on her own.

Then Philippe showed her a skill that she'd never learned in J school. "Can you help us out?" he asked their bartender politely. "We write for Levy Media—it's a national online entertainment syndicate—and we're working on a story about the best hangouts in all the major cities. Any suggestions?"

The bartender, a young man who looked like he was waiting to be discovered as the next *Top Pop Idol* contestant, giggled and chatted with them for a while after that before turning to another customer.

"Why'd you do that?" Sandy asked. "We can just ask Lori again if you want to go somewhere else."

"You'll see," said Philippe. In the blink of an eye their bartender was back with a round of shots.

"Here, you guys," he said. "On the house. Tell me more about your site. Are you going to cover South by Southwest? I have a band, and..."

And so it went, from club to club. Philippe had a knack not only for scoring free drinks, but also for promoting the Nacho Papi brand. People fell over themselves to give Philippe and Sandy their cards and suggest stories to them, and to make note of the site's name. "So they can check it tomorrow and see if we mention them," Philippe explained to Sandy later. "So be sure to give shout-outs to the people and places you really liked, and you'll be hooked up for life."

At one thirty they met up with Lori at her bar and had yet another free round. Then, at two, she punched out and joined them for an after-hours breakfast at a diner on South Congress. She and Philippe got along just as well as Sandy had known they would, and the three of them talked and laughed through many, many songs on the jukebox.

Sandy climbed the stairs to her apartment at four thirty in the morning, dead tired but elated by the instant memories of the most exhilarating night she'd had in months. She dutifully undressed and washed her face, but was too tired to transform her sofa into a bed and so fell asleep facedown on top of it.

On the coffee table, inside her purse, her phone kept up the weary flashing it'd repeated all night. One, two, three, four voice mails and text messages from Daniel. But Sandy had been too busy to notice, and was now deep in neon-lit dreams.

24

Girl, where in the hell have you been?"

That was Veronica, on Sandy's cell phone. Sandy took her macchiato and a bottle of water from the drive-through clerk of a chain coffee place before answering. She was hungover and didn't have the strength to endure her usual coffeehouse, Calypso, on a Saturday morning, when it would doubtless be crowded and noisy.

"I've been working. You know, running around looking for stories, like I always do."

"I guess," Veronica said, as if that didn't quite explain it. "I just haven't heard from you. I have to get online to find out what's going on. Oh, my God!" Her voice modulated up into a higher pitch here. "Sandy, *who* are these crazy people talking about you on Nacho Papi? About seeing you naked and stuff? Do you *know* them?"

Sandy winced at the shrillness of her friend's voice, and at the memory of the comments left by Donny the Man and others. She had pulled into the parking lot of an old-fashioned mall that no one ever visited because she couldn't drive, talk to Veronica, *and* drink coffee simultaneously. But she needed to drink the coffee immediately. So she sat behind the wheel of her parked car, enormous bug-eye sunglasses shielding her from the unmerciful mid-morning sun, and double-fisted her macchiato and water while using her shoulder to press the phone to her ear. A hundred feet away, the mall entrance sat sullen and dark. Sandy could just make out poster-board signs attached to the glass doors. They proclaimed "Say NO to GIGA-MART" and "Keep Austin WEIRD, DAMMIT!" It wasn't an inspiring scene.

"No, I don't know those people," she sighed into the phone. "They're just random people who read the site. Some of them are crazy, I guess."

"God, Sandy. Don't you worry about them seeing you on the videos and maybe stalking you or whatever?"

"No." Sandy took a long pull of water to counteract the dehydration caused by her hangover and espresso, and considered the question. "No. I mean, what's a stalker going to do? Follow me back and forth to work? Watch me type stuff on my laptop? He'd get bored after a while and go back home."

"I *guess*," Veronica said again. "What about your blog, though?"

"What about it?"

"Don't you worry that people will find out that it's you writing it, and they'll—I don't know—get jealous and kill Daniel or something?"

Sandy laughed. "Not even." But it made her stop, again, and imagine the potentials. "Why would anybody do that? They wouldn't even be able to figure out Daniel's real name, first of all. And I don't even talk about him that much. If anything, I'd be worried that a stranger would take pity on me and call my mom to tell her to get off my back." She laughed again at this thought.

"Well, I saw that you're not mad at Danny Boy anymore. That's good, huh?"

"You read that on my blog?" Sandy couldn't keep from sounding surprised. Veronica never mentioned her blog.

"Yeah. You know how I read Nacho Papi every morning, right after I read Hate-O-Rama. Then, after that, I like to go check on your blog and see if anything you're saying there relates to what you said on Nacho Papi. Kind of like getting the inside scoop, you know?"

"Well, you already have the inside scoop, right? Since you're my friend in real life and all?" Sandy didn't know whether to be amused or annoyed. It sounded as if Veronica hadn't been interested in her writing until it'd been validated with Hate-O-Rama's stamp of approval.

Veronica laughed. "Well, yeah, of course. But you know what I mean."

Sandy didn't, exactly, but she decided to let it go. She was probably overreacting because of the hangover, she told herself. So what if Veronica had only started reading her personal blog recently? At least she was reading it, which was more than Sandy could say for her other friends.

"Oh, hey, I wanted to tell you. I have a huge show coming up. June ninth. Can you come?"

"That's two months from now," Sandy pointed out. There was a pause, and Sandy realized that Veronica was expecting her simply to say yes. "I mean, yeah. I'll be there. Where's it going to be?" Most of Veronica's shows were at restaurants and coffee shops. They'd let her display her art there, usually with other people's, and then hold little "openings" that were basically excuses to sell food and coffee to the artists and their friends. It wasn't exactly the big time, but Veronica had sold a few of her collages at those things and was gradually building a fan base in the Dallas area.

"This is a really *big* show. There's a new gallery opening up in Oak Cliff, and my boss knows the owner, and
he got me in!" Her voice pitched higher again. "It's a real
gallery, Sandy! With real art! I get to show my stuff there
for six weeks!"

Veronica's enthusiasm was contagious. Sandy was glad
to hear she was finally catching a good break. "That's
awesome, V. That rocks. I can't wait."

Sandy made a mental note. She'd put Veronica's show
on her calendar first thing, then cross her fingers that
Angelica wouldn't have something more important for
her to do that night.

25

Post from Nacho Papi's Web Site

Selling Out and Selling Back In
by Sandy S.

Shawna Douglas has just joined the list of undercover Latinas who've decided to come out of the closet in the hope of making money. On the cover of her new reggaeton [This should be italicized, I think—DT] album, "Todo Mi Cuerpo," [This should be italicized as well as in quotes—DT] Douglas writes:

> The album title means All of My Body, but I want this
> album to reflect all of my mind and soul, too. Not just
> the black part of me but my Ecuadorian heritage, as well,
> which I have always cherished but which my fans haven't
> yet gotten to appreciate. I hope you enjoy this new me.
> [This quote is a little vapid and doesn't present the subject
> in a flattering light. Maybe find another quote?—DT]

Bravissima, Shawna. Way to cash in. Not since Linda Ronstadt's "Canciones de Mi Padre" (which translates to "Finally, Being Mexican is Marketable") has anyone so blatantly de-cloaked for dollars. [On the whole, this piece is clearly written, but slightly inflammatory. Watch tone.—DT]

26

They were back at Samurai Noodles, but this time Sandy was trying the tuna and Daniel was eating a bowl of fried rice. He picked out and set aside everything in his bowl except the rice itself while waiting for her to read the edits he'd made on her post. He kept grinning at her, as if he were being an especially good boyfriend who deserved some recognition, if not an outright reward.

Sandy read the first few pages—there were about ten, total—and then had to stop because her temper was rising. "I don't get it."

"What? The part about the tone being inflammatory?"

"No." Sandy felt herself losing patience. "That's the part *you* didn't get. The tone of the whole site is inflammatory. It's supposed to be. That's what readers expect from us. Didn't you read their comments on this piece?"

"No. I didn't have time to read the comments. I only printed and read your posts." He added in a defensive murmur, "I barely had time to do that."

"Well, I don't know what you expect me to do with this. The piece has been online for a week, and, last time I checked it had almost thirty comments from people who obviously enjoyed reading it. You didn't see that my tone is right in line with the rest of Nacho Papi, and you didn't notice that we don't italicize Spanish on the site at all because it's supposed to be bilingual. You didn't even say whether you *liked* the piece." The words came hurtling out of Sandy's mouth. She paused for breath, then added, "You know what, Daniel? If you couldn't say something nice, maybe you shouldn't have said anything at all."

Daniel sat up indignantly, spilling a little rice from his fork onto his shirt in the process. "Oh, right, I shouldn't have said anything. Sure. With you giving me the silent treatment for weeks now, and then oh-so-casually asking if I've read your latest post, every time we talk? You know, Sandy, I'm really busy at the university. I know you don't think so, because you don't really take an interest in what I do there, but you could at least appreciate that I took the time to comment on your work. That"—he pointed to the pages in her hands—"is more than I'd do for my best students."

"Oh, so you spend more time on me than you spend on your best students? Wow, Daniel, that's great. I would *think* you'd spend more time on your own girlfriend. What'd you do—stay home one night from drinking beer with your friends?" Sandy felt her blood race hot and saw that diners around them were starting to glance in their direction. But she couldn't stop. She had more to say, built up for a long time now. "You know, when I think of all the times I read your work and strained myself to come up with constructive comments on the spur of the moment…And now you're acting like it's some big sacrifice to return the favor. That's really selfish of you, Daniel. Really self-centered."

Daniel never got hot-angry, like she sometimes did. Instead, he got cold-angry. He had the cold expression on his face now. When he spoke, calmly and quietly, she could tell he was also somewhat hurt. "I didn't realize it was such a 'strain' for you to read my work. I apologize for that. I won't put you through the trouble anymore. But I hope you understand that my writing is my career, so it's a little different."

At this, Sandy became so upset that she literally bit into her tongue trying to keep from yelling at him outright while everyone at Samurai Noodles watched. Instead she stood and said, "Well, my writing is my career, too, whether you think it's as important as yours or not."

With that, she gathered her things and left, leaving his printed pages behind her.

THE LAST THING Sandy was in the mood for, when she got home that day, was a long conversation with, and questions from, her mother. And yet that's what she got.

"Oh, Sandy, guess what." Mrs. Saavedra apprehended Sandy as she emerged from her car with purse and work bag dangling from her shoulders. Sandy only raised her eyebrows in answer. She was too tired to respond, having spent the five hours since her argument with Daniel sitting in the Nacho Papi office maniacally typing toward deadlines. Her mother continued talking, oblivious. "It turns out Aunt Ruby does know about this Tío Jaime, after all. She said she's met him a couple of times, but do you know that Aunt Linda would never say what was going on between them? Can you imagine? Isn't that crazy?"

"Yeah." Sandy was relieved to hear that her other great-aunt knew Tío Jaime. Somehow that made him almost family. Therefore, he'd be willing to help her out with her work by consenting to be interviewed. She wouldn't have to worry, then, about the possibility of him refusing to sign the release form. At least that's what she hoped her mother's words meant.

Sandy turned to the garage stairs and the relative serenity of her apartment, but her mother protested. "Aren't you going to come in for a little bit?"

Sandy sighed. "Can I go up and change first? I'm really tired."

"Why, what happened?" her mother was quick to ask. "Did anything happen at work today? Did your father call you?"

"What?" At this unexpected question Sandy turned back to her mother. "No. Why? Did he call you?"

"He left me a voice mail. I guess you know that he's finally gotten engaged to that skinny girlfriend of his."

"What?" Sandy practically bellowed. She hadn't known. She'd had no idea.

"Oh," said her mother, whose distaste-filled expression stood in sharp contrast to Sandy's surprise. "Well, sorry. Why don't you call him tonight, in that case? Then come down and tell me everything he says. I can't believe he's doing this. He's such a bastard."

Sandy turned and hit the garage stairs with a stomp. But it wasn't the phone that she turned to when she got to her room.

27

Blog entry from *My Modern TragiComedy*, Sunday, April 9

That's it.

The last time I posted here, I retracted the ranting I'd done about my boyfriend.

But now I see that I was right the first time, and that he's the wrong man for me. It is with regret that I inform you that HeartThrob GeekBoy and I are through. I just can't deal with it anymore.

Let's change the subject, please

to another one that's just as annoying, actually. My mother has pissed me off so badly that I don't even know what to do about it, short of moving to another city.

And you know what? My father's pissing me off, too. He's getting re-married and didn't see fit to tell me. My mother told me, but in terms of how embarrassing it was to her, not with any consideration of how I might feel, seeing as how I'm his daughter and—hello!—as previously explained, he didn't tell me.

I'm tired of the two of them living in their own petty worlds, doing things to spite each other and never worrying about the effect it might have on their own daughter. I don't know why it surprises me every time, though, seeing as how that's how they behaved when they were married and all throughout their divorce. But it still hurts. It makes me feel like I'm nothing. You know? Like I can only rely on myself.

Luckily, I know that I am more than just nothing. I have my writing career and all the success that's come with it lately, even if my parents and my boyfriend are too self-involved to notice or care.

It's just you and me, then, readers. Thanks for being here for me for so long.

Love,
Miss TragiComic Texas

28

Two nights later, Sandy waited in Daniel's bedroom while he went to get her a glass of water. She hadn't actually wanted anything, but she'd accepted his offer so that, while he was in the kitchen, she'd have more time to plan what she was about to say. She hadn't expected his housemate to be home, either. Matt was watching television in their shared living room, which left Sandy to do her talking in Daniel's bedroom—not the ideal place for a breakup. But it was now or never. She'd already said on her blog that it was over, and now she had to follow through.

He walked in carrying the University of Texas Longhorns coffee mug she'd always hated, not saying anything or even looking at her as she stood by his bed. "Would you close the door behind you?" she said.

He did and then set the mug on his nightstand, using a folded envelope for a coaster. He looked nervous. Sandy wondered if he knew what was coming.

"Daniel, we need to talk."

"I know. That's what you said on the phone. That's why we're here, isn't it?" His testy tone made her suspect more than ever that he already knew.

"Well, I guess you realize that things between us have been kind of...strained lately."

"Is that was it is? Strained?" He practically snarled it at her. This was going to be difficult, Sandy thought. He knew, and he was upset. She hadn't exactly pictured an ideal way to do this, but in her imagination he'd been more shocked and sad and less obviously angry.

"Yes. All we do lately is argue, or else try to avoid arguing. And...I just feel like, ever since I've started this new writing job..."

"What? I haven't been supportive enough?" Daniel crossed his arms and took what Sandy couldn't help but see as a childishly defensive stance. He acted like he already knew what she was going to say even before she did, and yet he was ready to deny it. She wanted to take a step back, but couldn't because she was already standing against his twin bed. If she hadn't been the one caught in this situation, it might have been funny, it was so ridiculous.

"Well, yeah. You haven't been supportive, and it makes me unhappy, but there's nothing I can do to change your mind about it, and I don't want to quit writing for Nacho Papi. And I know how you feel about it, so I can't be around you without being aware of your feelings. How you feel about me, for what I'm doing." Sandy strained to speak calmly and state her case without emotion.

"Oh, okay—so it's *my* fault because I was honest with you, like you wanted me to be?" His words were shaky, with more than just anger. "I guess I should have pretended to think this stupid Web site was great, so you'd be happy? So we wouldn't be at this point now, having this 'talk' about our relationship? It's all my fault, is that it?"

Sandy became afraid that he was about to cry, and

then felt teary-eyed herself. "No," she said. "I'm not saying it's your fault, or that you should have said anything different. I'm just telling you, I think we've grown apart. We want different things out of life, and we can't expect each other to change our lives to conform with the other person's ideals."

Sandy stopped talking. The first tear had rolled down Daniel's cheek, and her first tear wasn't far behind. She wished, suddenly, that she hadn't started this. It was way more difficult than she'd expected.

"Okay, well, just stop right there." He started talking loud and fast, words spilling out of his mouth like he was trying to keep her from interrupting. "Because I need to talk now. You're saying all this stuff about me conforming to your ideals, and me not being honest, and you can stop right there, because I've been having some problems with you, too. I haven't wanted to say it, because I didn't want to hurt your feelings, but you haven't exactly been the ideal girlfriend lately, either."

Sandy started in surprise. She opened her mouth, but Daniel didn't let her speak. He became louder. "One, you're always rude to my friends. And they notice. And I'm tired of it, and I can't cover for you anymore. Two, *you're* the one who's not supportive of *me*. You've never liked my writing, and it's pretty obvious, and I don't really appreciate your lack of honesty about it. And, three, yes, your writing for that site embarrasses me. My friends have been talking about it. I didn't want to tell you, but now you're forcing me. Yes, it's embarrassing, and I wish you wouldn't do it, but you don't care about my feelings, so I think we should break up."

He finished practically on a shout that Sandy knew Matt would be able to hear from the other room. Tears were streaming down her face now, but they were tears of anger. She couldn't believe he was making these accusations. She knew he was only saying these things because his feelings were hurt. But still, he was hurting her now, on purpose. And he was trying to break up with her before she could break up with him. It was obvious.

And she was glad now. She felt like she was seeing his true colors, in all their ugly, mismatched glory.

"Oh, and another thing—we never have sex when I want to," he blurted. "And you're…you're not good in bed."

At this, Sandy finally blew her top. "You know what, Daniel? I felt bad about coming here to break up with you, but now I don't. Thanks for being a complete asshole about everything and making me realize that I should have dumped you a long time ago." She turned and walked to the door. He stood there frozen, arms still crossed on his chest and the frightening sneer still on his face. Sandy gave him one last look and decided against saying anything else. She opened his bedroom door, went through, and slammed it behind her.

Matt jumped in surprise as she walked through the living room. He had the TV on mute and had obviously been eavesdropping. But Sandy didn't care.

She exited the apartment without another word, leaving it for the last time. And it was a relief. She was bitterly happy that she'd never have to be there again.

29

The worst part about breaking up, Sandy found herself thinking the Sunday after the break up she had initiated, wasn't that she missed Daniel. She didn't, at all.

As she drove south on I-35, back toward the scene of the Chupacabra to interview the man himself, Sandy mused over the past weekend. It wasn't that she missed Daniel's conversation, or his lack of it, or the mediocre sex. It was that now she didn't know what to do with all her spare time. And not because she'd spent so much of it with Daniel before, either. But she'd devoted a lot of time to him, so to speak. Waiting for him to meet up with her. Waiting to hear what his plans were before she could make her own. Waiting for his opinion before she could make a decision.

Saturday, the day before, for instance, she'd felt burned out and didn't think she could write one more word—not for Angelica, not for QBS, not even for her blog. So she'd gone to the bookstore. Through force of habit, she'd started with the literary fiction, picking up titles by the same authors she always sought. After a few minutes of this, she'd realized that she wasn't enjoying herself, one, and that, two, it was because most of the authors she read had been introduced to her by Daniel.

Feeling rebellious, she'd gone back to the front of the store where the brighter-colored selections were piled on tables. As she perused the popular novels, she imagined Daniel disapproving. "A little lowbrow, don't you think?" he'd say. Or "Sandy, *please*."

She'd ended up curled in a chair, devouring something Daniel would never approve of: a romance about a plus-sized Latina vampire who had fallen in love with a disabled African-American werewolf from the wrong side of the tracks.

In the end, she'd left the romance at the store and gone home with slightly more serious stories. But it'd felt good at the time, indulging in something that wasn't on Mister MFA's recommended reading list.

Sandy took the turnoff that led to the middle of nowhere. Having this Daniel-shaped space in her life to fill, she reflected, wasn't the worst problem a girl could have. Not by a long shot.

As she neared Tío Jaime's house, she slowed down to make sure she wouldn't miss her turn amongst the masses of cacti that bordered mini-forests of scraggly trees. She was going back to interview the old man, this time with questions from readers. Her plan was to do a feature called "Ask the Chupacabra," sort of a video advice column. Tío Jaime's first video interview was one of the site's most popular posts to date. Angelica loved Sandy's advice column idea and was already talking about building it into something more—something they could sell.

Thinking of Angelica made Sandy remember that she needed to get Tío Jaime's signed release form. She made a mental note to ask him for it as soon as she got to his house.

When Sandy drove up, the old man was walking out from behind the house in his usual uniform of jeans, plaid shirt, and straw hat—with a shovel in his hand. He recognized her car immediately, again, and waved hello. Sandy waved back.

After exchanging pleasantries and small talk about the weather, the goats, and Cano's diet, Sandy cut to the chase. "Tío Jaime, my boss really liked that last interview I did with you, and so did our readers. I was wondering if you'd be interested in doing another."

The old man squinted into the distance with a slight frown on his face. "You know, m'ija, I'd really like to, but…"

Now Sandy frowned. Here it was. He was going to say no. He was going to say he wished he hadn't done the first one.

"…but I have so much work to do while it's still light outside, and I don't think I'll have time to do it all if I sit around talking for an hour. You know?"

Sandy did know. Suddenly she felt guilty about show-ing up in the middle of the day and imposing on Tío Jaime in this way. It'd been very presumptuous of her to assume he'd have nothing better to do.

He turned to look at her. "Unless…"

"Unless?"

"Maybe you could help me?"

The next thing she knew, Sandy was behind Tío Jaime's house helping him dig holes and stuff tomato and chili pepper plants into the ground. He said he didn't mind shoveling, but that bending down hurt his back. After a few rounds of planting, Sandy knew what he meant. Feeling lucky that she'd worn jeans and flats that day, she kneeled on the ground so he wouldn't have to. Then she plugged four-inch blocks of dirt into the ground until her fingernails turned black and her hair stuck to the perspiration on her face. "Tío Jaime," she finally said, "how many tomatoes and chili peppers do you *need*?"

"Oh, not that many," he said. "But I like to grow extra and give them to Mrs. Sanchez down the road. She makes them into picante sauce and gives me a few jars every year."

By the time they were done and Tío Jaime had led her into the kitchen to wash her hands, Sandy felt like she had literally earned the right to interview him again. He seemed to concur, because he asked if she was ready with her questions.

"Do you mind if we record outside this time?" she asked. "The porch makes a better background, I think."

"Whatever you need to do, m'ija."

They moved one of the kitchen chairs out next to the bench on his porch and Sandy set up her camera so that the sun was behind it.

"Tío Jaime, like I was telling you earlier, the readers really liked your first interview." He smiled at this, completely bemused. "I didn't tell them your real name, but we're calling you the Chupacabra." At this, the old man laughed aloud. "So now we want to do a feature called 'Ask the Chupacabra.' The readers send in questions, and you answer them."

"Well, I don't know what they could ask that I would know the answer to," said Tío Jaime. "I'm just an old man ranching goats. I never went to college or anything."

"No, don't worry about that. I'll just ask, and you answer naturally with the first thing that comes to mind, and if you don't feel comfortable we'll stop. Does that sound okay?"

He smiled and shrugged. Encouraged, Sandy pressed Record on her camera and began. "Okay, first question. This is from a man calling himself the Wild Juan. The question is, 'What do chupacabras eat?'"

"Well, that's dumb," said Tío Jaime. "They eat goats." After a pause, he added, "Goat tacos, with chile and lime. And preferably a Tecate on the side, also with lime. Next question."

"Next one's from La Sirena, and it has two parts. One, she asks if chupacabras get married. Two, she asks, if she and her boyfriend have been living together for five years and he hasn't proposed yet, should she wait around any longer?"

Tío Jaime sat back and looked into the distance. By his side, Cano came to attention and waved his tail attentively. "Well, not only do chupacabras get married, but sometimes they get divorced, too. As for this woman's boyfriend, I'd have to know more about the situation. I guess I'd have to ask what *she's* waiting for." There was a pause, and Sandy wondered if he was consciously putting in dramatic timing or just thinking up what to say next. The Chupacabra continued. "If he's been living with her for five years, obviously he's too lazy to go out and find anybody else. It sounds like he's just waiting for her to get good and mad and force him to pop the question. That way, if it doesn't work out, he can always blame her and say it was her idea. So, the *real* question is, does she want to marry a man who's lazy and doesn't take responsibility for his actions? If so, she should start nagging him right away."

This time, Sandy turned the camera right in time to catch Cano bark his agreement. She smiled to herself as she pulled up the next question. Her readers were going to love this interview.

AFTER THEY WERE done recording and Tío Jaime had served them another glass of lemonade, Sandy asked if he needed any more help around his property. She didn't want to do any more physical labor but felt that it was the least she could offer, considering that he was helping her to do her job.

"No, m'ija, not right now. But come back in a week and you can help me weed that garden."

Sandy said she would. A slight breeze blew by and lifted her hair. Strangely, the otherwise hot and still day had become breezy on Tío Jaime's property. Next to them on the porch, Cano had surrendered to the impulse to take a quick nap. His nose made little whistling sounds in time with the rise and fall of his ribs as he slept. Sandy wondered if she should leave and let the old man get back to his work. But he seemed content to sit there quietly with her, and she felt content that way, too. It was peaceful, here on his porch. In a little while she'd have to get up and drive back into town and back to work. But not yet.

"You know, you remind me of your aunt in some ways. Your great-aunt, I mean."

Sandy knew he meant Aunt Linda. She waited to hear what else he'd say.

"You have a profile sort of like hers, and you remind me of her when you smile. Plus, you know, she was a writer, too."

"She was?"

"Yes. In fact, I thought when you and your mother came here, you would see…"

He stopped talking and Sandy turned to see what had caught his attention. It was a black car pulling into the long, dusty drive. A black BMW, in fact. Sandy watched curiously as it rolled across the gravel.

"Oh, good. You'll get to meet Richard," Tío Jaime said. "I didn't think he'd be here so soon."

Before Sandy could ask who Richard was, the man

himself stopped his engine and emerged from the car. He wore a disassembled suit: pinstriped pants and a white shirt with collar and silk tie pulled free from his neck. He was a good-looking young man with thick black hair and black eyebrows to match, a nice firm chin, not too short—but Sandy noted that he looked upset. Or uptight. Or just plain uppity, maybe. Like a self-important politician. Or maybe like a lawyer. Yes, a lawyer, she thought. And then she was even more curious. She and Tío Jaime stood to meet him.

"Sandy, this is my nephew, Richard," Tío Jaime said. "He's a lawyer. He's here to visit me from California. Richard, this is Sandy. She's Linda's niece's daughter. You remember Linda."

"Pleased to meet you," Richard said, taking Sandy's hand and looking at her suspiciously. "Tío Jaime, are you busy? Should I come back later?" He looked at them as if wondering what they could possibly be doing. As if he'd caught Sandy in the act of preying on his elderly uncle in some way while sitting there drinking lemonade.

"No, stay. Sit down with us. We're just talking. Do you want some lemonade?" His uncle turned toward the door, but Sandy turned to go.

"Actually, Tío Jaime, I need to be going now. I have to get back."

"Back?" Richard asked.

"Back to Austin," Sandy said. "Back to work."

"Oh? Where do you work?"

Sandy paused, wondering how she could explain it quickly without exciting more suspicion from this uptight, suspicious-seeming lawyer. But Tío Jaime answered for her. "She's a writer. She's been interviewing me."

"Oh, really? About what?" The nephew's voice was all charm, but Sandy could just tell that he had a temper and that he probably didn't have the sense of humor to understand what she'd been doing.

"Um . . . about local legends. Chupacabras." She smiled weakly and Richard raised his eyebrow. "And about his life experience, living here on this land, and about his friendship with my great-aunt."

At this, Richard's eyebrow went even higher and he turned to his uncle for confirmation. Sandy hoped Tío Jaime would go along with her version of the facts. He said, "I was telling Sandy about how Linda used to write. And she helped me put in the chile and tomatoes, so you don't have to do that now. You're not dressed for it, anyway."

At this Richard looked down at his outfit in mild chagrin, as if the last thing he'd expected to do that day was manual labor. Tío Jaime crossed over to Sandy and gave her a hug. "All right, m'ija. Go back to work. I'll see you next week, okay? Wear some stronger shoes."

Sandy said goodbye to them both and hightailed it out of there with her bag and the camera it carried, feeling like she was escaping with stolen treasure. Her Malibu blew puffs of dust at the BMW as she pivoted in the gravelly yard and then drove away.

She had a feeling of foreboding as she headed back to town. How long, she found herself wondering, would Nephew Richard be in town?

It wasn't until she was miles away that she remembered the release form, and the fact that she still hadn't gotten it signed.

30

They were at a party in Atlanta, and Sandy didn't even know why. She stood with Lori and twenty other people in a blurry line around a fountain that emitted Toro vodka from the mouth of a bucking metal bull. Lori held a plastic cup with two fingers of cranberry juice and was waiting to top it off. Sandy still hadn't finished the dirty martini in her hand. Loud rock-and-rap music blasted from the speakers of the DJ on the other side of the warehouse-like club. All around them suited men and sparkle-sheathed women jostled against each other to the beat.

A young woman wearing red shorts, a red bikini top, and red bull horns in her long black hair walked up bearing a lighted tray of colorful test tubes.

"Shot? Shot?" she offered, smiling at each of the party guests in turn.

"What do you have?" Lori shouted, then leaned in to hear the girl's answer.

"Toro Berry, Tropi-Toro, Pom-Toro, and Buttery Toro Nipples," the shot girl shouted back.

"Mm! Two Buttery Toro Nipples, please!"

Lori reached into her pocket and retrieved a ten-dollar bill, but the girl shook her head. All drinks were on the house. Lori winked at her and tucked the ten into her bikini top before accepting the test tubes. The girl gave Lori her first genuine smile.

"Want one?" Lori offered the test tube to Sandy, who shook her head.

"Can't. I'm still working on this."

Lori shrugged, downed both shots in succession, then replaced the test tubes on the girl's tray, upside down. The girl glided away. Sandy couldn't help wondering if it made sense for her to be wearing those horns. Did female cows have horns too, or only bulls? She brushed the ridiculous thought from her mind. What did it matter?

Lori yelled "Woo!" for no reason that Sandy could see. But several of the men who'd been watching her yelled back, as if in approval.

They were jostled up to the Toro fountain. Lori filled her cup and said, "Come on. Back this way." She threw smiles and winks to the men still waiting as she and Sandy departed for another corner of the warehouse.

Angelica had given them this assignment, along with their plane tickets, the day before. She'd said simply that they'd been invited to this party, and that Toro vodka was considering purchasing a sponsorship package from Nacho Papi.

"Should we take our cameras, then?" Sandy had asked. "Or is there anything in particular you want us to cover at the party?"

"Not necessarily," Angelica had replied. "Just go and have a good time. But be ready to write about it, just in case."

Sandy, Lori, Philippe, and George had arrived in Atlanta at 5 P.M., right in the middle of a Thursday rush hour. They'd cabbed it to a café Philippe knew near the center of town and had then taken another cab to their hotel to check in and prepare for the party. Sandy put on a white tube dress from an Austin boutique owner who'd sold it to her at a deep discount in the hopes of seeing Sandy wear it on the Internet.

"You're lucky you can wear white. And a strapless bra," Lori had said as they dressed in their shared room. "I'd look like a giant freak monster in that dress." She was wearing a black backless number from her own collection. It showed off her tiger tattoo.

In the middle of the party room there was a series of high, circular stages on which girls danced in various costumes—cheerleader, schoolgirl, referee—all with the red bull horns on their heads.

"This is so nineties," a familiar voice said behind Sandy. She turned to see that Philippe had joined them. As usual, he made her laugh and feel a little more comfortable. She had no way of knowing whether he was right; she'd spent the tail end of the nineties in pubs and coffeehouses and had never been to a party like this. But now that Philippe said it, she could totally imagine that this scene was already passé.

"At least it's open bar," said Lori, who was now finishing the contents of her plastic cup. Sandy knew from happy-hour experiences during the LatinoNow days that Lori could drink way, way more than that, the only result being that she'd act even perkier than she had before. Sandy, however, had to intersperse her cocktails with water and food to keep from blacking out. That was another thing she'd learned at UT.

Philippe led them to a side room Sandy hadn't noticed before. They'd arrived at the party at 11 P.M. and it was 2:45 now, Sandy noted by glancing at Philippe's elegant TAG Heuer watch.

Inside the much smaller but still large room, there

was quieter but still loud music piped in through hidden speakers, and low, plush seats everywhere. It was a sort of lounge, Sandy saw, and people were definitely lounging in it. A woman lay with her blond hair spread out on a round, oversized leather ottoman, her dress barely hanging on to her body, seemingly asleep with a smile on her face. Next to her, two men sat in earnest conversation, one of them idly stroking her hair, as if she were a pet.

On a fur sofa in the far corner, not even very much in the dark, a couple made out languorously. Sandy noted this and then turned her eyes elsewhere. But they weren't the only ones.

She and Lori followed Philippe to a group of satin settees where two men and a woman, apparently acquaintances of his, were talking with bored expressions. Philippe introduced everyone and they all took seats, Sandy ending up on the outside of the circle.

"Who is that up there?" Philippe asked one of the men, whose name Sandy hadn't understood.

"No idea. Isn't it sad? I thought they were going to get Sergio, but he left for Ibiza at the last minute."

"He looks terrible," one of the women said. Sandy didn't know who they were talking about—Sergio in Ibiza, or whoever it was "up there."

"Wait. Sergio, as in DJ Thirty-One Flavors?" Lori said.

Philippe and his friends nodded.

"Oh my God!" Lori's slight Texas drawl made Sandy notice that none of these Atlanta people had accents. They all talked like people on TV, just like Philippe. She wondered if they'd look down on her friend for that. But Lori went on, "Thank God he isn't here—he hates me."

"Ex-boyfriend?" one of the men asked, as if he couldn't care less.

"God, no," said Lori. "But he was living with Josie, who owns Glass Tangerine, and I was dating *her*, like three years ago. So he showed up at the bar where I was working at the time and threw a bottle of Goose at me. It was so *wrong*."

The others had leaned forward in interest. "I thought I recognized you!" said the woman. "You were on Sailor Girls, with Rachel and Abby. Right?"

"Right," said Lori. "But that was, like, forever ago."

Obviously, everyone else sitting there had a working knowledge of all the proper nouns being used. But Sandy had no idea. Subsequently, she began to space out, looking around the room and taking in the details. The blond who'd been asleep was now sitting up and asking for water. The make-out couple was now rising to leave, probably to escape to someplace more private. A young woman standing near them was offering something to her friends. It was a brown pill bottle, like the ones from the pharmacy, Sandy saw.

As if on cue, the Atlanta woman sitting with them and now listening in fascination to Lori's stories lifted her silver clutch and took out what looked like an aspirin container. But Sandy knew that what she offered them next probably wasn't aspirin. One of the men took a pill, and so did Lori. Philippe shook his head politely, saying "Can't. Antibiotics." Sandy followed his lead, smiling and saying only "No, thanks."

Now one of the men started sharing gossip about someone else Sandy had never heard of, and she decided not to stick around any longer. She turned to Philippe and whispered, "Rest room?" He indicated with a wave that it was back in the warehouse somewhere. Sandy took that as her excuse to set down her martini and leave the group. None of them seemed to notice.

Back in the big room, which sounded so much louder to her now, Sandy looked for the ladies' room in earnest. By the time she found it she really did have to go. She burst through the door, which had a female Precious Moments figurine glued to it, crossed the dingy floor, and pushed open the first unlocked stall. Unfortunately, it wasn't vacant. Two women looked up blearily from the white line of powder that was balanced on one of their forearms.

"Oops! Sorry!" Sandy let the door bang closed again and left the rest room just as quickly as she'd entered it.

Back in the warehouse she saw that the circulating shot girls had gotten rid of their trays and were now offering bottles of Pure NRG water. The Toro fountain had been turned off, leaving the metal bull dribbling. The lights above the bars were dimmed, indicating that the party was ending, but no one had told that to the DJ or the crowd around him. Young women danced with young men who'd removed their jackets and ties. Older men stood along the walls and watched the young women. The DJ who wasn't Sergio had the party guests yelling and raising their hands at his command. Sandy stood and watched for a while, but remained uncompelled to move along with the crowd.

"Boring, huh?" an unfamiliar voice said at her side. She turned and saw a guy with his tie loosened and jacket still on. He had a nice smile.

"Yeah, it is, kind of."

"I'm Jeremy," he said. "I'm with Ad Reps."

She recognized the name from press releases she'd been seeing since her LatinoNow days. He was in marketing, then. "Oh, I know Ad Reps. I'm Sandy. I write for Nacho Papi."

"Oh, hey. Isn't that one of the Levy Media sites? I'm impressed."

His smile seemed genuine, and Sandy was struck by how good it felt to be recognized for her talent. There were only a few select people writing for Levy Media, and she was one of them. Hell, yes, people should be impressed, Sandy thought. Not everything had to be judged by Daniel's snotty "literary" standards. For the tenth time that week alone, she congratulated herself for having dumped him.

"Can I get you a drink?" Jeremy from Ad Reps asked her.

Sandy looked around. "Probably not. Looks like they're closing everything down."

"You're right." He looked around. "Do you want to dance?"

She didn't. "I'd rather just talk. Is there someplace we can..." She wanted to sit down for a while and get off the high heels that were starting to pinch her toes, but there were no chairs in sight. She didn't want to go back to the drug lounge.

"I think there's a deck or something," Jeremy said.

"Yeah, there is. It's that way." George had walked up behind them and was pointing in the direction from which he'd come. "Hi. I'm George Cantu. Levy Media." He held out his hand to Jeremy, who shook it and re-introduced himself. "So, Jeremy, what's going on at Ad Reps? How's business?"

"Not bad," Jeremy said politely. His smile didn't waver, but Sandy could see that he didn't want to talk to George. George, however, was firmly planted next to Sandy now and seemed in no hurry to leave or to take a hint.

"Well, Sandy, I have to go." He reached into his pocket and, in one smooth motion, pulled out two cards and handed her the first. "It was good talking to you. Why don't you give me a call? George." He handed George a card with a nod, then disappeared.

"What was he, trying to pitch a story to you?" said George, taking a sip from the sweaty bottle of Bud Light in his hand. Without waiting for Sandy's answer, he went on. "This is getting boring. No opportunity anywhere."

Sandy didn't know what he meant. Was he talking about stories or business deals, or was he admitting to her that his attempts to hit on the Toro girls had failed? She'd been about to snap at him for driving off the man she'd been talking to, but the dumb way he stood there, completely oblivious, made her realize that he hadn't even done so maliciously. He simply was *that* self-involved.

"Where are the others?" he asked.

"Uh, I don't know." Sandy didn't feel like explaining what was going on in the other room.

"Hmm." He took another drink of his beer, and then walked away just as abruptly as he'd shown up.

Sandy looked around for Jeremy, but he'd melted away into the crowd.

"Put your hands up in the air *again!*" the DJ shouted into his microphone. He was starting to give Sandy a headache. She moved away from the crowd, toward the wall that didn't have the hidden room, opposite the entrance, thinking that the deck had to be in that direction. She passed shot girls counting their tips and janitors scooping empty cups into trash bags, and did eventually find a glass door leading to a second-story deck. There was a uniformed security guard waiting right outside the door. "No drinks outside," he told her gruffly. She showed him her empty hands and he nodded. She walked out among benches and tables made of the same wood as the deck, some occupied by couples in conversation. The rail that edged this overgrown balcony was surrounded by the tallest magnolia trees Sandy had ever seen. The wind was starting to cool, but it felt good after the stuffiness of the club. She leaned against the railing and looked out. Below her, the street was peppered with people who'd recently left the nearby bars and hotels. Above her were the stars that'd been strong enough to shine through the dusty, lamp-lit air.

She stood there alone for quite a while, thinking about everything that'd been happening to her lately. If you'd asked her a year ago, or even a month ago, what she'd be doing today, she definitely wouldn't have said "Drinking free liquor in an expensive gown, at a party in another city." And yet that was what she was doing.

Her phone buzzed within the little bag strapped to her wrist, indicating that it was time to return. "Duty calls," she told herself. Philippe would probably take them to another club or restaurant. Sandy sighed. It was tiring being fabulous for a living. But she wasn't about to trade it for the future she would have imagined a year ago.

31

Post on Nacho Papi's Web Site, Monday, April 24

Can someone get me some coffee?
by Philippe

What a weekend, kittens. Your faithful servants, Lori, Sandy S., George and myself, were completely caught up in a social whirlwind. From the Miscreant Show in Dallas to the Toro Vodka bash in Atlanta to the grand opening of Cova right here in our own backyard, we covered all the important happenings so you wouldn't have to. And, if you haven't yet seen Lori and Sandy in eveningwear, I have to tell you that you're missing out. Oh, wait—no you aren't. See pictures, below.

READER COMMENTS ON **CAN SOMEONE GET ME SOME COFFEE?**

God, seeing those pictures makes me wish I had been there. I'm so jealous of all those people who got to go! I wish I could meet you guys!
Chilly Rellena

That Philippe is hot. When are you going to introduce me, Sandy??? You always did like to keep all the hot ones to yourself.
V for Verguenza

I've met Lori. She was in Austin one time, at Roca and my
brother-in-law had VIP, and I met her there. She's even hotter in
person.

Tobster

They're all in Austin, menso. They live there. And, V for
Verguenza, I'm pretty sure Philippe is gay. Am I the only one who
actually reads all the posts? Jeez, people.

The Wild Juan

I know who Sandy S. is. She was in my Physical Science lab at
UT. She was always stuck-up. Her boyfriend's a total tool.

Darky Dark

Sandy and her boyfriend aren't together anymore. Not only do
I read all the posts, Wild Juan, but also Sandy's other "secret"
blog. You should check it out. It's hilarious.

Misty

32

Monday afternoon, Sandy drove South on I-35, which was starting to feel like her personal pathway of self-therapy. Every time she took this drive it forced her to mull over what was happening in her life.

This time, no matter how hard she stared out the windshield or how many times she changed the radio station, she couldn't stop thinking about the comments on Nacho Papi.

V for Verguenza was her friend Veronica. She knew that because Veronica had told her. But all those other commenters—she had no idea who they were.

She'd already become immune to these strangers' remarks about her looks, her intelligence, and her writing. Positive or negative, they no longer had much effect on her, and she could skim over them without getting very emotional. However, now that the site was gaining ever more popularity, there was a whole new level of personal remarks within the comments. People were coming out of the woodwork now, talking about meeting Sandy and her fellow staffers at events, or seeing them on the streets of Austin, or knowing them in real life.

Sandy couldn't imagine who this guy was who'd taken her physical science lab. It was true that she'd kept to herself in that class, but it bothered her that he'd called her stuck up. She had never been stuck up. Concentrating on the subject matter, yes. Tired from her part-time job, yes. Hungover from the night before, maybe. But never stuck up. And it bothered her to have her real-life personality construed that way.

Sandy felt self-conscious now, everywhere she went. She was always mindful of what she did, and how it might look to others, because someone might recognize her and criticize her behavior on the site. Just the day before, for instance, a waitress at a local café had left a comment about George, saying he was a poor tipper. George had laughed it off, but Sandy had been mortified on his behalf. She promised herself to avoid that sort of situation at all costs if she could help it. She'd be on her guard. Always tip well, always drive well, be nice to everyone, and never pick your nose in public, she reminded herself every hour or so. It was as if she was constantly on camera, even with no cameras in sight.

Not only that, she had to make sure her hair and makeup were done, too, even if she was only going to the grocery store. She never knew who might be watching, waiting to comment.

Really, though, as she drove down the highway toward Tío Jaime's house, all those worries only served as a distraction from what was *really* bothering her: Who the hell was this Misty person, and how did she know about Sandy's blog?

She'd called Veronica and Jane first thing, of course, and asked them if they'd told anyone about it. At first they'd both said no. But then, under pressure, Veronica had admitted to telling two or three other friends. But those friends lived in other states and didn't know Miss TragiComic Texas was also Sandy S.

Jane had told her boyfriend but assured Sandy that he couldn't care less. Then Jane had pointed out that Sandy hadn't exactly been careful about her anonymity. "Anyone who really wanted to find out who you were, could," she'd said. "Anyone reading on a regular basis would figure out that you live in Austin, you went to UT, you had a boyfriend who was in the creative writing program."

Sandy didn't want to think about it. She couldn't imagine anyone going through that kind of trouble in order to dig up the details of her life, or what their purpose would be in doing so. Instead, she decided that this Misty person must have gotten Sandy confused with someone else. Or else she was making idle accusations, for attention. Things like that happened all the time. Sometimes their readers seemed deluded or mentally ill. Maybe Misty was just off her meds. One could always hope, Sandy thought.

As she neared Tío Jaime's house, she willed herself to forget about the commenters and concentrate on the task at hand. She was going back to interview the old man for the third time, and this time she had a surprise for him.

Francisco had designed a Chupacabra T-shirt to sell from the site. They were already doing well with the basic "Nacho Papi's T-shirt." Now they were offering one that featured a picture of Tío Jaime, with Cano in the background, under the words THE CHUPACABRA IS MY HOMEBOY.

This gave Sandy a whole new set of worries. According to her boss, the release that Sandy made all her interviewees sign gave Levy Media carte blanche to use Sandy's digital imagery as they wished—including making it into T-shirts with catchy slogans.

But Tío Jaime hadn't signed the release. And what, Sandy wondered now, would the old man say when he found out? Sandy imagined he'd probably laugh. He had a pretty easygoing sense of humor. But what if he didn't laugh?

In actuality, Sandy told herself, she could probably get away with not telling him about it. So what if there were a few hipsters walking up and down the drag wearing T-shirts with the old man's picture on them? How would Tío Jaime even find out about it?

But she knew that was wrong, and that she *would* have to tell him. That's how she'd been raised: to be honest and to respect one's elders. She had no choice. If Tío Jaime became upset, she'd have to deal with it, one way or another. And, either way, she'd have to get his signed release form.

This time she'd called ahead to make sure that, one, he was home and, two, that his nephew Richard was no longer in town.

She arrived at the old man's house ready for work in tennis shoes and her oldest jeans. He met her at her car with a glass of minty lemonade, a tonic to prepare her for the work ahead. Sandy noticed Cano waiting on the porch behind him and, to the side of the porch, a single goat fastened to a tree with a length of rope.

"Meh-eh-eh-eh!" the goat said to her.

"What's he doing here?" Sandy asked, her voice not nervous as much as hesitant. This wasn't one of the goats from the petting zoos of her childhood. He was bigger than a big dog and had full-size horns on his head.

"He's sick," said Tío Jaime. "He's staying here for a while so I can give him medicine."

"What kind of sick?" Sandy asked.

"They got into some trash that someone dumped on the side of the road, and this one ate some glass. So he needs to take a break until his stomach heals all the way."

Sandy made a wide circle around the goat, wanting to steer clear of a creature that could eat glass and still stand there meh-ing. She was struck by the sudden thought that, if goats could eat glass and chupacabras could eat goats, then chupacabras weren't something you wanted to mess with.

Sandy spent an hour and a half helping Tío Jaime weed his vegetable patch, strengthen fence posts, and give the sick goat his medicine. The goat's green eyes, with their minus-sign-shaped pupils, widened with fear and unnerved the hell out of her. But then Tío Jaime showed her how to pet the goat, scratching around his horns where the animal couldn't reach. The poor thing calmed down and closed his eyes halfway, which made him look more like a contented cartoon character and less like a crazed beast associated with Satanic rituals. Sandy and Tío Jaime petted it until it lay down at the base of the tree, and then they retired to the house to wash their hands and fortify themselves with more lemonade.

In the kitchen, Sandy opened her bag and brought out the bag of croissants she'd picked up from Calypso that morning.

"What's this?" asked Tío Jaime. "Bread?"

She tore open one of the croissants, showing him the cinnamon and almond filling. Then she showed him one of the others, which was filled with chocolate. He said something in Spanish—obviously an expression of pleasant surprise—and took the cinnamon croissant.

After they were settled on the porch, Sandy opened her bag again. "I have another surprise for you." Without further introduction, she pulled out the Chupacabra T-shirt.

It seemed to take Tío Jaime a while to realize that the man pictured on the shirt was him. When he did, however, he laughed. "What an ugly mug," he said.

"Do you like it?" Sandy asked, nervousness evident in her voice this time.

"What is it?" he asked. He read, "'The Chupacabra is my homeboy,'" then asked, "*Whose* homeboy?"

"Whoever's wearing the shirt," Sandy said.

"But who would want to wear it?" He was genuinely puzzled, as if Sandy had just shown him some piece of advanced technology, or something in another language.

"Your fans. You have a lot of fans." Sandy let that sink in, then said, "Everyone who reads our Web site loves your videos and the advice you give. They e-mailed about a hundred more questions for me to ask you. They call you the Chupacabra, and one of our readers said he wished you were his homeboy. And then all the others started saying it, too, so we made this T-shirt for your fans to buy."

The old man shook his head. "No. You're playing a joke on me."

"I'm not. Here"—Sandy opened her bag and pulled out her laptop this time—"let me show you...."

"No." He waved away the laptop and turned his head as if he were going to refuse even to look at it. "Don't tell me. Whatever it is, I'm okay not knowing."

Sandy frowned. "But I just wanted to show you a screen shot of comments written by your fans."

Tío Jaime shook his head again with a grimace. Sandy couldn't figure it out. He wasn't angry, obviously. It was almost like he was fearful. Or...disgusted?

"What's wrong? Are you upset? Do you wish we hadn't done the videos?"

"No," he said. "It's not that. I just don't want to see these people who call themselves my fans. They don't know me. And it's not good for a man to walk around with his head all swelled up. Like a false idol."

His words made no sense to Sandy. She couldn't

understand what he meant, or why he wouldn't be happy to have fans hanging on his every word. None of the Nacho Papi readers had requested T-shirts with Sandy's picture, or with pictures of any of the other staff writers. Tío Jaime—the Chupacabra—had managed to win more fans than any of them, and he didn't even have to write a thing.

"Well…" Sandy knew the probable answer to her next question but had to ask it anyway. "So, is it okay with you if we sell the T-shirts on the site? I could…We'd give you a cut of the profits." That wasn't true. Angelica had strictly forbidden her staff to offer any kind of payment to their interviewees. That was what the release forms were for—to make sure no one would ask Nacho Papi or Levy Media for money. But Sandy made the offer, figuring she could pay Tío Jaime out of her own salary if that was what it took.

"No." He shook his head even harder than before. "I don't want any money. Listen, m'ija, I didn't mind doing the interviews or the questions or whatever. That part's okay. If people like it, and they get to read it for free on your Web site, that's fine with me. But I don't want to be selling stuff with my picture on it like I'm some kind of movie star. I'm not. I'm just a regular man, and I want to keep it that way."

Sandy didn't know what else to say. The reporter in her wanted to push for the story, the info, the lead—whether or not it made her source dislike her. But the human being in her wanted to respect this other human being, her friend. He was more than a source or an interview to her now. He was a real-life friend, wasn't he?

She decided to compromise. "Okay. We won't sell the T-shirts. I'm sorry. I didn't want to make you uncomfortable."

"It's okay," he said, already looking calm again. "I'm not uncomfortable. I just don't want to do it." He turned and looked her in the eye, then. "That paper you wanted me to sign—does it say that I give your bosses permission to sell T-shirts?"

Sandy nodded sheepishly. "That, and other things, yes."

"Then I won't sign it. Sorry, m'ija."

"No, don't be sorry. That's fine. I...I respect your choice." Sandy thought fast, trying to come up with a way to salvage what she could from the situation. "But, Tío Jaime, can we keep doing the advice column? Recording you answering the questions?"

"Sure, that's fine," he said.

As quickly as possible, Sandy pulled out her camera and her notes, hoping the previous conversation hadn't soured the mood enough to ruin the advice segment she needed to record for her weekly quota. She glanced at Tío Jaime. He had reached for a chocolate croissant and was regarding it meditatively. The first thing she'd have to do when she got back to the office, she realized, was get Angelica to draft a new release form. One that gave permission for the interviews but nothing else. Explicitly stated, and easy for Tío Jaime to understand. Because she wanted him to be able to understand and feel comfortable with what they were doing. Not only because she needed the interviews to generate page views for her salary, but because he was her friend now, and she didn't want him to be unhappy.

She would fix everything. Everything would be fine. But first Sandy needed to get her story.

"Okay. First question is from Junior Senior. He asks, 'Chupacabra, please tell me once and for all what women want.'"

Tío Jaime turned and looked at Sandy in surprise and undisguised annoyance—so much so that Sandy was almost afraid. "What?" he said. "Somebody asked that? You're telling me I have a lot of fans on your Web site, but then they ask me stupid questions like that? These people don't need to be reading Web sites. They need to go back home to their mamas' houses and do some more growing."

Sandy stifled a giggle, then prompted the Chupacabra to continue. "What would Junior ask if he were grown?"

"Nothing, because he'd realize that there's no 'women.' There's only the woman you want to be with, and I can't tell you what she wants because I don't know her. If he wants to know what a certain woman wants, the best thing to do is ask that woman herself. But if he's thinking all women are the same—that they all want the same thing out of life—then he needs to go back to school and pull on little girls' pigtails until one of them hauls off and smacks some sense into him."

He scoffed in disbelief and took a bite of his croissant. Sandy zoomed in on the goat tied to the tree, who gratified her with a well-timed "Meh!"

"Next question," the Chupacabra commanded. And Sandy obeyed.

33

Time: Thursday, May 4, 12:47 PM
To: Nacho Papi Team
From: Angelica Villanueva O'Sullivan
Subject: MEMORANDUM

As discussed in our last meeting, George's sudden resignation means that each of us needs to take up his slack with two additional posts per day. I'm holding interviews for his replacement starting next week. Please continue to refer your friends as appropriate.

Per yesterday's meeting, the new salary structure goes into effect today. That means page views matter more than ever. Francisco, you were lowest last week—spice it up a little. No more posts about G-Phone apps. Readers are tired of those, and Zoom Phones just purchased an Elite Sponsor Package.

Sandy, you were highest. Great job with your last Chupacabra piece.

In general, all of you are doing very well.

Attached please find your updated itineraries and flight information for this weekend's launch party. Let me remind you again that this is a working party—you will be meeting potential sponsors, so pack appropriate clothing and stay on your toes.

I'll see you all in LA. Please notify me immediately upon your arrival.

Oh, and please be advised: I cannot approve requests for customized release forms. You are only authorized to use the ones provided by Levy Media Legal.

> Cordially yours,
> AVO

andy sat on a hotel bed that Friday evening trying to finish texting a paragraph onto her new phone's mini keyboard while Lori wiggled and bobbed beside her.

"God, these phones they gave us are so freaking awesome," Lori enthused. "Okay, are you ready? I'm going to hit Record."

"Ready," Sandy said. She didn't actually want to be recorded anymore because she still had a deadline to meet. And now that that idiot George had left Nacho Papi for its newest competitor, Buzz News, Sandy had even more posts to write in order to meet her quota each day.

Lori had already used the new phone supplied by their latest sponsor to record Sandy and herself at the Austin airport, on the plane, at LAX, and in the taxi all the way to their hotel. Her technique was to record as much as possible and then send it all to Francisco, entrusting him to edit out the boring parts and highlight the gems. So far, the gems included their flight attendant recognizing them as Nacho Papi's writers, and their taxi driver serenading them with traditional Peruvian love songs while staring at Lori's cleavage and scorpion tattoo. Sandy hadn't been able to write many posts at all that day, and made a mental note to ask Angelica if appearing in videos with Lori counted toward her daily quota. She felt a little guilty about doing that, since Francisco was the one doing the bulk of the work on the videos. And especially because Sandy was pretty sure he only did it because he was in love with Lori. But that wasn't her problem. She needed as many page views as she could get, and Francisco needed to learn to look out for himself.

"Smile," Lori whispered as she huddled next to Sandy and held out the phone at arm's length so that its lens would encompass them both. "Hi! Here we are, Lori and Sandy, in our hotel room in Los Angeles. It's a good thing I have my Zoom Phone with me so you guys can be here with us. Sandy, which bed do you want?"

"I'll take the one by the window."

"Then I'll take that one too!" Lori giggled lasciviously and Sandy gave a cool smile. She always played the straight man in Lori's posts, and Lori always played it bi.

"We're about to get ready for the big launch party tonight. I hope you guys can make it, but, if not, you can watch it live, here on the site. Post comments and let us know how you like my outfit!"

Sandy held her cool/smart/sophisticated expression steady until Lori hit Stop and dropped her phone. "Oh my God, I am so nervous. I think I'm gonna puke," she said, grabbing a pillow and clutching it to her torso.

"You're not going to puke. It's going to be fine," said Sandy, for what felt like the fortieth time since they'd left Austin. "We'll get to the party, they'll turn on the cameras, and you'll turn into Lori the Star. Everyone will love you, Angelica will be happy, and you'll be just fine. You can always throw up when you get back to the hotel if you need to." That was usually how it happened. The more nervous Lori became, the better she did on camera, and then she ended up being physically ill afterwards.

Sandy felt sorry for her, but not sorry enough to let it affect her own work.

She was nervous too, because they were going to meet Angelica's boss, Jacob Levy, tonight, but not nervous to the point of gastric disorder. After all, no one was expecting Sandy to be the life of the party. She'd been gaining social experience, as Angelica was always sending them to various events and club openings, and Sandy had found that standing there looking just the way Angelica had designed her was all she ever needed to do. Sometimes people walked up—men, especially—and tried to engage her in conversations about politics or things she'd said on the site. But they were usually so nervous or self-conscious themselves that Sandy could dispatch them with a few remarks. It was almost like magic. The fact that she appeared online regularly, was almost a celebrity, made people feel intimidated by her in person.

Sandy had been afraid at first, thinking that strangers at these events might make the sorts of remarks to her that strangers made on the site, commenting on her looks or her intellect or conjecturing about her personal life. But in real life, outside of the anonymity of the Internet, no one was rude at all. No one had the nerve to be.

It made her feel powerful, in a way. Way more powerful than she'd felt when she was only a writer for LatinoNow, or a tech writer for a bunch of bossy engineers, or a struggling student. Now that she worked for Nacho Papi she felt, for the first time, like she was really somebody. More and more lately, when she showed up at events around Austin, and even at the State Capitol, people knew who she was. Or if they didn't know exactly who she was, they could tell that she was *somebody* and that they had to treat her with respect.

And she knew that Lori felt the same, at least on some

level—when she wasn't retching in a bathroom somewhere or sitting in a corner chewing her nails, like she
was doing right at that moment.

"Come on," Sandy said. "Let's get ready to tear this
town up."

A couple of hours later, Sandy's prediction came true.
Lori stood in the middle of the Cadillac Club, which
Angelica's boss, Jacob Levy, had rented for the occasion. Admirers surrounded her three men deep, and she
shone in the light of the live-streaming camera that fed
her every move to their Web site for her fans around the
country to see.

Sandy, meanwhile, was navigating through waves of
silver balloons and waiters bearing trays of champagne
to meet and pose for pictures with Cleo J., Cuoc X., and
the other writers from their sister sites. She and Cleo J.,
whose real name was Kendra James, hit it off very well
and spent half an hour marveling over how much they
had in common, upbringing and career wise, before
Angelica came over and reminded them to mingle with
the other guests. And there were plenty of them to mingle with. Sandy met the writers and editors for all of
Nacho Papi's sister sites, plus the New York team who
sold ad space on the sites. Then there were tons of other
people: media people and publicity people and business-
people and the all-important sponsor people. And then
just plain people—and Sandy was glad that Philippe was
there to show her the ropes. She stayed close to him all
night, and he made sure she knew who was who. And
he also made sure she had a good time. She always had
fun with Philippe. He made her laugh and made her
feel sophisticated, just by standing next to her and looking interested in what she had to say. She noticed that
Lori did just fine by herself, but Francisco mostly stayed

with the other techies from their sister sites. Angelica, meanwhile, was completely in her element, scheming and laughing with her fellow editors and each of the Elite Package sponsors.

An hour into the party, Sandy met Jacob Levy himself. It was only for a few moments. He was a lot shorter than Sandy had expected, but also exactly how she assumed a media mogul from New York would be, attitude wise. Talking to him simultaneously made her feel like a yokel from the sticks and inspired her to move to New York herself, one day. He spoke with each staff writer there very briefly, telling each of them the same thing: that they were doing a great job and he was glad to have them as part of his organization.

After a while the music stopped and all the guests turned to look at the ska band that had been playing on a small stage in the corner of the club. The musicians all looked to the opposite corner of the club, causing everyone else to do the same. Sandy saw that there was a podium and microphone set up there, and that Jacob Levy was making his way up to it to make a speech.

"Thank you. Thanks to everyone for coming," he said in response to a smattering of tipsy applause. "As I've been saying, you guys are doing a great job. Page views are through the roof!" There was a louder smattering of applause and hoots. Sandy couldn't help but notice that Mr. Levy didn't seem to be very practiced at public speaking. He held his hand up until the noise abated and then continued. "So, I guess it makes sense, what I'm about to say. What I'm about to say is good news for Levy Media and for all of us here."

The crowd got even less noisy at that, and Sandy leaned forward a little to hear what her boss's boss would say.

"Levy Media is launching a cable television station.

It's going to be called Hate Station, after our flagship site, and each of the sites represented here will contribute to the programming."

A gasp rippled through the crowd like wind through a field. Sandy gasped, then turned to Philippe, who was standing next to her. For some reason he didn't look surprised at all.

"That's right. That's right," said Mr. Levy, nodding. "So, congratulations to us all! There'll be a full press release forthcoming, of course. And, of course, all of our sponsors will be made fully aware of new partnership opportunities." With this he winked at the crowd and stepped down from the podium, stumbling a little as he went.

Realizing the speech was over, the partygoers broke into applause over the announcement. Simultaneously the band struck up a fast dance song. A troop of waiters emerged from the walls of the club bearing champagne reinforcements, and the guests eagerly helped lighten their trays.

Sandy turned to Philippe again. He was shaking the hands of the people on the other side of him. When he finally turned back to her, Sandy leaned close and whispered, "Did you know about this already?"

He smiled in reply. "I had reason to suspect" was all he said.

Then Sandy saw Jacob Levy sneak out the club's exit. She wondered if he had a more important party to attend or if he just didn't like parties. Either way, his absence didn't mean this one was over. If anything, the club became louder and more crowded after Jacob Levy left. Everyone was in a frenzy to congratulate each other and themselves, and to toast the hell out of the occasion.

Lori managed to break away from her admirers long

enough to run up to Sandy and squeal "Oh my God, oh my God!" And then, "George is going to be *pissed!*"

She was right, Sandy realized. George was going to be very sorry that he'd chosen to leave them right before this development. But he deserved it. That's what he got for leaving them for a competitor, with zero notice.

Across the room, Francisco huddled with his fellow tech-heads, looking more anxious than excited. Sandy felt a brief flash of pity for him. But it faded as the new editor of *Mujer* magazine, who'd been introduced to her as one of Angelica's friends, appeared at her side and said, "Sandy! Congratulations! We'd love to interview you right before the station debuts...."

By the time Sandy and Lori cabbed back to their room, evening bags bursting with business cards, it was long after 3 A.M. and Sandy wasn't feeling nervous at all. In fact, she felt completely fabulous—like her life had just taken the turn that it'd been destined to take. Like everything she'd done so far had been preparing her for and leading her to this moment.

She was going to be on television. Everything that had been bothering her lately—the annoying commenters, the missing release form, Daniel, her day job, her parents—evaporated to make room for one momentous thought.

She was going to be on TV. She, nerdy little Dominga Saavedra, who'd worked her way up to becoming blogger Sandy S., was now going to become a star!

35

On Saturday at noon, Angelica asked the staff to convene for a brunch meeting at her hotel, a much nicer hotel than the one where the writers were staying. Sandy, Lori, Philippe, and Francisco sat around their boss at a semi-secluded table in the tastefully decorated restaurant with various breakfast items piled on their plates. They talked in excited whispers while Angelica gave the waiter his orders and dismissed him. Sandy saw that Francisco still looked as anxious as he had the night before. Angelica noticed it too, after a while. She turned to him, sitting there at her left, and gave his shoulder one of her friendly hard pats. "We're going to get you new glasses," Sandy heard Angelica say quietly. "And new shirts." Francisco swallowed hard and nodded, seemingly somewhat comforted. Sandy wondered if he'd been afraid that he wouldn't be part of the TV show team.

Now that she thought of it, though, did she know for certain that any of them would be?

"All right. Attention, everyone." Angelica paused until everyone faced her, like a kindergarten teacher waiting for her students to quiet down. "You heard Jacob last night. This is fabulous news for all of us. I have your new contracts back at the office. Someone from Levy Media

Legal will meet us in Austin and go over all the details with each of you. In the meantime, I want you all to congratulate yourselves. Your hard work over the past few months helped contribute to this development. Levy Media wouldn't have been able to sign this deal without all your page views."

She gave them all her radiant smile and took a bite of the prosciutto on her plate.

Sandy decided to start with the questions. "Are we all going to be on camera, or will we just write for the station?"

"Good question. For now, I think it's safe to assume that all of you will be on camera. Of course you'll be writing the content, too. Nacho Papi will have its own half-hour segments on the station. Levy Media is setting up a studio near our Austin office for recording those segments. We'll create two or three sets for in-studio news commentary and interviews, and we'll also continue to record the same kind of video material we did for the Web site."

Sandy let her mind absorb these facts. Now that she was hearing the plan, she realized that she'd been assuming they were all going to move to New York. Or to Los Angeles. She smiled inwardly at her own ignorance and directed her attention to her breakfast of fruit and yogurt.

Lori spoke next. "There are only"—she paused and counted under her breath. "Only five Levy Media sites. If they each get an hour, how are they going to fill up the rest of every day?"

Angelica smiled at Lori, whose pink-streaked hair glowed softly under the branch-shaped chandeliers above them. "The satellite stations will start with an hour each. Hate-O-Rama, as the flagship site, will of course have a bit more time than that. The rest of the day will be comprised of paid programming."

Lori spent a moment visibly thinking about Angelica's answer. Then, she said, "You mean, like, informercials?"

"Yes. To begin with. Until we build our audience," Angelica replied.

Francisco asked, "Am I—I mean, are we going to be expected to edit the video for the show? And to do the...whatever extra graphics are required?" He looked equal parts defiant and miserable, and Sandy understood then why he'd been anxious. He was already doing all the graphics and video for the site, in addition to his post quota.

"You, Francisco, will oversee the graphic content. It will be created, however, by a team of interns."

Francisco sighed as if Angelica had just given him the best news possible. Then, smiling with relief, he tore into his huevos rancheros.

Philippe, Sandy noticed, had no questions. He ate his breakfast in perfect serenity. For a few moments, they all followed his example. Then, unable to contain herself any longer, Lori exclaimed, "I'm so excited, I think I'm going to die!"

"Well, don't die yet," Angelica told her. "We need you for the show."

They all laughed, more from the release of tension than anything.

"I'm excited, too," Sandy said. "I'm going to miss writing for the Web site, of course. But I won't miss the commenters."

Her co-workers laughed again.

"Really? Some of them aren't so bad," Francisco said.

"Right, *yours* aren't," Lori retorted. "Sandy and I are the ones who get all the psychos now that George is gone. All those guys wanting to see us naked—and then the one chick who keeps obsessing over Sandy and asking her on dates, V for Vendetta, or whatever her name is."

Francisco nodded, conceding the point.

Sandy felt herself flush. Lori meant, of course, her friend Veronica. She could see, now, how Veronica constantly dropping Sandy's name would look a little strange to the other writers. She decided not to tell them that V for Verguenza was someone she knew in real life.

"People," Angelica interrupted. "I hate to disillusion you, but we aren't discontinuing the Web site."

"We aren't?" they all said at once.

"No. We're going to do the television program in *addition* to the site."

They all fell quiet again. Philippe smiled wryly at Sandy over his egg-white omelet. It was obvious that he'd known all this in advance.

Sandy let her mind readjust to the facts. Again. She was going to be a TV star, yes. But in a little satellite studio in Austin. In addition to the full-time job that she was already doing. And with the same commenters still commenting on her every move.

This is still a good thing, she told herself. Isn't it?

Yes, it is, she decided. She would *make* it a good thing. Just like she'd done when LatinoNow had become Nacho Papi. And just like she'd do when the television show eventually became something even bigger.

She smiled at Angelica and her co-workers then, and lifted her latte in salute.

36

May 8, 2008
Re: Contract renewal
To Whom It May Concern:

It is with regret that I inform you that I will not be renewing my technical writing contract with QBS, Inc. I'm grateful for my experience here and wish you all the best of luck.

Sincerely,
Dominga Saavedra

37

Sandy felt like a bird—a free, feather-light bird without a boring day job any longer—floating her way through Calypso's brown velveteen ottomans and worn rattan chairs. As she approached the counter her phone buzzed. She checked and saw the name Jeremy. She opened the text and read, "Coming to Austin next week. Can we have coffee?" She smiled in remembrance of the cute marketing guy she'd met in Atlanta. She would check her calendar for space as soon as she got to the office.

At the counter, she recited her usual order to the barista on duty. The young woman stared at Sandy for a moment before letting out a slow "Hey-y-y-y," of recognition.

Sandy looked at the barista's face and immediately regretted having ventured so close to the university. She hadn't seen Daniel since their breakup and now, here she was, face-to-face with one of his fellow TAs' girlfriends. But Sandy couldn't remember her name.

"You're Sandy S.," the cashier said. "From Nacho Papi's Web Site!"

Sandy felt her smile fall into place, as if she were on camera for the site. It was okay—this was one of her fans.

"Remember me? Kristy? We met at the Fat Man and

talked about Ann Radcliffe being the grandmother of Goth? You were with Daniel."

"Right, right," Sandy said. Concentrating on the girl's light brown bangs falling over green eyes made Sandy recall her name. Kristy. And Kristy had been with...

"I was with Adam," she supplied, then added, "but I'm not anymore."

"Oh, really?" said Sandy. "I'm sorry."

"Oh, don't be. I'm better off. We both are, right?" At this, Kristy gave Sandy a mischievous smile. She leaned forward conspiringly, her long hair falling out of its cap and over the shoulder of her pale blue uniform shirt. This caused Sandy to lean forward too, and Kristy lowered her voice. "I laughed my ass off at your parodies of Daniel's poetry."

Sandy smiled with pleasure. It was good to have her talent recognized. But then, replaying Kristy's compliment in her mind, she realized something. "Wait, what? What do you mean? That wasn't on Nacho Papi."

"No, right. It was on your other site, My Modern TragiComedy."

Sandy stood straight and felt the hair on the back of her neck quiver. "You know about that?"

Kristy laughed. "Yeah. But don't worry—Daniel didn't know that I knew. He never read the site at all, right?"

"No." Sandy's mind raced over possibilities before she came out and asked. "How did you find out about it, though? That it was me writing it, I mean?"

Kristy laughed again. After glancing at the other two customers in the corners of the shop and assuring herself that they were both immersed in their respective laptop screens, she explained. "It was the funniest thing. Adam asked me to look up one of Daniel's poems online. He was always comparing his work to Daniel's and wanting me to tell him his was better. You know?"

Sandy nodded. She knew, all right, exactly how insecure grad-school poets could be.

Kristy continued. "So I searched for this one cheesy line about 'a string of bloody hearts,' thinking it would come up in one of the online journals, right? But instead I found that entry where you made fun of that line, last summer. And I started reading your site, and it was pretty obvious that you were Daniel's girlfriend, you know? I didn't say anything when we met at the Fat Man because I didn't want to freak you out. You know, I didn't want to come off like a stalker or anything."

Sandy was completely dumbfounded. It was a big coincidence, but the story made perfect sense. Of course someone would be able to find her site by looking up Daniel's worst lines. It was stupid of her never to have considered that before.

At that moment, a younger barista emerged from a door behind the counter. "Hey, Amy," Kristy said to her, "this is Sandy S., from Nacho Papi!"

"Hey!" said Amy in pleasant surprise. "Oh my God! I love your site. You're my favorite writer on it. I'm a writer too!"

Sandy asked the girl what she wrote and then nodded knowingly and encouragingly at her answer. Inside, though, she was still reeling from what she'd just heard. Amy chattered hard and fast, telling Sandy that she herself was a journalism major and asking if she could become a Nacho Papi intern.

"Hey," Kristy interrupted. "Tell her what happened the other day, in Daniel's class."

"What? Oh!" said Amy, her blue eyes rounding in sudden revelation. "Oh, that's right! You're the one!"

"The one what?" Sandy asked, bracing herself for more. Apparently Amy was one of Daniel's students.

"Oh my God, it was so lame. So Mr. Thomas—Daniel—had been missing class a lot, right? And blowing up at some of the other students and stuff? And then, the other day, he sent us all this e-mail, right? It said he was sorry he'd been so out of it, but that he'd suffered"—here she made her voice low and serious, in a somewhat competent impersonation of Daniel—"'a personal blow in the form of a romantic disappointment.' And he tried to make it seem like *he'd* been the one to dump *you*. But it was *so* obvious that he wasn't. He said that he and this woman were, like, torn apart by 'a difference in personal ambition.' It was so lame. We were all laughing about it."

"Wait, *what?*" Sandy said. "He told his *students* about our breakup?"

"He totally did!" Amy continued. She wasn't as careful about keeping her voice down. Out of the corner of her eye Sandy saw one of the other customers glancing their way as Amy went on with her story. "And then when Kristy told me about your blog, and I sent everybody the link, we were totally *dying*, it was so hilarious! And, like, he keeps assigning all these poems about breakups and evil women now, and it's so hard to get through class with a straight face—"

Right then, the door bells chimed. Kristy turned to greet the new customer and then, with a comically exaggerated look of panic, said, "Oh—hi, Daniel!"

Sandy and Amy spun to see that it was, indeed, the same Daniel they'd just been discussing.

"Oh, hi, Mr. Thomas," Amy said, more casually than Kristy had.

But it wasn't any help. Daniel froze in an awkward stance, staring at Sandy. Then he turned and left the shop, prompting his student to say "Awww!" Whether it was because she felt sorry for him or because she was disappointed that the drama had ended early, Sandy couldn't tell.

After getting Amy to make her iced mocha as quickly as possible, Sandy drove to work in an emotional debate with herself, torn between feeling pity and absolute triumph.

It served Daniel right, being humiliated like that. It was the least he deserved after having spilled his guts to his students about their private lives. Sandy may have mentioned a few things about it on her blog, but she'd never intended for anyone who knew them in *real life* to read it. Daniel, on the other hand, was obviously trying to drum up sympathy from his young co-ed fan club. Sympathy, and who knew what else? Maybe a rebound relationship or two?

Maybe she would have felt bad about the students reading her blog entries if Daniel had been any other guy. But he wasn't. And now he was finding out how she'd felt the whole time she was his girlfriend. Ignored. Pushed aside. Unappreciated.

Now *he* was the one being pushed aside, and *she* was the one with all the fans. It served him right, she told herself again, so there was absolutely no reason for her to feel guilty.

And the little voice in the back of her mind that kept telling her, as she drove on, that she'd done something wrong? Sandy told it to shut up. She was going to enjoy this reversal of fortune, at least for a little while.

38

She made it to the office at noon. Their flight back from LA had arrived a mere thirteen hours before that, so she didn't expect any of her fellow staffers to be slaving away at work just yet. Francisco proved her wrong, though. He was sitting at the conference table clicking back and forth between two laptops when Sandy walked in.

"Hey, Sandy, guess what. Your friend's T-shirt is highest-grossing this week."

"What friend?" Sandy assumed he meant the disgusting Official Nacho Papi Nalga Inspector T-shirt George had come up with. And it was no secret among their co-workers that she and George had been anything but best friends forever.

"You know. Your friend the Chupacabra. Everybody's homeboy. They're selling as fast as we can have them printed," Francisco said.

Sandy felt the color drain out of her face. "Really?"

"Yep. We've sold almost two hundred of them since yesterday."

Sandy said nothing in reply. There was no use feeling guilty about *that* now, either, she told herself. She had made this decision and now she had to live with it.

She had almost forgotten about the whole thing amidst the excitement of Los Angeles and the news about the TV station. Could anyone blame her? Here she was, about to make a career transition that most people only dreamed about. And then, flitting through her brain like a mosquito, there was this petty problem with a T-shirt and a piece of paper.

Not for the first time that week she reminded herself that Tío Jaime would most likely never discover they were printing the shirts anyway. Who would he know who would buy a joke T-shirt from a gossip Web site? Nacho Papi's readers were people with boring corporate jobs who surfed the 'Net all day. Or else they were students. But they definitely weren't goat ranchers or cactus farmers. So there was nothing to worry about, was there? And, really, if Tío Jaime had actually understood how much this T-shirt thing was helping Sandy in her career, he probably would have gone ahead and given his permission.

That was what she told herself—again—as she set up her laptop to review Francisco's edits on her latest video. Before long she became engrossed in her work and the Chupacabra went back to lurking in the dark corners of her mind.

Later that day, however, she couldn't avoid it any longer. It was time for another edition of "Ask the Chupacabra." Sandy packed up her equipment and started the long drive out to Tío Jaime's house. She had to face him as if she hadn't done anything wrong.

She *hadn't*, she reminded herself as she sped down the highway. He *had* given her his permission to use his image, right from the beginning. How was she supposed to know, back then, that he would later change his mind and get picky about *how* she'd use his image?

Besides, he would never find out anyway. He would never find out, she told herself, over and over again like a yoga student chanting. How could he ever find out?

She drove south faster, wanting to get it all over with.

Eventually she reached the gold-green fields of cactus and mesquite. Chupacabra Country, she named it in her mind. She slowed her Malibu and began the sequence of twisty turns that led to the old man's house.

At the second turn she rounded the corner and almost ran smack into a turquoise VW Bug that had stopped in the middle of the road. Sandy slammed on her brakes, then pulled over to one side to see what was going on.

Two young men stood in front of the Bug examining a sheet of paper. Sandy could tell by their skinny jeans and kooky hats that they were hipsters—maybe UT dropouts. Their Bug's bumper stickers, including the inevitable KEEP AUSTIN WEIRD, confirmed her impression.

What were guys like that doing out here? she wondered.

They turned to see who had driven up behind them. Their facial expressions practically shouted "We're lost!"

Then Sandy noticed their shirts. Specifically their brand-new THE CHUPACABRA IS MY HOMEBOY T-shirts recreating Tío Jaime's smiling face in double vision.

Oh, no.

There was only one reason they could be all the way out here, in the middle of nowhere, wearing those shirts. They were fans. As in short for *fanatics*.

She had to drive away before they recognized her. She put her car back into gear, but it was too late.

"Hey!" one of the hipsters called. "Sandy S.!"

They ran over to the front of her car, keeping her from being able to drive away. One of them put his hands on her hood. "Hey, Sandy S.! Don't leave! Help us!"

Sandy held her foot on the brake wondering what to do. Her heart was pounding all of a sudden. She was a little afraid. More than a little, actually. What were these guys doing out here? She was alone and they knew who she was. What would they do to her if she didn't drive away right now?

"Sandy!" They ran up to her window and motioned for her to roll it down. She did, but only an inch.

"Don't leave! Help us, please! We came out here to meet the Chupacabra. We want to interview him for our site! It's an arts organization! Can you introduce us? Please?"

The shorter one in the trucker hat did all the talking, and the taller one in the fedora nodded his head furiously in support. After examining their faces for insanity and their hands for weapons, Sandy put her car back into Park. Their jeans were too tight to conceal guns or knives. She opened her door, thinking fast all the while.

"Listen, guys," she said as she emerged from the car and then leaned against it as casually as she could. "I'm sorry, but I can't help you."

"What? Aw, man. Come on, Sandy S.! We're not trying to steal your gig. We want to ask the Chupacabra about his politics. And, like, about living off the grid and stuff," the shorter one said.

"No, I get you," Sandy said, making her voice as placating as possible. "I feel that. What I'm trying to tell you, though, is that the Chupacabra doesn't actually live out here."

"What?" said both guys.

"Right. He lives in Austin. We just come out here to film his segments." Sandy saw their faces fall in disappointment and felt a little bad about lying to them, but not bad enough to quit. "In fact, you just missed him.

He just left the set and drove back to his apartment, off Riverside."

"Wha-a-at?" they said again, slower and with more sad disillusionment.

"Yeah. We film the interviews at this house out here— it's my brother's friend's house. And the Chupacabra— Well, I shouldn't be telling you this, but the man we call the Chupacabra is actually an actor."

"Aw, man," the shorter one said. The taller one just stood there looking downcast.

"I'm sorry, guys," Sandy said, feeling relieved that her story was obviously working. "How'd you find our set, anyway?"

They looked down at the piece of paper they'd been studying, which Sandy now saw was a printout from a mapping site. "We have this friend," the shorter guy began. "We showed him your site—your interviews with the Chupacabra. He, um, recognized the area. Because, um, he, um...used to do stuff out here. Sometimes. So, um, he told us where it was. The general area, I mean. And so, um, we came out here to look."

Sandy nodded sympathetically. "Well, that was pretty smart of you. You guys are pretty good reporters."

They muttered thanks but were obviously completely broken-hearted.

"I'll tell you what," Sandy said, suddenly thinking up the perfect way to end it. "Do you have a card? For your Web site?"

"What? Uh." They searched their tight pockets without luck. Then the taller one ran to their Bug and retrieved something from the backseat. He brought it to Sandy and she saw that it was a flier for an event, printed on red construction paper. The hipster folded it so that the blank side showed, and then they began searching their pockets again. Intuitively, Sandy opened her own car door to get a pen from her bag.

After asking them to write their Web address and contact information on the backside of the flier, Sandy promised she'd contact them about doing a segment for Nacho Papi. They thanked her again, much more cheerfully now. They turned back to their Bug, but Sandy stopped them. "Guys, everything I just told you, about the Chupacabra being an actor? And about his house being my brother's big weight-lifting jock friend's house? I need you guys to keep that secret, okay? I need you guys not to blow my cover. Reporter to reporter. You know what I'm saying?"

They nodded and said they knew what she was saying. "Don't worry, Sandy S. We'll say that we found his house and he pulled out a shotgun."

"Good. That's good. All right. I'll be contacting you guys about the interview for your organization, then."

And with that, they left. Sandy stood watching and waving until they were gone. And then she stood there for a while longer, congratulating herself for handling the situation so well.

She got into her car, turned it around, and drove back north. She couldn't do any more work today, she decided. Because, all of a sudden, she felt sick to her stomach.

39

Post on Nacho Papi's Web Site, Thursday, May 11

It's the Sensitive Ones You Have to Watch, G-Friends
by Sandy S.

For Part 32 in the eternal saga that is their breakup, Lawrence Villalobos is now claiming that he was the one to break up with Sara Milan, and that he did so because of her drug use and "reckless behavior."

Come on, Laurencito. We all loved you in that movie about Cesar Chavez, but you're eroding that goodwill faster than you snorted those lines on DJ Kabuki-O's yacht. We all know what happened between you and Sara, and the best you can do now is accept it, haul yourself through rehab, and then call your agent and try to get booked for another tear-jerker.

Speaking from recent personal experience, there's nothing more pathetic than a man who can't take a breakup like a man.

40

Time: Thursday, May 11, 4:02 PM
To: Dominga Saavedra
From: Daniel Thomas
Subject: your words

Sandy,

I have to say that I'm disappointed, to say the least, in your decision to discuss our breakup in a public forum.

I understand that bitterness may be eclipsing your better judgment. But I would ask that you endeavor to take the high road, as I have.

Sincerely,
Daniel Thomas, Ph.D.

41

Time: Monday, May 15, 10:54 PM
To: Dominga Saavedra
From: marco.saavedra@tcminc.com
Subject: Hi from your dad

Dear Sandy,

How've you been? Sorry I haven't written much lately. Things have been busy at work. And with other things...

I've been trying to read your website when I get the chance. It's kind of confusing but I did see some of your articles and thought they were good. You have a biting wit that I envy. Wish I could write as well as you.

Hope to see you soon. Hope you're doing well. And your mother.

Love,
Dad

42

It'd been another long working weekend. Now that Toro vodka was officially an Elite Sponsor, Sandy was obliged to attend their functions and be videotaped, wearing a different borrowed dress and coming up with creative, not-obviously-sponsored posts to write each time. She'd figured out that the best method was to drink one Pure NRG water for every two Toro vodkas and to befriend the Toro girls, who gave her the best story leads.

It was still tiring, though. She'd flown to Phoenix on Saturday and then to San Antonio on Sunday for the Latino Literature Conference. Because, along with everything else, she was Nacho Papi's designated literary expert. Which was ironic, in a way, considering everything.

Sandy was finding that she had come to rely on her weekly visits with the Chupacabra. For one thing, his advice was comforting to hear. The Chupacabra's down-to-earth sensibility reduced the angsty-est problems to simple matters that were easily solved with a little bit of honesty and common sense. Listening to Tío Jaime dispatch their readers' questions made Sandy feel what it meant when old people said, "This, too, shall pass." It made her feel like everything was going to be okay, like it was possible to take a break from your problems and enjoy simple things, like gardening. Or lemonade.

Adding to this was the setting. Something about Chupacabra Country, with its long green horizon and constant mild breeze, made Sandy feel at peace. It was funny—she'd already known that, of course, but wouldn't have thought that it had translated to the videos she made for the site. Obviously it did, though. Her readers commented on it all the time and joked about buying homes next to the Chupacabra's.

The week before, when she'd missed their appointment because of the hipsters, Sandy had reviewed all the previous "Ask the Chupacabra" episodes. When she watched them over again, she saw just how different they were from the rest of the content on the Nacho Papi site. They formed a sort of oasis from all the gossip, the criticism, and the "hate-o-rama," as Mr. Levy would have termed it. She could see why those hipster boys had driven out to find the Chupacabra. She totally understood what they'd been looking for.

And she was the one who'd shown it to them. But for now she was the only one who knew how to find it. And she'd try to keep it that way, for the old man's sake. She didn't want to upset him. She couldn't afford to, of course. If she stopped doing "Ask the Chupacabra" she'd take a considerable hit to her page views, and therefore to her salary.

She'd felt a little bad about the T-shirt thing, which didn't even count toward her page-view credits after all, because it had gone against Tío Jaime's wishes. But it turned out that the first week of sales had been a fluke. They'd sold a few hundred Chupacabra shirts, and then their fickle audience had dropped them like last year's G-Phones, moving on to Francisco's bumper stickers that read KEEP AUSTIN WIRED. So it was almost like the T-shirts had never happened and Sandy didn't have to worry about it anymore.

As she drove, her mind worked in Shuffle mode. Thinking of work made her think of the e-mail Daniel had sent her after she wrote the Lawrence Villalobos breakup post. It was funny to her that Daniel had finally started reading her Nacho Papi posts after all this time. Of course he had; he wanted to see if she'd make reference to him, the way he alluded to her in his classes. She almost wished she hadn't made that crack about breakups in her post about Lawrence Villalobos. It'd brought her down to Daniel's level. But she hadn't been able to resist. It was a hilarious post. Even her dad thought so. And he almost never e-mailed her for anything.

And, really, as long as Daniel never found out about her personal blog it was no big deal.

Maybe it was time to take it offline, she mused. Or at least remove all the entries about Daniel.

But then she remembered Kristy telling her how much she'd enjoyed Sandy's parodies of Daniel's work. She remembered all the comments she'd gotten from readers on those entries, too. Those were some of her funniest, most heartfelt entries.

Why should she take them down? she asked herself. It wasn't like she'd used Daniel's actual name. And even if she had, she was well within her rights to discuss her own life and describe things that had happened to her, wasn't she? Daniel was free to start his own blog and tell his side of the story if he wanted.

But he never would, because he considered himself too good for that. And that was ironic, because the genre he found so lowbrow was what had won Sandy a bigger audience than Daniel's poetry ever would have.

It wasn't her fault that people wanted to read about her life, in her down-to-earth writing style. She was giving her fans what they wanted, and she couldn't help it if Daniel hadn't found a way to do the same.

Having neatly reasoned her problems away, all within an hour-long drive, Sandy pulled into Tío Jaime's driveway with a clear conscious and a light heart.

43

"What'd you bring me this time?" the old man asked as she emerged from the car laden with snacks.

"Jalapeno sausage kolaches and a Peppermint Coffee Cooler." Sandy handed him one of the two drinks she was carrying and took the bakery box to the small table on his porch.

They ate and chatted a bit before beginning the interview. Sandy vented a little, telling Tío Jaime about a couple of readers who'd started to criticize the Nacho Papi staffers' writing and suggest that they, themselves, would do a better job for less pay.

"Well, m'ija, you know how people are," Tío Jaime said, sitting back and taking a sip from the drink she'd brought him. "They're like crabs in a bucket. The minute one crab starts to climb up, the other crabs reach up and try to pull her back down. You know what I'm saying?"

Sandy nodded. She definitely knew what he was saying, and had met plenty of crab-like people lately.

"You kids don't realize how lucky you are, though," he said. "Back when I was young, nobody even thought about writing anything or trying to be on TV. Your aunt, for instance..." He paused and looked up, as if at something flashing over his head. At his feet, Cano lifted his ears. "That reminds me. I've been trying to remember to give you this forever." He got up then, and went back into the house. Sandy stayed seated, not knowing whether she was supposed to follow. Sometimes, lately, Tío Jaime had sudden memories and walked into the house, only to come out after a few minutes as if nothing had happened. At first she'd assumed he was going to the bathroom, but now she wondered if his memory was starting to erode.

This time, however, he returned to the porch with a book. Actually, Sandy saw as he slowly moved closer, it was a journal.

"Here," he said, handing it to her. "I've been wanting to give you this. It was your aunt's."

Sandy took the book from his hand. It was bound in dark green cloth, so old that the corners were rubbed bare and the cover itself had buckled slightly. The yellow-edged pages had numerous gaps, indicating things tucked between them. "What," she said. "When...?"

"It was her journal. The only thing of hers I wanted to keep. But I've never read it. I didn't feel right."

Sandy ran her hands over the journal. She was torn between wanting to open it right then and wanting to hold it safely closed, within her hands, forever. She had never really known her great-aunt—hadn't met her more than two or three times—but already she felt that this journal contained an identity. It radiated warmth and— Sandy felt cheesy for thinking it—also a life of its own.

"Are you lending it to me?" she asked.

"I'm giving it to you. I've been meaning to give it to you ever since you first came up here. Your aunt should have been a writer, and she was always proud that you became a writer, and I know she would have wanted you to have it."

"Thank you." Sandy felt warmth and then moisture

rise to her eyes. She didn't know if she could really believe Tío Jaime—he might have been exaggerating a little, to be nice—but it certainly was a comforting idea to imagine her late aunt being proud of her accomplishments and passing down a heritage, so to speak, in the form of a desire to write. "I think I'll wait and read it when I get home," Sandy said.

Tío Jaime waved dismissively as if he were already through with the subject. "Do whatever you want with it. Read it when you're ready to."

Sandy tucked the book carefully into an inner pocket in her bag, among the tools of her trade.

The old man said, "That reminds me. You probably shouldn't visit me next week. My nephew Richard is coming to town again."

"Really?"

"He's staying for a while, but not at my house. He says he can't go without air conditioning, so he'll be at one of those big hotels in Austin."

Sandy let her curiosity get the better of her. "Why is he coming here if he's not actually going to stay with you?"

Tío Jaime shrugged and made a face. "His mother makes him check up on me, I think. But he probably has some work to do with lawyers here in town, too. Otherwise I don't see him coming all the way out from California just for me."

"Where in California does he live?"

"Los Angeles. The big city."

"What does he do there? I mean, what kind of lawyer is he?"

"Immigration law. But he mostly works with people from England and Bermuda and the Middle East, so he's making good money. He's single. I would try to set you up with him, m'ija, but he just broke up with someone a year ago and I think he still needs time to get over it."

Sandy quickly demurred. She hadn't meant to seem interested for *that* reason. "Well, I hope he doesn't get angry about our interviews. If he thinks you should get paid for them, I'm willing to—"

Tío Jaime interrupted. "Don't worry about that. What he doesn't know won't hurt him. I'm not so old that I need other people making decisions for me. I know I can trust you not to write anything embarrassing about me or do anything wrong."

And that, Sandy thought, settled that. "Well, in that case, I'll go ahead and ask you this. Tío Jaime, would you be interested in appearing on a TV show with me? Doing the same thing you do now, answering questions and giving advice, but on TV instead of on the Web site?" She didn't like springing it on him like this but figured there was no time like the present. Angelica had suggested it, and Sandy knew from experience that Angelica's suggestions were actually polite demands.

"I don't know, m'ija. I like answering your questions and visiting with you here, and I don't care what you do with the answers, since I don't have a computer anyway. But I'm thinking a TV show would be too much for me." He looked out into the distance and shook his head. "I don't want to be famous."

After their visit was over, Sandy drove home and reflected on what the old man had said. He had the right idea, she thought. Being famous, even just a little bit, wasn't all it was cracked up to be.

Yes, it got you free drinks and free clothes. And fans and compliments. And, most importantly, recognition for your hard work.

But it also got you things you didn't expect. Like people

who definitely *weren't* fans criticizing you in public. And you had to worry about every little thing you did in case someone was watching. There'd always be someone with an ax to grind and anonymous access to the Internet.

However, for Sandy, the benefits outweighed the inconveniences. She was just famous enough to have plenty of fans reading her work but not yet so famous that anyone would ever write articles about her.

And that, she decided, was the ideal balance. That was the way she planned to keep it.

44

Sandy walked into her regular nail salon, which was tucked into an obscure shopping center on the north side of town. Now she felt less like a carefree bird than a weary carrier pigeon with a weight dragging in the bag at her side.

She was carrying an invitation, and not for another club opening or media party. It was the invitation to her father's wedding.

There was nothing else in the envelope—no letter, no note, not even a scribbled explanation on the card itself. Just the same impersonal invitation hundreds of other people must have received. As if Sandy were just one of hundreds, no one special.

She took the massage chair the white-coated ladies indicated, letting them remove her sandals without speaking. The smell of acetone and the whine of tiny belt sanders applied to fake nails barely reached her consciousness. Sandy sat back into her chair's noisily vibrating tough love, closed her eyes, and tried to remember the last time she'd even heard from her father.

It'd been a few days ago. He'd left her a quick voice mail asking if everything was okay and if she needed any help making her student loan payments. And that was it. No mention of his upcoming wedding.

Of course Sandy could have gotten more information from her mother. But she'd been avoiding Mrs. Saavedra as much as possible, not wanting to hear any of that news from those lips.

"Excuse me," said the woman in the seat next to her. She sounded annoyed, probably about something the nail techs were doing. Sandy stayed still and eavesdropped while her own tech drained the water in the foot bath below her. "Excuse me," the woman said again, louder. "Do you work for the Web site called Not Your Pappy?"

Sandy opened her eyes and turned to look at the woman. "Me?"

"Yes. I recognize you." The woman was in her mid-forties or early fifties. She had puffy brown hair streaked with blond and wore a brightly colored T-shirt decorated with what looked like graffiti and rhinestones. It clashed with the displeased look on her face. She turned toward Sandy as well as she could without disrupting the paint job going on at her feet. "You're Sandy S. You wrote that article about Hispanic vampire romance novels."

Sandy nodded, not sure whether to say any more. Who was this woman? Not a vampire fan, surely? And she certainly didn't look Hispanic. So what was her problem?

She didn't keep Sandy in suspense for long. "You made fun of Lucia San Lucas's series, *Hot-Blooded Suckers*. You said reading it was a painful experience, and not because any 'knock-off Lestat' had bitten you. You called her writing 'horrid' and said her syntax was a 'satanic force'!"

Sandy felt herself cringing in her massage chair as the woman's voice got louder and louder. Those were the words she had written about that particular author, yes. But somehow they sounded much uglier coming out of this woman's mouth than they had when Sandy was typing them.

On either side of them, customers and nail techs alike were turning to see what was going on. This, Sandy thought, was one crazy fan. She glanced nervously at the nearest technicians, who were beckoning to the salon's manager.

"Listen, ma'am," Sandy said in what she hoped was a soothing voice. "I understand that not everyone is going to agree with my opinions—"

"Lucia San Lucas is my sister-in-law!" the woman yelled. She was now trembling with passion and had pulled both feet out of her pedicurist's reach. "She may not be the best writer in the world, but she's a good person. She worked hard to get those books published, and she deserves all the success she's gotten with them!"

"I'm sure she does," Sandy began again, but to no avail.

"What have *you* ever written, besides a bunch of hateful words about people you've never met? My sister-in-law gets hundreds of letters from people whose lives were changed by her books! She's a role model for young Hispanic and plus-sized girls. Can *you* say that? What do you do, besides criticize women who are more successful than you?"

"Well…"

What could Sandy say at that point? She did plenty. Maybe she wasn't a role model, but she did inspire her readers, in certain ways. At the very least, she entertained them.

But even if she'd had a good answer to the question, this woman was obviously not in the mood to hear it.

The manager had come over and was now trying to soothe Lucia San Lucas's sister-in-law back into her seat.

Although the staff obviously didn't understand why the woman was angry, they clustered around her and coaxingly murmured, "You get discount, okay? You get discount," until her breathing had slowed back to normal. Finally she thanked them and handed over her credit card. Two technicians kneeled and gently eased her feet into disposable flip-flops. Then, with one last glare at Sandy, the woman got up and marched imperiously out of the salon.

Sandy couldn't help noticing that her left pinky toe was still unpainted.

"You okay?" the manager asked her.

"Yes. Thank you," Sandy said.

"You know that lady?"

"Um...kind of," Sandy replied. She couldn't think of a way to explain that would make sense to people who weren't native English speakers. She imagined herself trying with "I write ugly words. She saw my words and got mad." But there was no need. The manager was already moving on. "You get discount, okay? You pick color? That's pretty color."

Sandy sat soaking in discomfort and awkwardness for the rest of her pedicure. Around her, the other patrons kept glancing her way. The technicians below her seat spoke a steady stream of Vietnamese. Whereas normally she'd brush off suspicions that they were talking about her brittle nails or lopsided calluses, Sandy knew for sure this time that they *were* talking about her. Conjecturing about what she'd done to enrage the other customer. Or who knew? Maybe they, too, knew who Sandy S. was and what kind of words she wrote for a living.

45

As Sandy drove from the salon to the office, her mind overflowed with the snappy replies she should have made.

Yeah, I bet your sister-in-law cried all the way to the bank. Her last advance could've funded ten scholarships for kids who want to write real literature!

Or: *I may criticize people for a living, but at least I know where to put my prepositions!*

Or: *You say her writing changed people? Into what, vampire bats?*

She wished she'd said any of these. Or anything at all.

The truth was, Sandy told herself, she'd been caught off guard. She hadn't expected to get yelled at for criticizing celebrities because—hello!—they were *celebrities*. They didn't need protection. Now that Sandy was removed from the situation and thinking about it with a clear head, she realized that there was no way Lucia San Lucas had ever read Sandy's Nacho Papi posts about her crappy writing. Or if she had read them, there was no way she'd cared. Why would she?

Ms. Lucas had hit the big time and was going to rake it in, no matter what someone like Sandy said. She undoubtedly got way more flak on a daily basis from critics who were way meaner than Sandy. What difference did one more voice in the fray make? Especially when the critics would never outweigh the adoring fans who were perfectly happy to spend their money on overwrought Latino plus-size vampire romance. So there was no use getting upset about anything that crazy woman had said, was there?

Sandy told herself all of those things, over and over, until she felt better.

SHE MADE IT to the office only five minutes late for the meeting. "Sorry, sorry," she called, waving at everyone around the table—Angelica; Lori; Francisco, Marco, the new tech assistant; and Michelle and Jasmine, the new interns; plus the phone in the middle of the table that represented Philippe, who was in Miami at the moment—before taking her seat.

"Let's get started," Angelica said. "We have a lot on the agenda today."

Sandy pulled out her notebook, eager to distract herself from the drama that had just gone down. And she was especially eager to hear this week's page-view count and see if she'd won the weekly bonus again. She was sure she had; her posts on Heather Santiago's rehab stint had done very well, and her last "Ask the Chupacabra" had been pure gold.

"Contract amendments," Angelica said. She put her hand on the stack of papers in front of her on the table, then passed it to Lori. "We have a new salary structure. From now on, you'll get fewer credits from page views and more credits for your TV segment ideas."

"For our ideas? How do you credit those?" Sandy asked.

"The ideas that are good enough to make it to the

air get the credit," Angelica replied. "You pitch your best ideas, and I decide which make it on. For our regular news segments, you'll take equal turns anchoring. Unless, of course, viewer feedback shows a preference for any of you. If that happens, we'll make adjustments as necessary."

There was a moment of silence while the staffers absorbed this information. Then the student named Marco piped up. "Do assistants and interns get credits for their ideas too?"

Angelica favored the boy with a smile. "That's a good idea. Why don't you come see me after the meeting and tell me what you have in mind."

Marco and his fellow interns practically bounced with excitement. Francisco, Sandy noticed, looked a little sick.

"I need you to sign these clauses and return them to me before you can proceed with this week's recordings," Angelica prompted them.

Sandy looked down at the contract amendment that'd been passed to her. It was five pages long and looked just like all the others they'd given her since she'd started working for Levy Media. With a sigh, she took out her pen and signed away.

Two HOURS LATER, Sandy was down the hall, on the set. The "interview set," to be precise, which looked a little like a college-dorm common room. It had three cheap loveseats flanked by potted plastic trees, and there were framed posters on the two fake-brick walls. One of them was actually Oscar's old Frida Kahlo print, the one that used to hang in what was now Angelica's office. The only other item of interest in the room was the giant monitor parked on a rolling TV stand between two of the loveseats. Its screen showed the Nacho Papi logo.

The room reminded Sandy of the sets you always saw on the cable music stations where the hosts sat around introducing music videos or interviewing small-time bands. And now she knew why those sets were so common: they were cheap and easy to make, and much smaller than they appeared on TV. This one had taken less than a week for Levy Media to create, and it was one of three other sets in the same building as the Nacho Papi offices. So, Sandy knew, the rent couldn't have been much.

She was about to record a segment on this set, interviewing small-time reality-show contestants. Two of them waited for her on the loveseats, young and nervous-looking in the light of the blazing lamps that the Nacho Papi lighting technician intern kept readjusting. Next to him, in the business corner of the room, camera technician interns adjusted their cameras. Angelica had even found a couple of intern directors—graduate students who worked for less than minimum wage and were grateful for the film credits, if you could call them that. The real director, of course, was Angelica herself. She supervised everything, either on the set as they taped, or after the fact from the editing room.

Sandy took her place on the loveseat farthest to the right, giving the two young women an encouraging smile that only one of them returned. She knew exactly how they felt. She'd been at least that nervous the first time she'd come to this set to film her first segment. She still was that nervous, in fact. But, unlike these girls, who were barely out of high school, she knew how to hide it.

The crew was ready within a few minutes. Unlike everything about TV Sandy had ever seen on the movies, this crew worked quickly and quietly. There was no clapper thing, no one yelling "Take one!" Instead, Angelica herself said, "Quiet, everyone," and then "Okay, go."

Sandy smiled at Angelica and the student behind the camera, still unable to bring herself to look into the actual lens. She had index cards on her lap but didn't refer to them as she began: "Hi, guys. Sandy S. here. I'm talking with Baby and Lola from *Video Girl Wannabes*, the Musi-Caliente reality show. They're going to give us the inside story on the show you've been loving to hate for the past few weeks. But don't worry—no spoilers. They won't tell us who wins at the end."

She turned to the young women. Again, one of them smiled—the one with orangey highlights and colored contact lenses who only looked fourteen years old to Sandy even though everyone on that show was supposed to be eighteen or over. The other, who had long black hair under a newsboy cap, didn't smile. She glared at Sandy and said, "Yeah, uh—my name is Lisa. Lisa Quintanilla. They just called us Lola and Baby for the show."

"Oh." Sandy was thrown off guard. No one had given her much background info on these people, and she'd only planned to ask them a few questions about the show itself. From the few episodes she'd seen she knew that this Lola—Lisa—was supposed to be something of a tough girl. But she looked to Sandy like a run-of-the-mill suburban poser. Sandy took the interruption in stride, turning to the other girl and saying, "So your real name isn't Baby?"

"No," she simpered. "But you can go ahead and call me that."

"Okay, Baby. Why don't you start by telling us where you learned to dance."

Above their heads, the monitor flickered into life, showing a clip from *Video Girl Wannabes*, in which "Baby" wore cut-off jean shorts and a wet tank top and danced as if she'd been stripping since birth.

Seeing herself on the screen, the girl laughed. "I don't know. I just watched, like, a lot of videos."

Baby wasn't the brightest bulb on the show, Sandy knew. She'd frequently been made the butt of jokes on the show. If Sandy wanted to, it'd be really easy to make fun of Baby now. But she didn't want to, not really. She felt an odd affinity for her. Maybe it was because she'd known quite a few girls who dressed and talked like Baby, back when she went to high school on the east side of town. It had always seemed ironic to her that these girls who wore the skimpiest outfits also wore crucifixes on their necks.

The monitor was now playing clips of Baby in a pillow fight with other contestants, Baby pretending to wash a car while dancing in a wet mini dress, and Baby kissing another girl.

At this point, Sandy was supposed to ask about the same-sex kissing. Instead, though, she said, "Have your parents seen the show?"

Baby laughed again. "Yeah."

"What'd they think?"

The girl glanced up at the monitor thoughtfully, as if trying to remember. "Well, my mom liked it, but my dad got kind of mad."

"Did he?" Sandy was genuinely curious at this point. In her peripherals she saw the crew at their silent work. And Angelica, watching with narrowed eyes. Sandy leaned forward a little. "What did he say?"

Baby's smile became slightly awkward. "He, like, yelled at me and stuff. When they saw the one with me kissing Lil Ruby, he got, like, super mad."

"What'd he do?" Sandy had an idea already, but she had to ask.

"He, like, called me some names. In Spanish. And he kind of, like, pushed me a little bit. And then, you know...I had to move to my friend's house." She stopped there and glanced at the crew, as if looking for approval.

All thoughts of making fun of this girl left Sandy's mind at that point. She didn't even want to ask the lesbian question. But Angelica was there, waiting. Sandy decided to try to lighten the moment. She said, "Well, so, is there going to be any more kissing on TV in your future?"

Baby shrugged. "I don't know. I mean, if they tell me to."

"Do you have anything lined up? Any videos?" Sandy wanted to throw this girl a bone, if possible. She noticed Lisa/Lola getting antsy next to Baby.

"Yeah. Big Daddy B, the rapper that was on the second episode with us? He liked my stuff and asked me to be on the video for his next single."

"What's the name of it?" Sandy asked.

"It's called 'Why U Such a Ho,'" Baby replied proudly.

"Well, congratulations on that. We'll keep an eye out for it." With that, Sandy shifted attention to the other girl. "Lisa. How about you? Any opportunities coming out of *Video Girl Wannabes* yet?"

"Yeah," she said, in a ghetto-esque drawl that, again, Sandy couldn't help but suspect was less than authentic. "Yeah, I got a few things goin' on. Nothin' I can talk about yet, you know."

"I understand. Let's talk about the show, then, and your role on it. You were something of an instigator, I noticed."

"Mm-hmm." Lisa slouched down farther in her seat and peered at Sandy from under the brim of her cap.

Sandy was instantly annoyed. Whereas before she'd been speaking out of turn, this Lisa character was now turning reticent. Sandy wondered if it was in reaction to

Baby's embarrassing admissions. Whatever the reason, she had to soldier on. "Who'd you have the most problems with?"

Lisa shrugged. "Nobody, really. I mean, me and Queenie got into it a few times, but they made it look worse on the show than it was in real life. She and I are actually friends now."

"Have you hung out with her since the show finished taping?" Sandy asked.

"Well, no," Lisa said. "We've been too busy, basically. With all the stuff going on."

"If you had the opportunity to say something to one of your former castmates, what would you say, and to whom?"

Lisa sat up a little and fixed Sandy with the same glare she'd given her at the beginning of the segment. "Actually, you know who I'd like to say something to?"

"Who's that?"

Lisa looked directly into the camera then, as if threatening the entire audience. Behind her, the monitor played clips of her shouting and shoving her fellow reality-show contestants. "Belinda B and that punk-ass Donny the Man!"

Sandy recognized the names but, for the sake of their viewers' edification, asked, "They aren't on the show. Who are they?"

"They're the people talking the most shit about us on your Web site." Lisa tried her best to look menacing, but Sandy could tell that she was getting a slight thrill from saying curse words on camera, just like she'd done in the reality show.

"So what would you say to them?" Sandy asked. It was time, she decided, to do a little instigating herself. "You went on a reality show in order to win parts in dance videos and other shows, presumably so you could get famous, is that right?"

"Well, yeah."

"And now people see you on TV, starting fights with Queenie and Moniqua and the other girls, and now some of the viewers don't like it. They're talking about the show online, and they're stating their opinions. What's wrong with that?"

Lisa paused, then replied, "What's wrong is that I'm trying to be a dancer, here. I'm not trying to have a bunch of fools talking about my clothes, my tatts, the size of my ass. It's not *about* that."

"So you're saying you want to be famous enough for everyone to talk about your dancing, but not so famous that they talk about anything else?" Sandy asked, unable to repress a smile. "Have you ever expressed your opinion of a celebrity? Like, say, rapper Sister Sonya?" Lisa didn't answer and Sandy pressed on. "Did you, for instance, say in the very first episode of *Video Girl Wannabes* that Sister Sonya was, quote, a 'washed-up, ugly-ass dyke?'" Knowing that the editor interns would remove the offensive words later, Sandy clarified, "Did you criticize her looks and use a homophobic term for her sexual orientation?"

Lisa shrugged and shook her head for a moment. "Man. That's different. Sister Sonya's a damned millionaire."

Sandy couldn't repress her smile now. "Do you want to be a millionaire, Lisa?"

Lisa shook her head harder, in obvious dismay at having embarrassed herself without any help from Sandy. "Man. Come on."

"Do you want to tell Belinda and Donny the Man to hold on to their opinions until you make your first million? Do you want everyone on the Internet to stop talking about you until that happens?"

"Man. This is some bullshit," was all the girl could say.

"It *is* bullshit," Sandy said. "I agree. But we're going to keep watching, Lisa, to see if you make it. I hope that you do."

46

Post on Nacho Papi's Web site, Wednesday, May 24

Nobel Horniate, or Latest in a Long Line of Latino Authors with Groupies
by Sandy S.

Some of you literary types may remember that Nobel Prize-winning poet Honorio Mendiola mysteriously bailed on addressing Cornell graduates a few weeks ago. Well, sources now tell us why. According to students, Mr. Mendiolo spent that day in his hotel room, recovering from a night of drinking, firing up Colombia's finest, and—no doubt—measuring verse with three young co-eds. For the record? Honorio prefers blondes.

See link to similar story about Jose Sonora Williams, below. What's up with these macho Latino writers, using our country's institutions of learning as hunting grounds for one-nighters? This takes me back to my own college days. I remember a visit from a celebrated young novelist who will remain nameless (his name started with G and ended with ilberto) who made it his business to pick off the saddest, least talented, and most attention-starved of our creative writing section for "special mentoring." Never mind that he, like his fellow horny scribes, was ugly as sin. The most annoying effect of the phenomenon was that we had to listen to his groupies reading Gilberto Gonzalez-inspired

second-person ramblings at every single class for the rest of the
semester. Boring! Young women, do us all a favor and call up
someone like Christian Ortiz, instead. I hear he's newly single.

READER COMMENTS ON **NOBEL HORNIATE**

Oh my God that is so funny! Please tell me Gilberto G hit on you
and you shot him down, Sandy!!
Luisa

Give me a break. Honorio Mendiola is a genius. Nobody at Nacho
Papi is fit to shine his shoes. Who cares if he has a few groupies?
　　Also, this is pretty rich coming from Sandy S, considering that
she slept with her own Creative Writing teacher until he got fed
up and dumped her. Bitter, party of one?
Watcher in the Wings

Sounds like Sandy is jealous that she's the ugly one on the site.
Show us more Lori!
Not Yo' Papi's Macho

Hey, Watcher in the Wings, get your story straight. He wasn't her
teacher, and Sandy dumped HIM. Take it from someone who knows
the facts first hand. What are you anyway? Mendiola's mom?
V for Verguenza

No, I'm not his mom. I'm just a fellow writer who can't stand
sour grapes from talentless hacks. I wasn't going to go there, but
now that you're questioning my credentials...Sandy S. is a total
starfish in bed, from what I hear. Two, she didn't look that good
until *after* she and my friend broke up. Third, she has a big
mole on her right cheek. (Not the cheek on her face, either.) And
she doesn't eat jalapenos because they give her gas. More than
enough reason for D.T. to dump her, as far as I'm concerned,

without even considering her crappy writing and condescending attitude.
Watcher in the Wings

Total BS! And, hello, spicy foods give a lot of people gas. D.T.'s the talentless hack here, and Sandy dumped HIM. Whatever he told you was obviously just the story he uses to cry himself to sleep every night.

(Hey, Sandy, sorry I didn't return your call the other day. I'll call you tonight, okay?)
V for Verguenza

Watcher, sounds like you have a sick fascination with Sandy's butt.

Verguenza: Tell us more! It's obvious that you have the *real* inside track! Private message me!

Oh, and Honorio's way overrated, fan boys notwithstanding.
Belinda B

Whatever, Watchate and Nacho Macho. Lori's cute but I definitely wouldn't kick Sandy S out of bed for eating jalapenos! Sandy, whether you dumped him or he dumped you, you can call me to console you, girl!
The Wild Juan

47

Sandy sat in a kitschy diner in South Austin, miles away from the university and Daniel's stomping grounds, where she read the latest string of anonymous commenters' vitriol and her loyal readers' defense. Earlier that morning she had parked her car at Calypso to get an iced latte. Right before she'd entered the coffee shop someone across the street had shouted, "Hey, Sandy S.!"

When Sandy turned she saw two frat types waving at her. "You suck!" one of them yelled. They weren't waving, she saw then. They were throwing her the finger.

Unsettled, she'd gotten back into her car and driven away. At that moment she had almost felt afraid. Now, however, she was just perturbed. And annoyed.

She couldn't tell if things had gotten worse since the big announcement that Nacho Papi was going to be on TV, or if the poison-pen letters had increased since she'd seen Daniel that day at Calypso. Maybe he had told his friends his own version of their breakup and they'd taken it upon themselves to avenge him publicly. Or maybe Honorio Mendiola was posting the comments, she thought with a rueful smile. Or any one of the other celebrities or demi-celebrities she'd written about over the past several months.

V for Verguenza was her friend Veronica, of course. Sandy was grateful for her support but sometimes got annoyed when Veronica dropped personal details into her comments, as if to show off to the other readers that she had inside knowledge on Sandy and the other Nacho Papi staff members.

Feeling the need for another ally, Sandy closed her laptop and called her friend Jane, with whom she'd been playing phone and e-mail tag for a couple of weeks now, figuring Monday at lunch time was as good a chance to reach her as any.

"Hello?"

"Jane, it's me. Hey, are you reading this stuff on the site?"

Jane paused for a second. "On your work site, you mean? Or on your personal site?"

"On Nacho Papi. All the comments under the post I wrote about Honorio Mendiola."

"Oh. No, I haven't read that one yet." Jane sounded the tiniest bit weary, as if she thought Sandy had called specifically to find out if her friend had been keeping up with her posts.

As soon as she'd said it Sandy remembered with brilliant clarity that, back at UT, Jane had been one of the students mesmerized with Gilberto Gonzalez during his visit. And that, sure enough, Jane had also tried her hand at writing some Gilberto-esque sonnets, although not for any creative writing class. She'd only shown them to Sandy and Veronica.

Sandy realized then that she'd been partly inspired to write that post, totally subconsciously, by Jane's temporary infatuation with Gilberto Gonzalez. She wished suddenly and fervently that she hadn't called Jane and brought it up. Because Jane probably wouldn't have read the post on her own. She didn't seem to read most of the site.

Sandy decided to change the subject. "Well, yeah. No, don't worry about it. I was just going to tell you something one of the commenters said, but it's not that interesting. What's going on with you?"

"Nothing much." Jane's short tone made Sandy worry, then, that maybe she *had* read the post in question and was upset about it.

"What's wrong? You sound...annoyed or something," she ventured.

"No. Not at all," Jane said, definitely sounding annoyed now. "Just busy. Listen, let me call you back, okay? I have to do this thing real quick."

"Okay." Sandy hung up, feeling defeated and regretful. Obviously Jane had read it, and there was nothing Sandy could do about it now. But she really hadn't remembered that stuff about Jane and her poems until after the fact. She couldn't help it if that had been in the back of her mind while she was writing, could she?

There was nothing she could do, she told herself again. Especially if Jane wouldn't even admit she'd read the piece. She'd just have to wait for her friend to get over it.

Sandy felt more alone than she had before calling Jane. She was sitting in a diner, surrounded by strangers, mulling over things strangers were saying about her. She couldn't talk to her two best friends about it, and she no longer had a boyfriend to talk to at all. She didn't want to call her mom, because every time they'd talked lately it'd been about her dad's upcoming wedding. Sandy's mother kept demanding that Sandy not attend as a show of loyalty to her, and then demanding that Sandy go to the wedding, after all, and act as a spy on her behalf. It was driving Sandy crazy—crazier than her mother usually drove her. Hence, she was sitting in a diner on the edge of town, avoiding her mother's company.

For the hundredth time that week alone Sandy thought about moving out of her mother's garage apartment. She wished she'd considered it more seriously before quitting her tech-writing job. Yes, Nacho Papi was paying her well right now—a pretty good salary for someone with only a token rent payment each month. But if she was ever going to move out of her mother's she'd have to find a way to make quite a bit more. Maybe the TV show would take care of that. Angelica had explained the latest, greatest salary and bonus structure, but it'd been too confusing for Sandy to take in during the meeting. She'd been planning to get Philippe to explain it to her over lunch when he got back into town.

Sandy felt a pull within her. A strong pull, starting in the area of her chest and radiating out toward her fingers, which drifted to her notebook computer's keyboard of their own will. She recognized the motion. It was a temptation to blog, to type her woes into a bottle and throw it out to a sea of unseen strangers who would send back their own messages of understanding, of sympathy, of resonation.

But that avenue was no longer open to her. The people who used to hang on Miss TragiComic Texas's every word were being replaced with people who knew her to be Sandy S., Journalist-slash-Gossip Writer and TV Star. They would no longer go to her site to read about *her*—the real Sandy, née Dominga Saavedra. And Sandy had to protect that self more than ever now. No longer anonymous, she could no longer trust strangers.

48

Time: Thursday, May 25, 9:02 AM
To: misstctx@misstctx.com
From: ronaldg1973@jumpmail.net
Subject: You don't know me, but

Dear Miss Texas,

My name is Ronald Green and I have an opportunity for you. I have an idea for a novel based on my life and I think you are the perfect person to collaborate with me on writing it. You have a pretty good style on this diary and I would like to see my ideas told in this style. I will pay you a reasonable fee once my book starts making profit.

If you are interested, please contact me immediately. I'll be waiting to hear from you.

49

The next day Sandy found herself sitting at yet another restaurant table alone. This time, at least, it was swanky. Luna de Miel, the new tapas restaurant in the medical center, was a former house, now all done up in carnations and candles. Afternoon sun slanted through the slatted blinds and onto the glossy walnut table where Sandy sat and resisted the temptation to pull out her laptop and get some writing done. She wished she were home, working, or even at work, working. Her boss, Sandy knew, rarely called one-on-ones in order to share good news.

Angelica was late, of course. By the time she strutted in, texting on her Zoom Phone and simultaneously talking on her old purple cell, Sandy had already demolished a pile of lavash with its accompanying plate of spiced olive oil. She set down the last corner of bread and waited for Angelica to give orders to the waiter. "Just a glass of chianti, please. Well, go ahead and bring me the smoked scallops with chorizo, too. And bottled water, with lemon." She turned to Sandy. "Have you ordered?"

Sandy requested the Moroccan chicken pie and an iced tea. The waiter swept away and Angelica, as always, got right down to business.

"Did you talk to your goat man? Did he agree to do the show?"

"No, he wasn't interested." Sandy said it calmly. She'd learned over the months that Angelica preferred to deal with people as direct as she was, and unconfident people made her suspicious. So she always told the truth without making excuses, whether or not she had the answer her boss wanted to hear.

"Okay." Angelica sank back into her booth seat with a sigh. "You'll have to try again, then. You'll have to convince him."

Sandy said nothing.

After a few moments Angelica went on. "The issue is, Sandy, that we need content. And by content I don't mean each of us sitting at a desk reading aloud the posts we've written for the week. It *is* cable, but we can't throw together just *any*thing."

Sandy nodded. She'd been thinking along that line herself ever since Angelica had made the announcement about the TV deal.

"I'm really annoyed that George left." The waiter appeared with their drinks and Angelica waited for him to pour a tiny decanter of wine into her glass before continuing. "I'd been thinking that the two of you could do a segment where you argue every week. You know how the readers were starting to pick up on the friction between you and liked to gossip about it. But then he had to run off with Tony." She meant the editor of Buzz News, the competition to which George had defected. "He's e-mailed me twice since we announced the deal." She looked at Sandy suggestively.

"Why? Let me guess—he wants to come back, doesn't he?" Sandy knew what a narcissist George was, and that he wouldn't be able to resist the opportunity to see himself on TV every week, as opposed to just seeing his own name in print. "*Would* you take him back?"

Angelica gave a ladylike shrug. "Possibly. It depends on what ideas he has to offer."

Sandy frowned. The idea of working with George again, after a month of enjoying his absence, was annoying. But she had to admit that since he'd left the site was missing a certain element that Philippe and Francisco had been unable to provide.

She got the underlying message in Angelica's words, too. Her boss was looking for people with ideas for television content. So far Sandy had provided none. Nothing out of the ordinary, at any rate. It was time for her to start brainstorming.

"Sandy, I'm sure you realize by now that you're my favorite Nacho Papi writer."

"I am?" Sandy was surprised. She'd always assumed Philippe was Angelica's favorite.

"Yes. As I've told you before, you remind me of myself at your age. Just a little less ambitious." Angelica seemed impatient as the waiter showed up again with their food, interrupting her again. "And you have to be a little more ambitious, Sandy, if you want to succeed. You have to stay one step ahead. Two, three steps. You can't just sit around waiting for things to happen to you."

Sandy listened intently but couldn't think of anything worthwhile to say. She wished a fabulous content idea would come to her right at that moment. But her brain didn't oblige.

Angelica leaned forward. "I'm being pressured to make choices I wouldn't necessarily make on my own."

Sandy held her breath. This was it, then. She was going to be fired. After all this time, she was finally losing the dream job. Just as she'd feared, she hadn't been able to measure up. She adjusted her glasses. She wondered if it was too late to beg for her tech-writing job back.

"I have to hire another woman for the site. Someone sexy."

"Sexy?" Sandy stared at her boss in surprise. "What happened to good writing? Did you tell them we're writing cultural commentary here, and not running an escort service?"

"I think if it were up to them, they'd prefer that we somehow do both." Sandy was struck by the resignation on Angelica's face. The older woman sighed. "Like you, Sandy, I have bosses. And sometimes those bosses ask me to do things I don't agree with."

Sandy exhaled audibly. She wouldn't have imagined Angelica being pressured or pushed around by anyone, even by the people signing her paychecks. But now that she thought about it, it'd been naive to imagine that Jacob Levy would let Angelica do whatever she wanted with his site.

"We've narrowed it down to two candidates," Angelica continued between bites of scallop. "One is a student from Houston, and the other is one of our regular readers who's willing to relocate from Boston."

"What? Which one?"

"She went by the nickname La Sirena. If we pick her we'll keep that name for her, because it'll excite the other readers to think that they might eventually be on the show, too, if they give us enough page views. But her real name is Tracy...Trixie something. No—Trisha MacLeod, I think."

"What? Is she even Latina?"

Angelica shrugged again. "I think her mother's half or something. Who isn't Latino, these days? Jacob liked her, though. Just between you and me, that's who I think they'll end up picking." She fell silent then and stared morosely at the window while sipping her chianti.

Sandy was silent, too. At least she wasn't being fired. Yet. She still had time to think up something fantastic in order to keep her job. She cut up her chicken pie into smaller and smaller pieces and waited for Angelica to say more.

Finally she did. "Sandy, don't lose this opportunity. I really want you to help prove what I've been working to prove all along—that we can be smart and successful without having to be sexy, too. I mean, we as Latinas."

Sandy raised her eyebrows at this. This was coming from the woman who'd made the two females on her staff undergo makeovers in order to retain their jobs. Looking at Angelica's bleach job, tightly fitted suit jacket, and long fake nails, Sandy wondered if she really meant what she said. Or was she just saying what she thought Sandy wanted to hear? Needed to hear in order to do what Angelica wanted?

"This is only between you and me," she continued. "I hope you understand that. But I mean it—I need you to come up with something good, as fast as you can. I'll try to help, but it would be better if you were the one to do it. Try again with the Chupacabra feature—the readers really love that and you're the only one who could make that work."

Not that again, Sandy thought. Like a recurring allergy, she was irritated by the fact that she'd never gotten Tío Jaime to sign the release. She didn't even have that part of it settled, much less any likelihood of convincing the old man to become a regular guest on their show.

Sandy nodded, wanting Angelica to know that she was willing to do whatever it took to succeed in this situa-

tion, whether or not it ended up involving the Chupacabra. Because she didn't want to lose this job. Not with so
many people dying to take her place.

She put her mind into overdrive, grasping for other
ideas. "Angelica, what if, aside from the Chupacabra
thing, we do a charity event? To win the public's good
opinion?" She thought of events she'd seen on television
and remembered the yearly public television auction.
"What about an auction?"

Angelica took a sip of wine, making a face as if it tasted
bitter. "What kind of auction?"

"You know, like the public television station does. We
could get our sponsors to donate stuff, and viewers could
call in to bid on it. Then we'd make a big show of giving
the money to some organization—maybe for Latino lit-
eracy or something."

The older woman frowned. "Do you watch the public
television auctions every year?"

"No. But I've seen them." Sandy tried to keep her voice
enthusiastic. "Once."

"Exactly. You've seen them. But you don't tune in spe-
cially to watch them. Why would you? They're boring."

Sandy felt herself slump a little in her seat. Angelica
was right, of course.

"It isn't a *bad* idea. It just isn't very exciting. We'd need
to think of a way to spice it up." Angelica narrowed her
eyes and peered into the distance.

Sandy mimicked her boss's expression, pretending to
join her in deep thought. Really, though, she had nothing. How did you make an auction exciting? With exciting donations, obviously. Maybe with…Lori in a sexy
outfit, updating the bids? No, Sandy told herself. That
was crass.

Before she could get much farther than that, Angelica's

thoughtful face turned to a smile. "I've got it! We can auction off dates with you and the other staffers!"

Sandy's mouth fell open in horror. "What?"

Angelica hunkered down like a football coach issuing orders and gave Sandy's arm one of her rough little squeezes. "We need to present to sponsors right away, to pay for the dinner and whatever entertainment...maybe a hotel...maybe evening wear for the staff. It'll be you, Lori, Philippe for sure, maybe Francisco. God, it's too bad we don't have a lesbian on staff, too. Although we *could* offer Lori to men *and* women. We could do that with all of you, actually. Yes." Angelica sat back, her mind obviously rushing through steps far beyond what Sandy would have been able to imagine.

"Angelica, no." Sandy was surprised to hear herself contradict her boss outright like that. But she had to put a stop to this before it was too late. "That's not what I meant. I didn't mean auctioning off ourselves."

"What's wrong, Sandy? It's harmless. We'll run background checks. We'll send cameramen along to keep everyone safe."

"It's not that." Sandy struggled to formulate the words that would change her boss's mind. "It's just—too personal. Some of the commenters are already getting out of hand, constantly talking about the way we look and their stupid sex fantasies about us."

"That's going to happen with any public figures, though," reasoned Angelica. "They see you as someone above them, something they can feel free to fantasize about. So winning an evening with you guys will be a fantasy come true for them." She smiled. Then, seeing that Sandy wasn't convinced, she added, "If anything, it'll make you more human to them again."

Her words were obviously meant to be comforting,

but they'd missed the mark. Sandy shook her head. "I just don't think—I just think this would be too much."

Angelica leaned forward. Her expression teetered between sympathetic and exasperated. "Well, Sandy, I'm not going to force you to do this. But I hope you'll consider it. It would be disappointing to our audience if everyone but you participated."

She was right. They *would* be disappointed. Because, Sandy realized, Angelica was going to go ahead with this idea. That's how quickly she decided things. And everyone else on staff would be more than willing to say yes. And they'd think she was being a big baby if she said no. And then the readers would catch on. And they'd talk about it in the comments. They'd know she was afraid—afraid of *them*.

Sandy didn't know which was worse, the constant comments about her or having the commenters know how much their words bothered her.

She would just have to do it, wouldn't she? If she wanted to keep up her front, she'd have to go along with the plan. If she wanted to keep her job.

Angelica went back into mental overdrive, planning days and weeks ahead. "I'm going to have to get this to Legal as soon as possible, but it shouldn't be too hard because Banana Nation did something similar last year with a contest prize and a staff dinner." She looked back at Sandy. "Oh, and we'll have to pick a charity to donate the money to. Do you want to handle that part?"

"Sure." For Sandy that would be the fun part—the only fun part, probably. And it would keep her mind off the frightening part: going on a date with a complete stranger crazy enough to pay money for the privilege.

"Good, good," Angelica said quietly, her thoughts obviously light-years away now.

Either because they were sitting in the afternoon sunlight or because the older woman had been working harder lately, Sandy saw now that her boss really was the same age as her own mother. They had the same wrinkles around their eyes, and the same eyes that seemed to guard against disappointment at every turn.

Seeing that made Sandy feel a little less dreadful about the situation for some reason. Angelica may have been a little manipulative, with the tendency to twist Sandy's ideas into something sensationalistic, scandalous, or downright scary, but she knew what it took to succeed, and she was willing to share that knowledge with Sandy. It was better than being nagged about her hair and her personal life by a woman who didn't even read her work.

50

So, does this guy record *everything* you do?" Sandy's latest interviewee said in a low voice, near her ear. "Or do you get to break away and have coffee, in private, sometimes?"

She turned and gave him what she could feel was a radiant smile. Her subject, Tony Ojeda—Tony O. for short—walked her out of his classroom and toward the side exit of the community college building. They were safe for now; they'd left Intern Marco several yards back, still fumbling with his camera bag. Sandy had a few moments of privacy with Tony O., with his handsome eyes and gorgeous Chilean accent.

"They do cut me loose, sometimes," she said to him. "Why, would you like me to interview you again?"

He laughed, looking down at her face with his nice smile as they walked faster, as if in silent agreement to make it out the exit door, down the steps, and to the relative intimacy of the parking lot alone together. "I'd love you to interview me again. Actually, I'd like you to come back and talk to the kids, without the cameras. They really liked you, especially the girls. You could tell them about yourself this time, and how you got this job. They really need mentors, these kids." He glanced back in the direction of the classroom where they'd just left his writers' group—the group he'd started for underprivileged kids. Sandy felt her heart melt a little at the thoughtfulness on his face. This guy was incredible. Was it at all possible that he was single, too? And interested in her?

Right on cue, he turned back to her and said, "But I was wondering if you'd like to get coffee sometime with me. Just the two of us. If you're interested, I mean."

"Oh, I'm definitely interested." Smooth as someone onscreen, Sandy reached into her bag and pulled out one of her cards, then handed it to Tony O. with a casual-but-electrifying brush of her fingers over his.

She felt like a person at a masquerade ball in Napoleonic times. Like she was wearing a sexy costume, along with a mask that made her feel free to go farther—flirt harder—than she would have in her normal clothes.

Dominga Saavedra, for instance, never would have handed her card to a man like this. Hell, she didn't even have any cards. But Sandy S....*she* had cards, she had guts, and she had men hoping to catch her attention.

She held her mask in place, smiling and going so far as to wish him goodbye with a half-hug and intercontinental air kiss very near the cheek. And then Intern Marco emerged from the building, ready to roll.

Perfect timing, Sandy thought. She wasn't sure she could hold on to the façade any longer.

But, she told herself, she'd be ready with it again the next time they met. Sandy S. had confidence and courage. That's who she'd be when she spent time with Tony, and with everyone else she was going to meet.

As Marco drove her back to the office to film her news segment for the week, Sandy lay her head back on the seat and allowed herself to daydream. Tony O. would go to her site—Nacho Papi—and read her words to find out more about her. He'd read her posts about other writers and realize she had excellent literary taste. Her posts about pop culture would show him she was whip-smart and didn't waste her time with trash. He'd see her conversations with the Chupacabra and realize that she was a good person.

He'd see the auction, eventually. He'd bid on a date with her. Sandy would have Angelica donate the proceeds to his teen writers' group. And then she'd go out with him for free.

Marco tried to beat a light by taking a corner a little too fast. Sandy was jolted back into an upright position, back into reality. It was too bad, she realized, that Angelica probably wouldn't want to use this writers' group footage for the show. She'd been way pickier lately and had said the other day that Sandy needed to keep the "feel-good, do-goody stuff" to a minimum.

It'd go on the site at least. Eventually. After Sandy turned in a few pieces about teen pop star Heather Lopez's sex tape. And a few about how much Toro vodka she'd drunk over the weekend.

Sandy had a lot of work to do. Too much, she thought, as she and Marco pulled into their designated area of the parking garage. She was taping segments, for the show and the site, five and six times a week now. Her post quota was higher than ever. Wasn't it time, she asked herself as she entered the office, for Angelica to show her a little appreciation? Maybe in the form of a raise?

She would ask Angelica today, maybe. Maybe right now.

"She's here," Philippe said as Sandy walked through the door into their maxi-office. The staff table was strewn with more laptops and interns than ever. Some of the interns looked at Sandy curiously, or with smirks on their faces. She ignored them. They were all a bunch of wannabes, constantly fantasizing about taking the place of one of the real staff writers.

"Call her in," Sandy heard Angelica say from the inner recess of her own office.

Philippe beckoned to Sandy and she walked the gauntlet of the silent, staring interns to Angelica's door. What was going on? she wondered.

As she passed Philippe, he put his hand on her arm and whispered, "Honey. Don't freak out, okay?"

That scared her more than anything else he could have said, she realized. Holding her breath, she passed him and went through the doorway to where Angelica waited, laptop open on her desk.

"Sandy, you need to see this," her boss said.

Bad news about the site? About Levy Media? They were going to get laid off, Sandy thought. This was the end of Nacho Papi.

Angelica stood, indicating that Sandy was to take her chair. Philippe had come in and closed the door behind him, so that the three of them would be alone. Angelica crossed over to where he stood. The two of them looked at the window. Then, looking back at Sandy, they realized that she'd been watching them.

"Read," Philippe said, pointing to the monitor in front of her.

Sandy looked down and saw a long block of black text on white. Then the headline caught her eye.

In sober silence, her boss and her co-worker stood and waited for her to take in the words on the screen.

51

Post on Buzz News, Friday, June 2

The Not-So-Secret Sins of Sandy S
by George Cantu

AUSTIN, TEXAS. When Daniel Thomas first met fellow grad student Dominga Saavedra, all he saw was a shy smile and moderate talent for writing prose. He had no way of knowing that he'd just met the girl who would eventually ruin his career.

"She was always asking for my help with her writing," Daniel was to remember, later. "She acted so innocent. I had no idea that she was writing all about me and our intimate relationship, all along."

Under the pen name Sandy S, Dominga Saavedra writes for online gossip rag Nacho Papi's Web Site. (Full disclosure: The author of this piece formerly worked for the same site for a very brief period—long enough to find out enough about Dominga Saavedra that the story told here doesn't surprise him at all.) Concurrently, however, Sandy S has been writing her own blog under another synonym, Miss TragiComic Texas.

"Apparently everyone at the University knew about it. It was an open secret, basically. Open to everyone but me," Dr. Thomas mused sadly when asked about the Web site where Sandy S systematically divulged every detail about her relationship with him to an audience of literal thousands. "My friends, colleagues, and students had been reading about me on the site for months before I found out about it. They knew she was going to break up with me before I did."

Even the most personal and humiliating details of Sandy S's planned break-up with Daniel Thomas were there for all to see. At the same time, rumors swirled among readers of her employer's site that Sandy S was romantically involved with fellow Nacho Papi staffer Philippe Montemayor, providing further grist for speculation about her erstwhile victim.

"I never saw it coming," says Daniel, who now faces his own coworkers and employers every day knowing that they most likely know personal, embarrassing details of his life with a former University student. He hasn't yet been laid off or otherwise discriminated against, but knows that it's only a matter of time before something like that could potentially occur.

Meanwhile, Sandy S continues to criticize other citizens of the city where she lives, as well as celebrities and fictional characters alike, under the banner of Jacob Levy's Latino-focused "entertainment" site. One can't help but wonder if it was all a giant publicity stunt, designed to gain readership for Levy's media empire, with Dr. Thomas serving as an unwitting victim. However, at the time of printing, neither Jacob Levy nor Nacho Papi's editor, Angelica Villanueva O'Sullivan, could be reached for comment.

"My advice is, never date a journalism major. Or anyone who writes for anyone else. Or any woman who seems shy but is drawn to men who are successful in her chosen field," says Daniel Thomas, who is now unfortunately older and wiser.

Good advice, Daniel. Readers, you've been warned.

52

Sandy's eyes sped over the words on the monitor once, twice, then three times, absorbing more of the horror with each pass. It was unbelievable. How had George interviewed Daniel? And *why?* Daniel's colleagues had known about her personal blog all along, the article said. And now—Sandy re-read again, to be certain—now everyone who read Buzz News knew about it too. Anyone who cared to could do a search for "Miss TragiComic Texas" and find it.

"So I'm guessing you turned down George's offer to rejoin our staff?" Philippe asked Angelica wryly over Sandy's shoulder.

Angelica responded with a dry chuckle. "I'm guessing he had this idea up his sleeve for a while. He probably had the whole thing written and was holding his mouse over the Send button while listening to me turn him down."

The two of them laughed while Sandy sat at Angelica's desk holding back tears of shame and rage that blurred her view of the monitor on which the life-ruining words had been written. "How could he do this?" she heard herself say under her breath.

"Who, sweetie? George or your ex?" Philippe asked.

"I don't know. Either of them. No one even knows

about the site....Hardly anyone even *knew* about my site, until now."

Angelica put a hand on Sandy's shoulder and gave it a little pat. "Well, you know what they say, then. No publicity is bad publicity."

Sandy sniffed to keep herself from sobbing aloud. "For Nacho Papi, you mean? Because this certainly isn't going to be good for me."

"Sandy." Angelica motioned above Sandy's head and, with a parting shoulder-squeeze on her other side, Philippe glided out of the office, closing the door behind him. Angelica pulled one of her visitor's chairs across the office to her visibly shaken employee's side. "Listen, Sandy. I know this must be an awful shock to you at the moment. But, if you'll take a few deep breaths and just let your head clear..."

"Then what? I'll find a way to delete all traces of my blog before it's e-mailed to everyone I know? I'll think of a way to kill them both and hide the evidence?" Sandy heard her voice getting uncharacteristically, unprofessionally loud, but she didn't care. She was being stared in the face by one of the worst things that had ever happened to her.

"No." Angelica tried to pat Sandy's knee reassuringly, but she was obviously unpracticed at that sort of thing. "But you'll realize that this isn't the end of the world. There are far worse things that can happen. You might even see this as a good thing. It'll definitely get you more exposure as a writer."

"But I don't want that kind of exposure!" Sandy said. "That site wasn't supposed to be part of my résumé."

"Why not? You have some good pieces on it."

"What? You've read it?" Had Angelica gone to her blog already, Sandy wondered, since reading George's article that morning?

"Not the whole thing—just bits and pieces, a while back," her boss said in a soothing voice.

"But—how did you know about it?" Sandy was genuinely perplexed now.

Angelica narrowed her eyes as if trying to remember. "I think Lori or Oscar told me. Was it supposed to be secret?"

Sandy stared at her boss in horror. "Yes, it was supposed to be secret!"

Now it was Angelica's turn to look puzzled. "Then why did you put it on the Internet?"

Angelica's office door opened and Lori's head poked through. She gave Sandy a quick look of sympathy before saying, "Angelica, Jacob's on the phone for you."

Both women stood and Sandy gave a quick swipe under each eye with her finger, under her glasses. "I have to go. I'm going to...work from home today."

"Of course," Angelica said, patting her one last time on the shoulder, this time more roughly, as if trying to encourage a soldier back into the fray. "Do what you need to do. Go relax. We'll see you Monday."

Sandy felt the interns' eyes boring into her back as she gathered her things. She pulled a pair of sunglasses from her bag and put them on before making for the exit. She opened the door and almost ran into someone coming in. A young, tiny, blond someone, with blue eyes and a tight, low-cut T-shirt stretched over a considerable expanse of bustline.

"Sandy S.! Hi! I'm so glad to finally meet you!"

Sandy smiled at the young woman and edged around her, trying to hide her immediate annoyance at being stopped by a fan.

"I'm Trisha MacLeod. La Sirena," she said. Sandy stopped in her tracks, unable to keep from staring. The younger woman went on. "I'm going to be working with you guys! I'm so excited! I'm such a big fan of your work!"

Sandy ended up mumbling something polite and shaking Trisha/La Sirena's hand awkwardly—the girl had tried to hug her—before getting out of there. She had enough drama going on already and simply couldn't process any more.

53

Reader comments on My Modern TragiComedy, Friday, June 2

Miss Tctx: I read that horible story online and I just want you to know that I can't beleive Papi chulo is such a jerk and also that Heartthrob Geekboy was never good enough for you and I'm sure he deserved what ever you did. They are both obviusly jelous of you

Comment left by: **Baby gurl!**

Well, now we see what you've been up to while on break. I had to come see what all the fuss was about and, all I can say is good riddance!

Comment left by: **Rocko**

Sandy: I don't care what anybody says. You're the best thing Nacho Papi has going on and George C is so obviously pissed that he jumped ship right before you guys hit the big time. As for your ex, I have to assume that you exaggerated his good qualities on this blog, because he sounds like a total douche to me. Gentlemen don't kiss and tell.

Comment left by: **Parker Peter**

What do you expect from a whore. I hope you get sued!

Comment left by: **Anonymous**

Wow. I just came here after reading the article about your ex and I have to say that I'm surprised. I thought it was going to be all about break-up drama, but I see it's much more than that. Glad I found you.

Comment left by: **Tomasina**

Sandy S., oh my gosh, I've been reading this site for months now but never knew that you were the same Sandy S. from Nacho Papi! Now I have to read everything all over again!

Comment left by: **silly putty**

54

Sandy sat in her darkened bedroom reading comment after comment. Hundreds of comments, taking up page after page in her blog. She read the good, the bad, and the completely ugly. She couldn't stop herself. It took her more than an hour, and all the while new comments were being posted.

She'd rushed home in order to delete her blog in its entirety. Or at least to password-protect the stupid thing. All the way there she'd cursed herself for having been dumb enough to post her personal problems on the Internet in the first place.

But when she got home and started seeing all those words—all those words written by strangers, about *her*—she'd found herself unable to go through with it.

She refreshed the page and found yet another comment. She read it. She hit Refresh again. Over and over.

In another browser window, she read comments on George's stupid, hateful article. It was the same story there: some readers bashed her, and some bashed George or Daniel. Some readers hated her, and some readers loved her.

Sandy flicked back and forth between the two pages, obsessively reading every comment that appeared. It was like watching a building blow up. Like watching a starlet fall down onstage. It was a veritable train wreck. But all about *her*. Sandy was mesmerized. She couldn't stop reading.

SHE WOKE UP at 10:22 A.M. on Saturday, eyes sticky and hungover from the night spent staring at electronic eight-point font. She felt vaguely nauseated. Nervous, even. She sat up from where she'd crashed on the couch, not even bothering to turn it into the bed first, and looked around the room. Something was tickling at the back of her mind. Something to do with something she'd left in this room.

Her eyes fell on a peach-colored rectangle facedown on the coffee table. The invitation for her father's wedding, which she'd completely forgotten.

AT 11:08 A.M., she was sitting in her car in the parking lot of a nondescript, nondenominational church, wearing a crumpled skirt and blouse and too much dry shampoo. Eight minutes late to her own father's wedding. She wondered if she should even go in.

The parking lot was filled with other cars, none of which she recognized. No, she recognized one. A gold Lincoln Town Car, its driver sitting at the wheel, staring through sunglasses at nothing. Holding a cigarette, which Sandy could almost smell from this distance, even though it'd been years and years since she'd smelled that brand burning in her mother's fingers.

As if by some familial telepathy, Mrs. Saavedra turned and looked right at Sandy. Then, moving mechanically yet quickly, she unlocked, got out, and locked her car. Click-clicked over to Sandy's Malibu, which Sandy hurried to unlock so her mother could slide into the passenger seat, silent as if on some assignation. Were they there to spy or to assassinate? Sandy wondered. *Bad joke.*

There was a long, long silence as the two of them sat in the glare, sheltered in their private thoughts. Sandy let her mother crack the window to smoke, knowing better than to complain about the scent messing up her car. She knew that her mother must have been very—sad, angry, something—to be smoking again, but especially to be quiet for so long. She felt sympathy, but also relief. She wasn't in the mood for conversation.

Then, finally, her mother did speak, and it was with a more sober, serious voice than Sandy had heard from her since the divorce, three years before.

"He didn't leave me, you know. He always said he would, but in the end it was me that left him."

That wasn't what Sandy had expected her to say. Her mother went on.

"He always thought I was such a dummy. That was his joke—that I was so dumb he didn't know what he was doing with me. Then everybody else joked about it too. And I just laughed it off. But then I started to see that it really did bug him, and I think I started acting dumber, just to bug him some more." She took a long, remorseful drag, looking like she already regretted this lapse into weakness. She flicked the ash hard out the window. "I would say, 'You're right, you should've married a college girl. Why don't you go find one?' But he wouldn't go. I think he liked telling everybody what a dummy his wife was. That was his excuse for when his own life went wrong. It was all her fault—his dummy of a wife."

Sandy couldn't do anything but listen. Never had her mother spoken about herself like this. Sandy was used to her talking about others, or spinning long fantasies for her daughter's future. She never would have imagined her mother observing anything so keenly, least of all anything that included herself.

"My mom—your grandma Petra—used to say 'There's two sides to every story.' I know my side, and I know his side. But now I see that there's more than just that." She turned to face Sandy. The sun shone through her darkened lenses, revealing puffy red eyes. "You've been seeing your own side of it this whole time. You think I ran your daddy away—forced him to rush out the door and leave you with your dumb old mama."

Shock hit Sandy like cold water over the head. It dawned on her then. Her mother wasn't this upset about the wedding. She had read Sandy's blog. Like a bad TV show rewinding too fast, she re-saw all the words she'd written about her parents. "Mom, I'm sorry."

"Don't be." Mrs. Saavedra chuckled dryly and took another drag. "You were right. Everything you said was right." She looked out the window, as if at everything in her past.

"Mom." Sandy reached for her mother, for the first time in recent memory. "No. I'm sorry. I was wrong."

Her mother shook her head. "No, you weren't. I read the whole thing. All of it. You were whiny, and you were spoiled. But you weren't wrong."

Another car pulled into the lot, peeling around the corner way faster than was appropriate for the occasion. A thin, balding man in a tuxedo practically ran out of its driver door, only to stop short of the church for a panicked search through all his suit pockets.

"It's Dad!" Sandy whispered, having recognized him only when he turned almost to face them. As one, she and her mother ducked down, eye level with the dash. What was he doing? Sandy wondered. Looking for the ring?

He finally found the right pocket and pulled out a pack

of cigarettes. After fumbling to light one, he smoked and paced jerkily back and forth like a video-game character. "What's wrong with him?" Sandy whispered as if he might hear them.

Her mother chuckled again, this time in what sounded like real amusement. She sounded kind of witchy, Sandy couldn't help but think. "He's nervous. He's worried he's making a mistake."

Sandy frowned, thinking this was a little uncharitable to be listening to on her father's wedding day. But her mother was right—he was incredibly nervous. Why?

"She's a dummy," her mother said. "She's a *real* dummy. She went to college, and she has a big-shot job, but she's dumber than hell. Dumber than *me*."

Sandy looked at her mother in surprise as the older woman began to shake with giggles. "He finally got what he deserved, and I think he's finally realized it."

Eventually her father went in to his fate.

"You'd better go in, too. You're going to miss it." Her mother seemed completely recovered now. "Go in there so you can tell me later what everybody's wearing."

Sandy shook her head. "I don't feel like it." She turned to face her mother directly. "You know, all that stuff I said on my blog, about you running Dad off and keeping him away from me, that was wrong. I know that now. It wasn't you, it was Dad himself. He never calls me. He barely even told me he was getting married." She sighed. "And...it hurt my feelings. And I guess it was just easier to believe that it was all happening because of you."

"Well," said her mother. There was a pause. "I was probably to blame a little, too. You were only telling it like you saw it." Sandy didn't say anything. Her mother changed the subject. "I'm sorry your dad's being this way, baby. And I'm sorry I didn't realize what a jerk that Danny was. I shouldn't have nagged you so much about him."

"It's okay." Sandy looked at the church one last time, feeling like its doors had closed on a chapter in her life. "Hey, how about we go get coffee?"

"At your fancy coffee place? Or you want to just go through a drive-through somewhere?"

Sandy thought about it for a moment. She couldn't go to Calypso. She was afraid she'd be recognized. "We'll go to a different fancy coffee place," she said. "I know lots of them."

Her mother threw the last of her cigarette out the window and reached for her seat belt. "All right, then. Let's roll."

55

Time: Wednesday, June 7, 12:34 PM
To: SandyS@nachopapiswebsite.com
From: vforverguenza@razamail.net
Subject: Don't forget this Friday!

Hey girl. You're still coming on Friday, right? I set everything up in case you want to bring a camera crew with you, and I'm attaching my bio and some other information in case you want to mention it ahead of time, maybe on Nacho Papi. ;)

Can't wait to see you there!

Oh and I saw that mess that happened with Daniel online. Hope you're not letting that get you down too much.

Veronica

56

Post on Nacho Papi's Web Site, Friday, June 9

Sorry if my personal problems are interrupting your attention whoring, but
by Sandy S.

If you're someone who's only been talking to me in public lately...who never calls me, personally, to see how I'm doing, but who always has time to drop a comment letting everyone else on earth know that you're my very best friend...then I can't make it to your event. And I can't bring a camera crew with me, either. Sorry.

I'm sure you'll find a way to talk about it where everyone can see. Break a leg.

READER COMMENTS ON **SORRY IF MY PERSONAL PROBLEMS...**

Whoa. I don't know who you're talking about, but it's cracking me up.
Miss Da Meaner

I think I know. Does her name start with V? :) :)
Carless in Detroit

Hello, how is this news? What is this, the Sandy S show now? If the posts have to be about her, can we at least get more details on what she does in bed?

Born Again Atheist

Who is this so called attention whore friend? Tell us more! We want to know!

Peachy

Sandy, I'm sorry to hear some of your friends aren't being supportive and only want to use you to get famous. You know who you can always call . . . . . .

The Wild Juan

andy regretted her post about Veronica's show within hours of seeing it on the screen. But, then again, she didn't, really. Veronica hadn't called or written to her since it went up. Best of all, she'd stopped posting those ridiculous comments to Nacho Papi under the name V for Verguenza.

Just to be sure all bases were covered, however, Sandy decided to call and explain it to their mutual friend Jane. She stood from her seat at the staff table, where she'd stopped at one of the open laptops to check page views and reader comments before filming the day's segment. There was only one intern in the main office at the moment, hard at work on another computer. Sandy walked into one of the mostly emptied side offices, one that still contained a desk and chair. Closing the door behind her, she pulled out her phone and dialed Jane's work number.

"What's up?"

Jane's short answer made Sandy wonder if she'd called at a bad time. "Hey, are you busy?"

"Of course. But I have a few minutes. What's going on?" Jane talked quickly and quietly. Sandy imagined her at the little desk outside her representative's office, pretending she was on a work-related call.

"Nothing." Sandy sat back in her chair. "Well, it's Veronica. You know her show's tonight."

"Right. And I know you're not going, because you're pissed at her for all those stupid comments."

"You saw my post?"

"Yeah." Jane said.

"Has Veronica seen it?" Sandy's emotional pendulum swung back to regret, and she wished again that she hadn't put those words online.

Jane sighed. "I don't know. Why don't you call and ask her?"

"I can't."

"Then why'd you write it? Obviously, you're hoping she *will* see it, aren't you?"

Sandy frowned. "Well…yeah, kind of. But you know why I wrote it, right? Have you seen the stuff she's been pulling?"

"No, but I can imagine. I know how she can get." Jane sighed again. "Look, Sandy, I don't want to get in the middle of this. You know she's going to freak out, and I'm not going to try to explain it to her. You need to call her yourself. Or take that post down."

"I can't. It has too many page views. It's already paid for my lunches this week."

"Well." Jane paused. "Whatever. I don't know. I have to go, okay? I'll call you back later."

Sandy hung up, feeling even more regretful. And alone.

She had run out of people to confide in. Veronica was acting like a flake, and Jane was being a hard-ass. Normally, at a time like this, she would have opened up her laptop and typed a nice, long entry to everyone else in the world. Then someone would have commented, saying she knew just how Sandy felt. And then Sandy would feel better about the whole thing.

But that was no longer an option. She'd been cheated out of it by George, and by Daniel.

The night before, Sandy had called Tony O., the Chilean writers' group leader, thinking he might want to get that coffee with her sometime this weekend. He hadn't picked up. He hadn't responded to the text she'd sent him the day before that, either. Sandy didn't know if it was because of George's article. Really, she didn't want to know. She deleted Tony's phone number and thanked God no one knew he'd ever given it to her. At least, she thought, she had learned her lesson as far as talking about romantic prospects online. Never again. Too bad the damage was already done, though. Would anyone with an Internet connection ever want to date her again? Maybe she could change her name.

"Sandy? Are you here?" Angelica's spike-heeled shadow filled the doorway.

"I'm here."

"We have space for an extra segment this week. You haven't done any extras in a while and I was thinking we could use the Chupacabra piece you just turned in. Francisco can intro it for you. I think the viewers would really enjoy it. What do you think?"

Sandy sighed. She didn't care anymore, honestly. "Sure. Fine."

As quickly as she'd walked in, Angelica swept away again.

Sandy heaved a quiet sigh. She couldn't wait until the stink from George's article blew over and she could go back to some semblance of a normal life.

58

June 17, 2008

Levy Media, Inc.
c/o Angelica Villanueva O'Sullivan
Sent via: Courier
Re: Unauthorized use of Jaime Escobar's image

I write as attorney for Jaime Escobar.

We have recently learned that you have posted various digital images and footage of Mr. Escobar on your site at www.nachopapiswebsite.com, and have used his image on articles of clothing sold on said site. In addition, you have used footage of Mr. Escobar on the Nacho Papi television program. In all these instances, you have used Mr. Escobar's image without his permission.

Based upon the foregoing, we hereby demand that you confirm to us in writing within ten days of receipt of this letter that: 1) you have removed all infringing materials from your site, and 2) you will refrain from posting any similar infringing material on the Internet, on television, or any other medium in the future.

Sincerely,
Richard Tallamantez

59

"Oh, no," Sandy said after reading the letter Angel-ica had handed her. "This is terrible. It's from his nephew. He's a lawyer."

"No, it's fine," said Angelica. "We're completely cov-ered. That release form the old man signed is iron clad. He doesn't have anything on us. Oh, that reminds me, Sandy. I need you to send a copy of his release to Legal. They need it for their files."

Sandy mumbled a response that Angelica could take to mean yes. Angelica gave Sandy one of her too-hard pats on the shoulder and swept away to oversee the day's taping.

This was it, Sandy told herself. She was going to get Levy Media sued, and then she was going to get fired. This was the beginning of the end.

She trekked to the studio on mental autopilot.

The moment she walked in Angelica had passed her the letter as if she were passing on a piece of fan mail, or a cookie. As if it was no big deal. Sandy supposed Nacho Papi's new television studio was too chaotic a place for its residents to take anything but the show seriously. Either that, or Angelica really *didn't* think the cease-and-desist letter was an issue. Sandy sighed. In Angelica's world there really was no such thing as bad publicity.

Co-workers rushed past Sandy like shoppers on Black Friday, leaving her standing there like a traffic island, clutching her letter. As quickly as she'd left, Angelica returned to Sandy with the new girl, Trisha "La Sirena" MacLeod, who was leading two very young women through the studio. One of them kept staring at Sandy, although she was obviously trying to be unobtrusive about it.

"Sandy," said Angelica, "this is your last chance. Are you sure you don't want to do this interview?"

"I'm positive." Sandy folded her arms across her chest and couldn't resist reaching to adjust her glasses again. Nor could she look into La Sirena's eyes or the faces of the girls with her. Angelica's latest idea was downright scandalous, and it involved Sandy, but that didn't mean that Sandy had to get involved.

"No, you're right, it's better this way," Angelica muttered. Then she turned back to La Sirena's guests. "Did you girls sign your release forms? We can't put you on the show without release forms."

They both nodded and smiled like twin dolls, and then La Sirena led them away. Sandy went to the editing room to watch, not trusting herself to stay quiet on set. On the monitors she watched La Sirena and her two guests settle themselves into the multi-loveseated interview set. The crew made last-minute adjustments to lighting and positioning. An older woman fluttered around La Sirena, powdering all the skin showing around her low-cut halter top. When the young director gave the word, La Sirena faced the camera and started.

"I'm here with Jenny Martinez and Missy Hawthorne,

two students at the University of Texas." The two girls smiled and waved at the camera. La Sirena continued. "And they have a story to tell us. Missy, I'll start with you. You were recently at a function for Lolita Boutique, correct?"

"That's right," Missy said with a slight blush. Then she faced the camera directly and explained, "I'm launching a career as a lingerie model."

"While you were at the party a man approached you and showed you a press pass, correct?"

"Yes. He said he was a famous journalist and that he could get me an interview and photo shoot with a top magazine."

"What magazine?" La Sirena leaned forward with a concerned look on her face, reminding Sandy of a real talk-show host.

"He didn't say. But he kept hinting around that it was something really big—that he'd fly me to New York or LA or something."

"And what was that man's name?" La Sirena asked.

"George," said Missy the lingerie model. "George Cantu."

La Sirena turned to face the camera. Behind her, George's old staff picture popped up on the screen. It was quickly replaced by a succession of unflattering photos of George in various settings. There was one of him eating at a party, with a bit of dip smeared on the side of his mouth. There was another in which he'd been caught grinning lecherously at a woman in a bikini. Sandy recognized it from the lowrider show they'd covered three months ago. It seemed like it'd been years.

"George Cantu is a writer for Buzz News in San Antonio. As longtime Nacho Papi readers will remember, he worked for us until a month ago, when he made a name for himself at Buzz by writing a character-assassination piece on our own Sandy S."

Behind her, the monitor dutifully switched to photos of Sandy. These, mercifully, were flattering. Sandy almost didn't recognize herself in them. There was one in particular in which she was wearing a strapless evening gown that had been lent to her by a local designer for a party in Atlanta. Sandy looked hot in that picture—she couldn't deny it. More than one man had hit on her that night. And yet she wondered if Francisco or one of the new tech guys had airbrushed it to smooth out her skin and add the smallest shadow of cleavage. She frowned at the thought.

"Missy, did George ever get you an interview or a photo shoot?" La Sirena asked.

The girl shook her head. "No. I had dinner with him twice, and he kept making excuses for why it hadn't happened yet. And he kept trying to get me to go back to his place. He said he wanted to take some Polaroids to show his producers. And, like, hinting that he could do more, if I did more for him. You know?"

"Oh, we know, Missy." The monitor went back to the picture of George leering as La Sirena turned to the other young woman, who was a more petite Latina with dark hair, and didn't seem like the lingerie modeling type. "Now, Jenny, you weren't so lucky, were you?"

Jenny shook her head, looking equal parts rueful and excited to have her turn in the spotlight. "No. I met George at a party downtown. I told him I was a singer-songwriter, and he said he could get his bosses to do a story about my band."

La Sirena nodded sympathetically. "And then what happened?"

Jenny did blush. "I went home with him that night, and we...uh...hooked up."

Sandy shook her head as she watched the monitor. *That poor girl.* Sandy decided to interview the girl and her band later, to make up for the fact that she'd had to sleep with George.

La Sirena said, "You told me, when we met, that something unusual happened while you and George were being intimate. Would you like to share that with us now?"

Everyone in the editing room with Sandy paused. Sandy was surprised by La Sirena's tasteless question, but found herself taking a step forward to hear the answer.

"When he, uh," the young woman said. "When he, uh, reached that point, you know...He called me a name."

"A bad name?" La Sirena pressed.

"No. Someone else's name." Jenny looked a little regretful now, as if maybe she was reconsidering her decision to tell this story on the air. Sandy felt even more sympathy for her.

But La Sirena leaned forward and urged her onward. "Whose name?"

"Sandy S.," said the girl. "He called out 'Oh, Sandy!'"

Right on cue, the picture of Sandy in the strapless gown went up on the monitor. There was a quiet gasp in the editing room. A couple of staff members turned to look at Sandy, who had been the one to make the noise. She felt as if a bucket of mud had just fallen on her head. She couldn't have been more shocked, disarmed, or disgusted if the answer had been his own mother's name. Or Angelica's. Or the current president's.

La Sirena faced the camera with a triumphant smirk on her face. "Wow, George. We knew you missed Nacho Papi, but we didn't know you missed it *that* much."

Sandy hurried out of the editing room. She wanted to

flee the scene but knew she had to stop Angelica from putting this segment on air first. La Sirena was wrapping up the interview when Sandy got there. She and her guests said goodbye and stood up, and then, fast as cartoon characters, the staff members and interns prepared the interview set for something else. La Sirena and her guests had walked a little way from the set with Angelica, who was congratulating them on a good job.

Sandy marched over and interrupted their conversation. "Hey. You didn't tell me you guys were going to talk about that. I didn't agree to that."

Angelica looked at her in surprise. "What's wrong, Sandy? It was a good story. It completely discredited that piece George did with your ex, and that picture of you looked fantastic. I thought you'd be happy."

"No, I'm not happy. I'm completely humiliated!" Sandy practically shouted it, then saw the two interviewees looking at her in open curiosity. La Sirena had her usual smile pasted in place. Why, Sandy wondered, was she the only one who saw how wrong this was? She stammered, "I just didn't think it was going to be so...*personal*."

Angelica laughed. "Oh, come on, Sandy. You, Miss TragiComedy Texas, are worried about a story being too personal?"

The other women laughed, and Angelica led the two guests away. La Sirena put a hand on Sandy's arm, reminiscent of Angelica's but less rough. "Sandy, I'm sorry. I thought you knew."

"I didn't know. I thought it was just going to be a story about George using his press pass to meet women. I didn't know it was going to turn into something so...creepy."

"Hey, don't worry about it. Just between you and me, the girl wasn't even sure he'd actually said your name. It was probably just 'baby' or 'mami.' But this way it's a better story, and we get him back for what he did to you, right?"

Sandy didn't answer.

"Listen," La Sirena said, her voice as sweet as a skinny latte, "you look stressed. Why don't you go somewhere and chill out? Go shopping or something. I'll cover for you with Angelica, and I'll take your news segment for the day."

Sandy pulled away from the younger woman's fake-friendly touch. "No, I'm fine. I can do my own segment. Thanks, anyway." She finished with a fake smile of her own, not wanting La Sirena to see that she was annoyed.

Get it together, Sandy told herself as she walked to the news set, smiling at the co-workers she passed. Now wasn't the time to fall apart emotionally. She didn't want Angelica—or that two-faced La Sirena—to think that she couldn't handle her job. Not after how hard she'd worked to get here in the first place.

60

Entry from Aunt Linda's journal, December 23, 1966

Jaime says if I wanted to leave Miguel, I could go up to the Hill County with him, where his cousin works on a goat ranch or some such thing. I'd have my own house, he said. No funny stuff. I told him there was no way. No, I'm not happy here. But I made my bed and now I have to lie in it. Besides, Rudolfo lives in Austin now and if I went up that way, he'd probably drag me right back home.

Mom says Ruby's doing good up in California. I'm glad for her. Even though we aren't close, I always wanted better for her. She's young. It's not too late.

It's almost Christmas. Think I'm going to try pyracantha berry jelly. That's what that bush is outside. Found a book about it at the library and they had the recipe, too.

61

Later that week, Sandy sat in her car in the parking lot of a south Austin diner. It was 10 A.M. on a Thursday, not a likely time for any Nacho Papi readers to be indulging in pancakes. There were only a few elderly types inside, in fact. But Sandy was reluctant to go in nonetheless. She felt shell-shocked, afraid to show herself in public and risk getting yelled at.

So she sat in her car with a drive-through latte, holding her aunt's journal. She'd opened it to a random page in the middle and was puzzling out the words. Rudolfo was her grandfather on her mother's side, of course. Miguel was her mother's late uncle, Miguel Trujillo, whom Sandy had never known. The Jaime in the journal was very obviously the man Sandy knew as Tío Jaime. But what had happened? Had her great-aunt left Miguel for Jaime? If so, no one in Sandy's family had ever talked about it.

Her thoughts were interrupted by her cell phone's ringing. It was a number she didn't recognize, area code 212. New York City.

"Hello?"

"Sandy?" A man's voice. "How are you? This is Jacob. Jacob Levy."

Sandy sat and listened to Jacob Levy talk. It was the first time he'd ever called her. He talked fast and clear, like a radio DJ hurrying through a sponsor's message. He was proud of the work she'd been doing. He was glad she was staying strong through the surprise publicity about her love life. He hoped she'd seen the latest page views and ratings, and that she was proud of how much attention she'd brought the show and the site. His voice reminded her of Angelica's: he was professional and upbeat, without any break in the flow.

"Yes, Mr. Levy. Thank you, Mr. Levy."

"Call me Jacob. Okay, Sandy, I have a meeting to get to now. You keep up the good work. I hope to see you in town soon."

"Yes, sir. Jacob."

He hung up and Sandy sat still, absorbing the moment. Jacob Levy was happy to be getting ratings and page views. It made no difference to him whether it was Sandy's life they were talking about or a made-up character who had the same name.

She looked at the time on her phone. It was just past 10 A.M. now, and she was scheduled to record her show segment, a quick overview of the news and then an interview with local activist Tito Z., at two that day. She really should have been on her way to the office right then, to check in with everyone and see what was going on. But instead she started her engine and drove off in the opposite direction.

THERE WAS A strange car in Tío Jaime's driveway.

"What are you doing here?" someone said through the screen door before she could even get close enough to make out the face behind it. The door opened and nephew Richard emerged. Sandy stopped in her tracks, in the yard. "You aren't supposed to be here," he said loudly, as if to keep her from coming any closer solely with the force of his voice. "My uncle has filed a cease-and-desist."

Sandy crossed her arms and swallowed hard. He was right. Of course he was—he was the one who'd written the letter on his uncle's behalf. But, at the same time, he *wasn't* right. He was wrong about *her*.

"Where's your uncle?" she said. "I came to visit him. *Not* for the Web site."

"Right. Where's your camera? In your bag? We don't want you here anymore, so you can go find someone else to mock for profit." He stood there like a tall, leafless tree. He wasn't wearing a suit this time, but even in a golf shirt and khakis he looked formidable. Righteous and ready to argue his case to the death.

But in this instance he was wrong. Sandy swallowed again and took a step forward. "I wasn't mocking him for profit, and I didn't come here for the Web site. I visit him all the time. You wouldn't know because you hardly ever visit. He's my…My great-aunt was his…He's my friend. You don't know."

Richard scoffed audibly. "Well, he can't see you, so you have no reason to be here."

Sandy was worried then. "What do you mean, he *can't* see me? Where is he?" He said nothing, only tightened his jaw and looked at the distant, omnipresent goats. Sandy took the few steps to the porch so she wouldn't have to talk as loudly. "Is he okay?"

"No, he's not okay. Ms. Saavedra, my uncle is very old. He might risk his health working outdoors all day, and he might perk up when pretty young girls come to visit him, but the truth is, he's in very poor health and the last thing he needs is the stress of being made into some kind of *online celebrity*."

The way he said that phrase, almost in a sneer, made Sandy wonder how much Richard knew about her. How much he'd read about her. Still, she wasn't going to back down now. "What do you mean, poor health? What's wrong with him?"

"What's going on?" Tío Jaime's voice came from inside the house.

Sandy exhaled slowly. He was here, then. "It's me, Tío Jaime."

"Sandy? Richard, why didn't you tell me Sandy was here?"

Sandy wondered why the old man hadn't come outside. And then the screen door was bumped open and she saw.

He was using a walker. For some reason Tío Jaime couldn't walk. Slowly—painfully slowly—he hobbled through the door in short clunks of the metal walker. He bent over the contraption in frustration, trying to force it through the narrow doorway.

"What happened?" Sandy gasped. "Why are you—?"

"Tío Jaime," said Richard, "you need to stay inside. It's almost time for us to go."

The old man wasn't wearing his hat, and his thinned gray hair fell over his eyes. He shook it away impatiently as he finally cleared the doorway and joined them on the porch. "I don't need to stay inside. I heard Sandy and came out to see her."

"Tío Jaime, this is the woman who sold the T-shirts with your picture. This is the woman who put you on TV without your permission. It's because of her that those boys came over here the other day. *She's* the one causing all the problems." Richard's voice had become loud again. He seemed to think Tío Jaime didn't understand what was happening—that he wasn't in his right mind and didn't know who Sandy was.

Did he?

Silence fell over the group on the porch and Sandy replayed Richard's words in her head.

Yes, she was the one who'd used Tío Jaime's image—who'd made him into a celebrity—without his permission. She had tried to rationalize it to herself but, at the end of the day, yes, it was her. She had done it all.

He was right. She was definitely the one who had caused all the problems.

Sandy felt her face heat up. She looked down at the floor and felt the two men looking at her.

It was true. She'd been the one to cause all the problems. Not just for Tío Jaime, but for herself. The hard realization of it made her face burn.

And what was she doing here now, Sandy asked herself. True, she may not have been planning to record Tío Jaime for the site or for the show—not *this* time—but she'd been about to interrupt whatever he was doing that day. She'd come to visit him because doing so always made her feel better ... about the problems she had caused for herself.

And here he was now, in poor health. The man was too weak to walk. And she hadn't even noticed the strain he was under this whole time. She'd been too self-involved.

Sandy felt tears well up in her eyes. She wished Richard wasn't here watching her. But, despite his presence, she looked up at the old man and said, "Tío Jaime, I am so sorry."

His eyes met hers, but he said nothing. Sandy had to squint to keep from crying outright. She had lied to him. He'd given her so much, and asked for so little in return, and she hadn't even been able to honor his wishes. Tío Jaime had been nothing but kind to her—and to her aunt—and she had used him for her own selfish needs. "I'm sorry," she said again. What else could she say?

Tío Jaime looked away. He turned away, dragging the walker in the direction of his front door, and began the long hobble back the way he'd come. Sandy stumbled forward to open the screen door for him, but Richard was already there. He held the door until the old man had gone inside, and then he closed it quietly before turning to face Sandy.

"You need to leave now."

With a sniff, Sandy nodded. She should leave. He was right. She had no right to be there.

But… "Richard, I just want you to know. I'm sorry for any trouble I caused your uncle. Truly, I am. But I need you to understand. I didn't do anything… I wasn't trying to do anything that would—"

"Save it," he said. "The damage is done, and the sooner you're out of here the better." He was staring into the distance again, like he always did when talking to her. As if she was too horrible a person to look at.

It hurt.

Sandy felt like she couldn't leave until she'd made him understand. "I'm trying to tell you that I didn't mean to cause your uncle any trouble. I know it's hard for you to believe it, seeing it from the outside, but I really care about him very much. I wasn't trying to use him to make money. I just thought that, if other people could get from him what *I* get from him—his words, his humor, his perspective on life—then maybe they'd—"

"Give you more money?" He did look at her now, and Sandy wished then that he hadn't. She could see it in his eyes: he *did* think she was a horrible person. She wished now that she had left when he'd asked her to. But because she hadn't, she got to hear what he'd say next. "Or maybe that they'll tune in to hear the latest installment of your sex life and make you more famous?"

Sandy was rendered speechless. He was so rude. So very hateful.

And yet what could she even say? How else could it look to him, what she was doing? Putting her personal life online and on the air for strangers?

It was no wonder he didn't want her anywhere near his uncle. In his place she would have felt the same way.

Finally Sandy turned to go. She walked down the steps and halfway to her car, and then she heard the screen door open again.

Tío Jaime came through, clutching a piece of paper in his hand, against the handle of his walker. Richard hurried to help him through the door, but his uncle pushed him away. He made it out onto the porch again and then, balancing himself against the walker with one hand, he held out the piece of paper for Richard. Sandy watched the whole thing, wondering what was going on now.

"Sandy, you wait," Tío Jaime said. Then, to his nephew, "Look. Look at this."

Richard took the paper and skimmed it with his eyes. He sighed in apparent exasperation. "Tío—"

"That's right," his uncle said. "I gave her my permission. So you can leave her alone now. It's not her fault."

Sandy was baffled. What was going on?

With a roll of his eyes, Richard walked down the steps and thrust out his hand at Sandy, handing her the crumpled, spotted paper. It was the release form she'd given Tío Jaime two months ago. He'd signed it. Sandy ran her finger over his signature, causing the blue ink to feather.

He'd apparently *just* signed it. For her. To save her from getting sued. To keep her from being a liar.

This time Sandy couldn't stop the tears, and she hurried to wipe her eyes before Richard could see. This was wrong, she knew. *She* was in the wrong, and now Tío Jaime was going back on what he'd said, on what he believed in, in order to help her.

"Happy now?" Richard practically snarled at her. "Would you please just leave? My uncle has things to do."

"Sandy, I have to go to the hospital," Tío Jaime called to her. "But I'll call you when I get back."

"But—" Sandy wanted to ask why he was going to the hospital, but Richard's look kept her from saying anything more. "I'll...I'll..."

Hadn't she done enough already?

Finally, under one man's glare and the other man's too-kind smile, she left.

62

Entry from Aunt Linda's journal, March 11, 1967

Lost another one. Didn't go to the hospital this time—the whole thing took care of itself. I couldn't even cry. I thought Miguel would be mad, but instead he used it as an excuse to go to the bar all weekend and leave me here alone.

Saw Jaime and told him what happened with the baby. He said he was sorry and I said I was sorry, too. I know he understood, since he lost Graciela before they could even have a baby. He's like me. He never complains.

That was all we said. I don't feel like talking to anybody lately, not even him. But I am glad that he's nearby, just in case. It makes me feel safer.

Went back to the library and got Jane Eyre again. Sister Jane. I know she must have secretly been a mexicana, because she was strong enough to go through everything she did.

Back to work now.

Entry from Aunt Linda's journal, September 8, 1967

I'm only going to feel sorry for myself here, for a little while, where nobody can see it, and then I'll get back to work. But lately I can't help spending a little time every day thinking about the way my life might have been.

What if I had married someone else? A good man, and not a handsome good-for-nothing. What if Jaime and I had met first, before he'd met poor Graciela and before I'd gotten stuck with Miguel?

What if I'd never gotten married at all? Maybe I could've gone with Ruby and Jose to California, to help out. Or told Mami I was going to California with them, and then gone somewhere else. Ohio, Wyoming, Oregon. New York City. Argentina. Spain. Paris. Africa.

I could have been a missionary. I could have been a teacher, at least. Instead, here I am. I can't even move a few hundred miles, no matter how much I want to. At first I thought Miguel would kill me if I left. Now I know he's too lazy, but my father would kill me, instead. Because everyone in town would find out, and he and my mother wouldn't be able to stand the gossip. It's less embarrassing for them to have a daughter who's unhappy for life, than a daughter who gets talked about.

And what would I be doing but trading one man for another? Every night I wish I could trade men, but what if it doesn't stop there? I trust Jaime, but I hardly trust myself. What if I leave with him, and then I can't stop? I don't want to hurt him but I don't know if I can keep from doing it, at this point. Sometimes it feels like I'm not a real woman anymore. I'm an animal. A witch. What if I get a taste of freedom and never stop leaving?

Where would it end? At the end of the earth...?

That's enough crazy talk. Back to real life.

Entry from Aunt Linda's journal, January 19, 1968
    Everyone is mad at me, and I've never been so happy.

Mami cried. Papi pulled my hair and called me a sin-vergüenza. But I stood my ground. It was going to take more than slapping and hair-pulling, from Papi, Mami or Miguel, to stop me.

Jaime came over to our house and told Miguel what we were going to do. I was afraid for him, but he said it'd be best this way—to tell the truth, face-to-face, without sneaking around like thieves.

At first I thought Miguel was going to fight him. But no, he was too much of a coward, or maybe he realized in his heart that we'd never belonged together. But he had to save face, either way. He told Jaime to go ahead and take me, that I was only half a woman, anyway, who couldn't bear children and didn't want to do anything but read all day.

If I'd still been 23 or 24, I would have flown into a rage, probably, and tried to tear his eyes out. Or at least spit in his sorry face. But now that I'm 25, I know better than to bother with worthless people. I let him say what he wanted while I packed my things and left. It was worth it, to get away.

We've been here two days now and it's just like Jaime said it'd be. One house for him, one house for me. Mesquite and cactus as far as you can see, and mercifully cooler than it was in the Valley. The soil is full of lime but I think I can do something with it. Already, I love the goats. They're so good and quiet. Jaime says we can drive to Austin or to San Antonio some weekend and see the sights. For right now, I'm glad enough to see my own little house. My own garden. My own life.

I'm happy. I can never go home again, of course. I'm going to miss Mami. But I'm happy. I'm free.

63

Time: Thursday, June 22, 3:36 PM
To: SandyS@nachopapiswebsite.com
From: anonymous@anonanywhere.net
Subject: straight to hell

you will go straight to hell. as He is my witness I can tell you that
you will burn in hell for what you have done. this is not the way
He meant for young women to serve, showing themselves to be
whores like "Sodom and gommorrah" and He will show you the
error of your weigh. you should give yourself over to Him and see
his Light. as God is my witness, repent right now and He will
forgive

Time: Thursday, June 22, 5:43 PM
To: misstctx@misstctx.com
From: jim.mayer@losangeleschronicle.com
Subject: Please contact me.

Dear Ms. Saavedra:
    Philippe Montemayor gave me your personal email address.
I hope you don't mind me contacting you. I've been following
your story on Buzz News and Nacho Papi and would love

to interview you for the LA Chronicle. Would you please
call me?

> Jim Mayer
> Online Features Editor
> Los Angeles Chronicle

Time: Friday, June 23, 1:47 AM
To: SandyS@nachopapiswebsite.com
From: nena81@happymail.net
Subject: thanks

Dear Sandy,

You don't know me because I've never written to you before
and my blog isn't famous like yours. But I had to write and tell
you that, no matter what happened with Geek Boy and Papi
Chulo and all that stuff, I'm glad you're online.

I've been reading your TragiComic Texas blog almost since the
beginning. I like it because you're a lot like me. My dad left my
mom when I was little, too. I had to work my way through school,
just like you. And I also want to be a writer.

When my friend told me you were the same writer as Sandy
S from Nacho Papi, I was so excited for you, but also for myself.
I thought, if you could get a job like that, maybe some day I
could, too.

When I see you interviewing the Chupacabra, it reminds me
of my grandfather, who recently died. So it makes me a little
sad, but also happy that you could find someone like that in your
own life.

I'm glad you didn't take your blog down after everything that
happened, because sometimes when I feel discouraged about
stuff, I go back and read certain things that you said, and that
makes me feel better. Sometimes when my boyfriend calls me
names or we fight, I think about you getting tired of Geek Boy

and not letting him put you down anymore. And I think that, if you can do that and come out okay, then maybe I can leave my boyfriend too and raise our baby on my own, and still have my dreams and know that they can come true.

Sincerely,
Mary Helen Molina

64

Sandy walked into the office at 10:45 A.M. on Friday, her eyes spazzy from reading for so long, going back and forth from her aunt's faded ink on yellowed paper to the e-mails on her computer and text messages on her phone screen.

She had spent hours reading over her online diary, agonizing again over whether to delete it. In the end, she'd deleted only the very personal parts about Daniel. Even though she'd never used his name, people knew it was him she was talking about. And now that that was the case, she removed everything about him that she wouldn't have said in public. Then she did the same for her mother and father. Then she did the same for herself.

In the end, she was surprised by how much was left. There was quite a bit she didn't have to be ashamed of. Maybe not the most interesting bits, but enough so that she didn't feel like she'd spent all her private time trashing her loved ones online.

This morning, she felt not *good*, exactly, but better. Definitely a little better.

"Hi, Sandy!" piped La Sirena as she entered the staff room. She was sitting with Lori and, as usual lately, the two of them looked giggly, like girls at a slumber party.

"What's wrong? You look tired. Want me to take your segment for you today?"

"No, thanks." Sandy kept her voice mild, hiding her annoyance with La Sirena's constant offers to "help" by taking Sandy's stories from her.

Lori, at least, seemed to recognize that her old friend might not appreciate her new friend's eagerness, and she hastened to change the subject. "Sandy, I guess you heard the news, huh?"

"What news?" Sandy heard a lot of news, all the time. It was her job. But she figured Lori was going to tell her something new about their jobs—probably that they were going out on location, or that they'd hired yet another staffer.

Angelica came into the room. "Sandy. Where've you been? You missed the big announcement."

Behind her, George emerged from her office. George Cantu, aka Papi Chulo, aka the man who'd ruined Sandy's life.

"George is back!" Angelica caroled. As if that was good news. As if that wasn't the last thing Sandy would ever want to hear at this point. "He's rejoining the staff. I was hoping you'd get here early so we could talk about doing a big segment on it today. You and George can have a big showdown on air. We can do a poll and let readers call to vote for which of you they like better. Or which of you should apologize on air. Or something. I was hoping you'd be here to contribute ideas."

Behind her, George stood there and smirked his ever-lasting smirk at Sandy. "I told Angelica we could take a few calls on air. You could answer sob stories from women who went through bad breakups, and I can take calls from guys who've been done wrong."

He didn't even seem angry about it, or malicious.

George was obviously only thinking about himself—his ratings and his popularity. And he expected Sandy to feel the same way, as if this were some publicity stunt and not her real life.

"And this will be the perfect lead-in to our charity date auction. We can charge an extra hundred dollars for the winners if they want to double-date with you and George!" Angelica stood there with an encouraging smile on her face, waiting for Sandy's reply. As if Sandy were going to agree instantly and start brainstorming more ways to put her life on display for the good of Levy Media.

They were all the same, Sandy realized then. George, Angelica, Jacob Levy himself. They only cared about publicity and profit. None of them cared about her dignity or even their own. It was as if they had no souls. They weren't a family at all. They were just—just characters. Badly drawn characters.

Sandy turned and walked out of the office without a word to any of them.

"Sandy!" Angelica called.

"Oh my gosh, Sandy!" Lori cried.

"Hey!" said George, who was probably most disappointed of all.

She walked out of the building and all the way back to her car. Then she got in and started the engine and began to drive.

She was going to the hospital, she told herself, to visit her friend. She didn't deserve a friend like him, she knew. But he was one of the few people she could trust right now.

AN HOUR LATER, a nurse was ushering Sandy into Tío Jaime's room. She was relieved to find that he wasn't in any ward identified as Emergency, Critical, or otherwise frightening.

She had driven to the hospital nearest his house, then gone to the information desk and told them she was Jaime Escobar's niece, and now here she was.

It was strange to see Tío Jaime in the cold, flat light of a hospital room, dressed in white and pale blue like a baby, without his hat or his dog at his side. It made him look old, Sandy thought as she took the chair at his bedside. But he was sitting up, wide awake, and looked just as alert as ever and like he was ready to continue where he'd left off, describing the world through the Chupacabra's eyes.

"How are you?" he said. "Did Richard tell you where to find me?"

Sandy gave him a sheepish smile. "No. You told me you were going to the hospital, and I did a little investigating."

The old man chuckled. "You outsmarted a lawyer. That's good."

"So what happened? Why are you here?" Sandy leaned forward in her chair to listen. She wished she'd thought to bring something with her, but she'd been in too much of a hurry to get here and find out what was going on.

"Nothing happened, m'ija. I just had a little trouble with my sugar and Richard got scared and had them stick me in here for a couple of days. He probably just wanted to get rid of me so he could have people come to my house and install a satellite or some damn thing."

"What do you mean, trouble with your sugar? You mean your blood sugar?"

"Yeah." Tío Jaime waved dismissively, jiggling the IV bag that Sandy now saw was connected to his hand by a long, milky tube. "The diabetes. It's nothing." He lapsed into one of his thoughtful silences, exactly as if they were relaxing at his house, talking about society and other people's problems.

Sandy thought of all the sweets she had brought to Tío Jaime's house during her visits. He'd never told her he was diabetic. She wanted to ask more about his condition but didn't want to be rude. She wasn't his family, after all, even if she did call him uncle. And he didn't seem at all interested in discussing it with her. "How long are you going to be here?" she finally settled on.

"Not too much longer, I don't think. Not more than two or three days." Sandy frowned. He looked fine, but it couldn't have been such a trivial health problem if he was staying that long. He saw her look and added, "It's nothing. They just want to watch me for a few days so they can run up my bill. But Richard wants it, and he says he'll pay for whatever my Medicaid doesn't, so I stopped complaining."

"Do you want me to bring you anything? Magazines? Books?"

He considered the question. Sandy could tell he didn't like asking for anything, but his room was the typically barren hospital room, and he didn't even have his TV on. He must have been bored out of his mind. "Could you bring me something to eat? Like some of those cookies? The ones with the peppermint, if you can."

Sandy frowned again. "I don't know, Tío Jaime. Should you be eating cookies?"

"No, he shouldn't." A nurse had bustled into the room and answered Sandy's question. "No cookies, candies, or anything sweet. You know that, Mr. Escobar. Don't be trying to get your niece into trouble."

The old man grumbled at the nurse but said nothing while she bustled about him, arranging his bedding and IV, making note of the information on various gray and beige monitors at his bedside. Then she turned and pulled the blanket off his feet, revealing to Sandy that one of them was in a fat, bulky cast.

"How's that foot feeling?" she asked.

"I can't feel anything," Tío Jaime muttered.

"Hmm. You're lucky you still *have* a foot to cause you trouble. If you'd waited any longer to come see us, we would've had to take the whole thing off." The nurse gave Tío Jaime a stern look, then turned to Sandy with a kinder one. "Good thing you and your brother are here to watch him now. Make him take better care of himself." And, with that, she left the room as briskly as she'd entered.

It was Sandy's turn to glare at Tío Jaime now, although he pretended not to notice. "What did she mean, take the whole foot off? What happened to you?"

"Nothing. They just took off a couple of my toes that'd been bugging me. Like I said, they just want to run up bills."

Sandy knew what was going on now. She'd heard before about old people with diabetes having their toes removed. It'd almost happened to her grandfather on her father's side, she knew. It only happened to very old people, who never went to the doctor. "Tío Jaime," she whispered, aghast. "Why didn't you tell me?" She thought back, again, to all the cookies and sweets she'd been bringing him. "And why'd you let me feed you all that candy?"

He shook his head stubbornly. "You didn't feed me anything. I ate them myself. And I can take care of myself. I know how much candy I can eat."

"Apparently you don't!" Sandy indicated his mummy-wrapped foot, which the nurse had left uncovered.

Tío Jaime grumbled again. "This isn't because of the

candy. It's because I didn't have my medicine. I got tired of going downtown and standing in those long lines, doing all that paperwork, just to see some smart-ass doctor and let him prescribe me more pills to stand in line for. I decided to just go without it. Nothing but a bunch of damn chemicals, anyway. It's all a racket."

Sandy got up and arranged the blanket over his feet, feeling guiltier than ever. She wished she had known he was so ill. Or that he'd needed help getting his medicine. He'd never *seemed* sick. He'd looked healthy as a horse, working outdoors, at one with nature and all that.

But, then again, she'd never asked about his health or anything else. She'd only talked to him about her own petty problems, and the petty problems of strangers.

What, she wondered as she took her seat back at the old man's side, would his uptight nephew say when he found out her part in all this? Maybe he already knew.

"Tío Jaime, I'm really sorry about what happened. About those T-shirts and the TV show, and people going to your house to bother you."

"That's okay," he said. "I gave you permission. I signed the paper."

Sandy frowned. "No, you didn't. You told me specifically not to do it, and I did it anyway. I let my boss do it without your permission. And then you only signed the paper to keep Richard from suing us. Why? Why did you do that?"

The old man shrugged. "Because you're the niece of my best friend. You made a mistake, but I didn't want to see you get in trouble for it. Besides, that was the chance I took. I knew what might happen. I could have stopped you from taking those pictures, but I didn't." He smiled up at Sandy wryly. "That's what I get for having a swelled head, thinking strangers needed my advice."

He was so good to take it this way. She smiled back weakly and shook her head. "I lied to you, but I'm going to make it up to you now. I'm going to get my boss to pay you for all your appearances, and for the shirts."

He shook his head. "No, m'ija. I don't want any money. Don't worry about it anymore. I was never mad about it. It was just my nephew. Speaking of"—he turned and looked at the clock on the bedside table—"Richard will be here soon."

"I'd better leave, then," Sandy replied. "He wouldn't be too happy to find out I'm visiting you."

"Maybe not. But..." He obviously had trouble forming the words of the request he wanted to make. "Would you come back again, maybe tomorrow?" He coughed and added in explanation, "It's kind of depressing, being here by myself."

Sandy sighed and leaned down to give him a hug that took him by surprise. "Of course I'll come back." She stood and took a notebook from her bag. She wrote her phone number on a sheet of paper, then hid it under the clunky bedside phone while he watched. "Call me anytime and I'll come back. If I don't hear from you, I'll come back tomorrow, anyway."

She gave him another hug then and left, wishing she could do more.

65

Entry from Aunt Linda's journal, April 2, 1968

We drove to Austin this weekend. They were having a carnival. It was beautiful.

The library there is so big. I think it has every book ever written. They let me get a card there and I checked out more books than I can read in two weeks. I was greedy, but it felt good. In two weeks I'll go back again, when I go to town with the eggs and the goat milk.

Ruby wrote to me. She said she's shocked, just shocked at my behavior. I had to laugh.

Sometimes I wonder what I did to deserve this happiness. Maybe God was too busy to see what I'd been doing, and he's forgotten to punish me for it so far.

Usually, though, I don't wonder. I just enjoy. Life's too short for that kind of worrying. Too short and too beautiful.

Entry from Aunt Linda's journal, September 8, 1969

I got a job. The elementary school needed someone who speaks Spanish, who can also read and write English, to help with the kids. So I'm a teacher's aide now. I ride there on my bike in the mornings. It's six miles.

They call me Mrs. Trujillo at the school, of course,

because that's still my name. But I tell the kids to call me Miss Linda, instead. They're all so sweet. I read to them and translate the stories so they'll understand. They're so smart and happy, most of them. It makes me wish I'd had my own. But God had another plan, so that's okay.

Jaime says that if I want to get married, we can just go to the church and say it, ourselves, in front of the altar. That God will understand, and we don't need any paperwork.

But I'm okay with it, either way. If God's going to understand, then he already does, I figure. I don't think of myself as married to Miguel anymore, and I don't think it matters whether I call myself Mrs. Trujillo or Mrs. Escobar.

I'm just Linda. I'm just me. Take it or leave it—I'll be fine either way.

I'm reading a book called The Age of Innocence. It's sad, but good.

66

Sandy went on vacation the Friday George was rehired. Not from writing her posts, of course; her contract made that impossible. Luckily, she was practiced enough by now to write Nacho Papi posts in her sleep. All she had to do was string together something about Amber Chavez's ass, some politician's hair, or a hint of what was going on in her personal life lately. She could whip up a whole batch of posts and e-mail them to Angelica from anywhere. But after visiting Tío Jaime, she called in and gave all her news segments for the following week to Lori and La Sirena. Then she went home. To hide.

"Sandy?" Early Saturday morning her mother quietly tapped at the garage apartment door, sounding like a cat scratching to get in. "Sandy, are you awake?"

Sandy rolled out of her sofa and unlocked the door, then went right back to her sofa to sit and endure her mother's conversation. Her eyes were blurred with sleep and old mascara. Her head throbbed in a low, insistent rhythm.

"What's wrong, baby? You look terrible. Did you stay up all night on the computer?"

Sandy shook her head. She hadn't stayed up *all* night on the computer. Half the night she'd read her aunt's journal instead. For a split second, she thought about telling her mother about the diary. But just as quickly she decided to keep it to herself. Aunt Linda had entrusted it to Tío Jaime, and he had entrusted it to her. There was no reason to tell anyone else about it. Besides, her mom still thought it was strange that Sandy had made Tío Jaime a mini-celebrity by interviewing him as the Chupacabra so many times.

Her mother joined her on the sofa and was unable to resist straightening the journal, the laptop, and Sandy's last few coffee cups on the coffee table as she asked again, "What's wrong, baby? Don't tell me nothing. I can tell something's bothering you."

"Nothing. I mean, it's no big deal." Sandy wiped under her eyes and ran her fingers through her hair, trying to look a little less pathetic than she must have seemed to her mother at that moment.

"Is it that thing with Danny? Are people still sending you ugly e-mails at your job?"

"No, it's not that. It's...my job, itself. You know the guy who wrote that article about me and Daniel?"

"Papi Chulo?"

It annoyed Sandy that her mother knew George's screen name, but she went on. "Yes, him. Well, Angelica hired him back. He's going to be on the TV show with us now."

"*What?* No!" Her mother couldn't have been more incredulous if one of her soap opera characters had admitted to killing another.

Sandy was gratified that she at least grasped the gravity of the situation. "Yes. He's back, and Angelica expects me to just show up at work like everything's fine and do a segment with George where we argue about relationships or something stupid like that."

Mrs. Saavedra looked puzzled. "Okay. So what's the problem?"

Sandy sighed in exasperation. She should have known her mother wouldn't understand. "The problem, Mom, is that I don't want to be anywhere near that jerk."

"Why not, though? Why not do the thing with him, and show everybody that he didn't get to you with his stupid article? Laugh it off. Make him look bad. Be the bigger person, like they say."

Sandy sighed again and fell back against a throw pillow, taking the other to hold against her chest. "It's not just that. It's..." How could she explain it so that her mother would understand? Her mother, who loved gossip and drama and was proud to have a daughter whose job embroiled her in gossip and drama? "It's that the show's not about other people anymore, Mom. Suddenly, it's about *me* and my personal life and my issues with George and the other writers. People are only watching now to find out more about my love life, or because they're hoping something bad will happen to me. It's like I'm a soap opera character all of a sudden, you know? Not a real person anymore."

"Well, you're famous now," her mother said matter-of-factly, as if she'd fully expected this trajectory to take place in her daughter's life.

"But I don't want to be famous for *that*," Sandy said plaintively. "Not for who I'm sleeping with or not sleeping with, not because people are arguing whether or not I'm a whore or a bad person. I wanted to be famous for my *writing*. And my reporting." Explaining to her mother, she realized, was helping her crystallize these thoughts in her head for the first time. "I wanted to be recognized for my *work*, and now it's too late to do that. I ruined everything. I went too far and I can't go back now."

Her mother made a sympathetic noise and put her hand on Sandy's shoulder. Unlike Angelica's recent gestures, her mother's hand was warm and somewhat comforting, even if it couldn't fix her problems with a single touch.

At least I'm not stuck in the Valley, in the sixties, with a husband I don't love and a lover I can't have. Sandy laughed bitterly at the thought. Some people her age had to endure *real* problems, she knew. But knowing that didn't make her petty problems any less unpleasant. She chuckled again, causing her mother to give her a worried look and to apply a hand to Sandy's forehead.

"Are you sure you're okay? Maybe you're coming down with something."

"I'm fine. I'll be fine." Sandy gently pushed away her mother's hand and stood. It was time to get up and get it together. "How're you doing, Mom? Have you heard any news about Dad since his wedding? Is he completely miserable?" It had been three weeks since her father's wedding, but so much had happened to Sandy since then it felt like only a few days.

Mrs. Saavedra shook her head and stood as well. "I don't know. I don't care anymore. I've stopped worrying about that man." She helped Sandy pick up the empty paper cups and crumpled napkins and carry them to the trash can in the kitchenette.

"Oh. Well, good." Sandy wondered what else to say. She wanted to keep her mom from worrying about her. "So what are you doing today?"

"Working. I traded shifts with Hazel today. I'm going in from two to ten."

"Oh." Sandy felt bad all over again. Here she was feeling sorry for herself, and meanwhile her mother had to spend her Saturday evening working at a bail bond office. "Well, that sucks."

Mrs. Saavedra laughed. "It's okay. Don't worry, baby. I traded with Hazel so I could have tomorrow off. I'm going to the movies." She glanced away, uncharacteristically shyly, and added, "With a friend."

"Oh, really?" Sandy's interest was piqued, but not rewarded.

Her mother hugged her and then turned to the door. "Take care of yourself, baby. Take a long bath—you'll feel better."

Sandy watched her mother hurry out of her apartment and back to her own life with all its little secrets. She wondered if she'd have that for herself, too, someday.

She turned and looked at her laptop, which sat innocently on the table. That was where all her trouble had started, and she'd been the one to start it.

Maybe, she thought, if she couldn't have secrets anymore, she could at least have a life she wouldn't be embarrassed to live under her real name.

67

She went back to the hospital Saturday evening. Tío Jaime had called and said that Richard had been there that morning and so most likely wouldn't be back until the next day. The coast was clear.

She was worried about Cano. It'd occurred to her the night before. How was the dog taking his master's absence? Was Richard going over there to feed him? To pet him? To sit on the porch with him, in the breeze?

She arrived at the hospital shortly after seven, when Tío Jaime was sure to have had his dinner. Bearing a gift of gourmet sugar-free chocolates, she rode the elevator up to her friend's room.

As she walked down the hall, her heels clacking past the nurses' station to his room, her phone shook and buzzed in her bag. Taking it out, she recognized the hospital's number. Instead of answering, she hurried to Tío Jaime's room and saw that it was, as she suspected, him calling her.

"Tío Jaime, I'm here."

Seeing her, he hung up the phone. "Oh. There you are."

"What's wrong?" she asked, taking the chair beside his bed and setting the candies beside the phone, on his nightstand.

"Oh, nothing." His voice was falsely casual. She recognized in it the tone of voice she used when she was trying to keep the truth from her mother. "I just called to see how you were doing. And to tell you that I might be going away."

"What?" Sandy looked into the old man's eyes to try to gauge the seriousness of his remark.

The evening sunlight coming through the window made a square of yellow around his head and torso, like a rustic halo. He sat there grimacing, looking like a medieval saint in his pale gown and tangled sheets. "Yeah. My damn nephew, Richard, has been nagging me to move to California with him. He wants me to stay with him or with my little sister, his mother. He says something about how having me in their household will be easier for the bills or the taxes or some such thing."

"But you don't want to move, do you? You don't want to leave your house. And your goats. And…your life!" Sandy knew he didn't. She could hear the reluctance in his voice.

"Not really, no. I wish I didn't have to. But I might have to, it looks like. I can't keep asking Richard to pay for all my bills here."

Sandy could tell that he was upset and embarrassed to be explaining this to her. But she wasn't worried about that. Her number-one concern right now was that he was being forced to leave against his will.

The sound of footsteps in the hall—loud steps caused by dress shoes, not squeaky nurse shoes—startled Sandy. Then a man's hand curled around the door, and she knew there was only one person it could be. She briefly considered hiding—ducking under Tío Jaime's hospital bed. But it was too late. He was in the room now, and he was looking right at her. She sat up straight and faced him defiantly.

Tío Jaime took the water glass from his bedside table and calmly sipped at it. He looked completely unperturbed, but Sandy knew he must have been holding his breath, waiting for his nephew's reaction to her presence.

"You again," was all he said. Nothing more.

He was cradling a basket of fruit in one arm. Somehow that made him look less wrathful than he had before, and Sandy felt herself relax a little. "Me again. I'm...Your uncle asked me to visit."

"I figured he would." Richard stood there looking at the wall. He looked tired, she noticed. Stressed. But apparently he had resigned himself to her existence in his uncle's life.

"That's right. I asked her to visit," said Tío Jaime. "How's Cano doing?"

"He's fine," Richard replied. Then he turned to Sandy. "Ms. Saavedra, may I have a word with you, in private?"

"No," said his uncle. "Don't talk about me behind my back. Whatever you want to say to my friend you'd better say right here in front of me."

Sandy had to hold back a giggle at the look of frustration on Richard's face. It was obviously warring with the respect he had for the older man. Tío Jaime, on the other hand, had his chin thrust out stubbornly, like a child's.

Richard took a deep breath and tried again to get his point across. "Ms. Saavedra, as I told you before, my uncle isn't well. He doesn't need any more stress in his life right now, or any kind of extra excitement. Please respect that and leave him alone."

Sandy went on the offensive. "You made me think Tío Jaime had a heart attack or something. You made me worry that I had done something to bring it on. But I didn't. And no one told me that he shouldn't be eating sugar! I never would have brought him cookies if I had known!"

"You brought him cookies?" Richard practically bellowed. "Why did you bring him cookies? Was that your bribe to get him to do your videos?"

"No!" said Sandy and Tío Jaime, simultaneously. "She brought me cookies because I like them," the old man added. "And because we're friends. Besides, I can eat sugar if I want to. I can control it."

"Obviously, you can't!" cried Richard and Sandy together this time, both pointing at his foot in its cast.

Tío Jaime looked down in chagrin. Richard glared at him accusingly. But Sandy had to laugh. It was finally too much for her. She laughed and the others turned to look at her in astonishment. Then Tío Jaime laughed, and Richard's brow smoothed down from anger to mere concern.

"Look, Mr....Richard," Sandy said. "I *know* what this looks like. I understand why you don't trust me. But please believe me when I tell you that I'm not trying to take advantage of your uncle. He's been a friend to my family—to my Great-Aunt Linda—since before I was born. The last thing I'd ever want to do is hurt him. In fact, I want to help him. That's why I'm here."

"What," said Richard wryly, "are you a doctor on the side?"

"No." Sandy ignored his sarcasm. "Tío Jaime told me that you need him to move to California because you can't afford to take care of him here. But he doesn't want to leave his home. So—" She paused, then heard herself say, "I'm going to help you pay his bills."

"No," both men said, shaking their heads in matching stubborn expressions that made Sandy see the family resemblance.

"I can't let you do that," Richard said. "This is a family matter. We can't take your money."

"But what if it's not my money?" Sandy had a sudden flash of inspiration then. "What if it's money he earned?"

"No," said Tío Jaime again.

But Sandy ignored him and told Richard, "Your uncle's helped make our site very successful. Our readers love him. But he's never let me compensate him for the features he's done. Let me do it now. If I can raise the money from our readers—from his fans—will you accept it and put it toward his bills?"

Richard opened his mouth to answer, but Tío Jaime cut him off. "If I make any money from work I've done, then, yes, I'll use it to pay my bills. Richard has no say in it."

Richard frowned, but Sandy gave them both a triumphant smile. It was settled, then. Now all she had to do was figure out how she was going to fulfill her promise.

"Let me...Tío Jaime, I need to talk to my boss. I have some ideas, but I need to clear them with her first." She stood awkwardly. She'd been sitting in the only chair in the room, and now that his nephew was here, she realized he had more of a claim to the seat than she did.

Feeling self-conscious, she hugged the old man good-bye, then passed Richard with a polite nod and exited the room in as graceful a hurry as she could muster.

"Sandy."

She heard him call to her as she rounded the corner by the nurses' station. She stopped and turned, and he walked out to her. He'd finally put down the fruit basket, she saw.

"I just wanted to say that I'm sorry if I seemed unnecessarily harsh yesterday. I was under some stress."

"Well. Yeah. Okay, thanks," Sandy said.

He went on. "I have to admit to you that, when I wrote that cease-and-desist letter, I hadn't yet seen any of the interviews you'd done with my uncle."

"You hadn't?"

"No. Only the T-shirts, and that he was on TV. And then, you know, I'd done a search on your name and found...that thing about you slandering your ex-boyfriend online. So I naturally thought—"

"What? That you should jump to conclusions, based on things you'd read online?" Sandy said. Her worst fears were true. He'd read George's horrible article about her relationship with Daniel. About her *blogging* about her relationship with Daniel.

"Well, no." He looked sheepish and didn't say anything else about it. But it was obvious to her that he'd drawn his conclusions from the article and had no reason to revise them now.

Sandy crossed her arms. "So you thought I was the kind of person who'd trash *anyone* online, no matter who."

"Isn't that what you do for a living?" he returned just as quickly.

Sandy had to admit to herself that he had a point. Still, she wasn't going to back down. Not with *him*. "I guess it is. Yes, you're right. I get paid to make fun of celebrities. Just like you get paid to defend criminals, I'm sure." She knew that probably wasn't the case if he practiced immigration law, but she said it anyway. He said nothing, so she'd probably hit the mark with that one. She continued, "I wonder what I'd find if I did a Web search on your name? Maybe I'll try that tonight."

With that, she turned and walked away.

"Hey," he said quietly.

But that was all he said, so Sandy kept walking. She didn't need this guy lecturing her. She already knew what she'd done wrong, and she was planning to fix it, whether he believed it or not.

68

Entry from Aunt Linda's journal, November 4, 1971

I voted for the first time. Isn't that funny, at my age? Afterwards, Jaime and I had lunch in Austin, near the University, and watched the students walking everywhere.

He's been after me to get a car. I might, and I might not. So far I'm okay with my bike, but it would be nice to have a car for when it gets cold. Maybe, when I save some more money.

Ruby says Papi isn't doing so well. I'm worried. I wish I could go visit, if only to make sure Mami's okay.

Entry from Aunt Linda's journal, December 18, 1974

Going to Del Rio for Papi's funeral, and to help Mami pack up to move to Ruby's in California.

Entry from Aunt Linda's journal, July 22, 1978

Where has this little journal been? Don't even know what to say here anymore. That's what happens when you get a TV, I guess.

I did get my car, and then another one. I'm a teacher now, at the same school.

Miguel is gone. He got in a wreck, drunk of course, and now I'm a widow, just like Jaime's a widower.

We could get married now, I guess. But we can't decide whose house we'd live in, his or mine.

Besides, he makes a good neighbor.

Ruby is doing good. Her husband bought them a bigger house and Mami has her own bedroom now. She loves watching Ruby's kids. I'm glad for her.

Rudolfo's oldest girl just got married. They don't live too far from here. I keep thinking that maybe I should write them. All that stuff in the past is the past. It's no excuse for not seeing my family.

Entry from Aunt Linda's journal, November 29, 1982
Going to California for Mami's funeral.

I'm not going to lie. I have regrets. Not for what I did, but for what I didn't do. I should have gone home more. I should have forgiven her face-to-face, and let her forgive me.

Entry from Aunt Linda's journal, June 8, 1987
Connie, Rudolfo's daughter, came to visit today with her daughter Dominga. We had a picnic outside. It was nice.

I told Jaime afterwards that the little girl reminded me of me, when I was little. Or maybe I just wanted to see it that way, because I imagined that's how it would have been if I'd ever had a daughter.

We had a ceremony at the school last week. Can't believe I've been teaching there for more than 10 years now. Time flies when you're having fun, I guess. The older kids gave me an award: Favorite English Teacher. That was nice, too.

Entry from Aunt Linda's journal, undated
Thought I had lost this.

Don't know what to write. Everything's the same, which is good.

We're happy.

Entry from Aunt Linda's journal, undated

Retirement ceremony today. It was nice.

Ruby says Connie's girl is going to college now, to be a writer. In a way it makes me sad that I never had my own child. Then I realize that God must have meant for me to concentrate on my children at the school.

Mostly, though, I'm very proud. Of course a girl in our family would turn out to be a writer. Loving books is in her blood. Even if she doesn't know it.

I'm just glad to see the way the world has changed since I was a girl. To see how everybody's freer now. I think about my great niece and my students, and how they're going to grow up in a better place and be able to do whatever they want with their lives. And I thank God for that.

Entry from Aunt Linda's journal, undated

I don't want to go to Ruby's, but I see now that I have to. I don't want Jaime to see me like this anymore. I want to leave him with good memories, only.

We've been happy here.

I'm glad. For everything, God, I'm glad.

69

Sandy finished reading the journal late Saturday night—very, very early Sunday morning, actually. It'd made her cry. It was a mostly happy story, of course, but she wished it had told more. She regretted, now, that she'd never really known her great-aunt. She wished that, at the very least, Aunt Linda had found time to write more in her journal.

On the shallowest level, Sandy found herself disappointed that there was no closure to the story as far as Aunt Linda's relationship with Tío Jaime went. Did they ever—hook up, for want of a better expression? Her aunt never said. But Sandy imagined they must have. It was obvious that they loved each other even though they never married.

She lay in her sofa bed late Sunday morning, hugging the journal to her chest.

Eventually her thoughts turned back to her own life. *Maybe I'll go to work tomorrow after all.* So what if George was going to be there? So what if Angelica wasn't really the caring mother figure Sandy had imagined her to be? This job was her life, and her life was what she made it, right? She could stay home hiding, or she could go back into the fray and show them what she was made of.

If she was going to leave a record of her own life online for future generations to find, the least she could do was work toward a happy ending.

ONCE ANGELICA GOT over her surprise that Sandy wasn't taking vacation after all, the rest was easy.

"So, let me get this straight," she said during their private meeting in her office on Monday morning. "You'll agree to participate in the date auction, and you'll even go on a double date with George and let us record it for use on the show, as long as the proceeds benefit your Chupacabra man?"

"Right." It filled Sandy's mouth with a bad taste just imagining it, but she reminded herself that she'd be helping her friend. Besides, how could it be worse or more humiliating than everything that'd already happened to her online? It couldn't.

"All right. Luckily, Jacob had the foresight to create the Levy Foundation last year for the Banana Nation charity event. So we can just funnel your auction money through the foundation and create a grant for the Chupacabra, and keep it all on the up-and-up."

"Sure. Sounds good." Sandy didn't care about the technicalities at this point.

"Well, we'll get the ball rolling, then." Angelica stood and gave Sandy her highest-wattage smile. "Glad to have you back, Sandy. You had me worried there for a minute, but I knew you'd come back fighting in the end. You're like me—you're too strong to let a little gossip get you down."

Sandy followed her boss out of the office, feeling like she'd just made a deal with the devil. She knew what Angelica was hoping for: a big blow-out with George, with every last detail caught on camera and granted in perpetuity to the Levy Media Money Machine.

No matter what, Sandy told herself, she'd go through it with her head held high. If there was any fodder for ridicule, *she* wouldn't be the one to create it, at least.

"Sandy! I'm so glad you're feeling better!" La Sirena caroled at her from a corner of the staff room.

Sandy returned her fake smile. "Me too!"

"Ladies, let's go. We have a show to record," said Angelica, leading the way out of the office and down the hall toward the studio. "Trisha, I want you to go ahead and do the segment on Tito Jimenez's steroid ring. Sandy, you'll pair up with George for the *Semana in Pictures*."

Two hours later, Sandy sat behind the counter on the news set, primped, prepped, and well lighted. Next to her, George sat on the other stool, forcing the prettiest intern to double-check the powder on his nose.

Show them what you're made of. Sandy repeated the sentence in her mind like an old woman saying the rosary. On the outside she looked serene as a saint, her legs crossed at the ankles as she patiently waited for taping to begin. Behind them, images of starlets, pop stars, and athletes flashed like playing cards on the big monitor.

"So, Sandy, long time no see, huh? I mean, not counting Friday, huh?" George's chatter was as inane as always.

"Right. I haven't seen you since you left for Buzz News," she replied calmly.

"Yeah. Listen, about that—" he started. But that was as far as he got. The director called their cue and it was time to begin working.

"Hey, hey, HEY," George said to the camera. "It's time for the *Semana in Pictures*, and this week my cohost is the lovely Sandy S."

"Good evening, everyone," Sandy said to the camera. Already she felt her persona falling into place. She was

Sandy S., internationally read Web writer and prime-time cable personality. Her viewers and readers were watching, and it was time to be pretty, witty, and bright for them.

"First up," said George, as he and Sandy swiveled to address the monitor, "we have a specimen of Amber Chavez and Husband Number Three, Carlitos Buenaventura." The monitor obligingly showed a photograph of the two celebrities on a beach, actress/singer/model Amber pretending not to pose for the camera and her husband standing behind her looking pale and sickly. "Ladies first, so I'll let you have first crack at analysis, Sandy."

Sandy struck a faux-thoughtful pose, then launched into the spiel she'd brainstormed an hour before. "The body language is very interesting in this one, George. Amber's says, 'Look at me, but please pay no attention to the hairy mole on my back. I'm having that removed next month.' Meanwhile, his gestures very clearly say, 'I need the blood of human babies to survive.'"

Someone behind the camera laughed. Sandy flashed a quick smile and noted that Angelica had come out to watch their segment.

"I agree completely, Sandy. And now—I know you hate it when I do this—but I have to make note of Amber's famous nalgas. She's not filling out that white bikini quite as well as she could be in the back. In fact"—the monitor switched to a Nacho Papi–made graphic, progressive views of Amber's backside over several years. Above the images were logos of brands for which Amber had served as spokeswoman. George continued, "I have to point out that, when she first modeled for Thuggin' jeans, Amber looked a lot healthier. Then, as you can see from our time-lapse photography, she lost a little weight for Solamente Amber perfume, then a little more for Vida water. And now that she's modeling for Prosecco bags, she's lost way too much." He turned to address the camera directly. "Amber, get back into your mamma's kitchen, girl. Eat you some arroz y frijoles!"

More chuckles from behind the camera. Sandy waited a beat and then did her bit. "Normally, George, I'd call you a disgusting sexist pig for pointing that out, but I have to say, instead, that the research shows Amber's only hurting herself." The monitor switched to another silly graphic, charting record sales along the curve of a woman's butt. "Nacho Papi has found that there's a direct, inverse correlation between Amber's butt size and her record sales. So, Amber, please—if you can't bear to eat the beans and rice anymore, at least have a little more caviar."

Sandy didn't get as many laughs as George, but she never expected to. She was the serious one on this show. She did the dry humor. She classed it up a little, if that were at all possible.

It was time for their next celebrity hazing. The monitor showed a photograph of actor Jared Rider holding up a cell phone and smirking in a crowded nightclub.

George said, "A sex video of Sabrina Lopez and Joe Villarreal mysteriously turned up on the Internet this week. The video was linked to Jared Ryder, another of Sabrina's exes. He denies responsibility, but it's pretty obvious that he had *something* to do with it. What do you make of it, Sandy?" He indicated the man on the monitor. "Is Jared trying to get revenge for Sabrina dumping him, or is it all a publicity stunt?"

Sandy turned to face George. She opened her mouth to say the lines they'd planned. But then, instead, she thought of something funnier. "I don't know, George.

Isn't that *your* department? Selling the details of a woman's romantic life just to get a little attention?"

This time, everyone behind the camera cracked up. There was a "Whoa!" and even Angelica laughed. Sandy held her "thoughtful" pose throughout the hoots and guffaws. George waited, too, for the laughter to subside, nodding his head and looking, finally, a little embarrassed.

"Touché, Sandy. Touché," he said. And then the control room put up the next celebrity target.

After the taping was done, George turned to Sandy with a rueful smile. "That was cold, Sand. I guess I deserved it, though."

"You did," she replied with a sweet smile of her own.

"You know, for the record, I have to point out to you that that article did us both a lot of good. It increased our page views by, like, a thousand percent. I'm sure you got hundreds of new fans who wouldn't have known about your writing before."

"Right. And hundreds of new anti-fans, too." Sandy kept her voice mild, but she wasn't going to let him off the hook so easily.

George shrugged. "Well, that's the price we pay, isn't it? If we want to be famous?"

"Great job, you two." Angelica walked over, beaming like a headlight. "I'm pairing you up again tomorrow."

70

Post on Nacho Papi's Web Site, Wednesday, June 28

But seriously, folks
by Sandy S.

As you've read below, Nacho Papi is hosting its First Annual Staff Date Charity Auction, and I'm one of the staff members you can bid on a date with, for better or worse. But, before the bidding starts, I wanted to tell you what your money will be spent on if you win the date with me.

Our beloved Chupacabra, Wise Goat Man and Viejo at Large, has suffered a health-related setback that's been distracting him from advice-giving and his outlaw life. The Chupacabra got his foot caught in the trap called diabetes, and he's been in a cast for a week now. Worse than that, he's having trouble with The Man and The System, and that's making it hard to pay his bills.

So I'm pimping myself out, so to speak, not for a non-profit full of anonymous faces, but to benefit our own Chupacabra, who's been like a grandfather or uncle to me these past few months.

See the video below, and see if you can bring yourself to bid on a date in order to help out our friend.

READER COMMENTS ON **BUT SERIOUSLY FOLKS**

Aw, man, that sucks. I'd bid, but I'm just a poor grad student
and it's already up to more than I can afford.
Toasty Toes

Somebody recap the video for me, please! I'm at work and can't
watch it!
The Girl Formerly Known as Maria

Maria: It's Sandy S, trying to interview the Chupacabra. But all
he says is "Turn that damned camera off! I'm not begging for
any damned hand-outs!" He has a cast on his foot. And Cano's
in the background, barking. Even when he's doing bad, that old
man kills me.
Boston Mike

Sandy, can we send donations outside of the auction? I want to
help out, but no offense, you're not my type. ☺
Julietta

Oh man, this is like my wish come true! Not that the Chupacabra
has diabetes, but that I might finally get to go on a date with
Sandy S.! I'm breaking my piggy banks now!
The Wild Juan

71

Within a few days of the announcement, Sandy had collected, in addition to her auction bids, several hundred dollars in separate donations for Tío Jaime's cause, as well as hundreds of cards and gifts delivered to him in care of Nacho Papi's offices. She drove to his house that weekend to give him the tribute from his fans.

"That's funny," he said, examining a stuffed chupacabra toy that someone had hand-crocheted for him. "I wouldn't think all these strangers would care about some old guy they never even met."

"Well, they've read and listened to your words for a while now. I guess that makes them feel like they do know you. Or like you know and care about them." Sandy stacked his get-well cards in a neat pile on the little patio table. She'd already presented him with a check from the Levy Foundation totaling all the readers' donations to date. Angelica had insisted they do it that way, for tax purposes and to protect the old man's identity. He hadn't wanted to take it at first, but she'd reminded him that this was payment, in essence, for the work he'd done for the site.

"Hmm," Tío Jaime said. "I guess that's why you do it, then, huh? To make strangers feel good about themselves?"

Sandy considered the question. She'd never thought of

it that way before. "Well, not really, honestly. I started writing for Nacho Papi because they bought my old company, then to get better known as a writer. And I started writing my blog to make *myself* feel better. But I have noticed that the blog helps other people sometimes. When I talk about stuff they've gone through, it makes them feel less alone." After she'd said all that, Sandy realized the irony of the situation. "It's too bad I'm not getting paid to write the things that help people."

Sandy offered to drive him to the bank to deposit his check, but Tío Jaime refused, saying it'd give Richard something to do later. So, after helping the old man put away his gifts and exacting his promise to deposit the check that afternoon, Sandy drove back into town. It was a beautiful day and she didn't want to hole up in her apartment anymore. She needed to run some errands and get her nails done, but before that, she had a caffeine habit that needed maintaining. She drove past Calypso, her old favorite coffee shop, and peered in the window. Not too crowded.

It was safer, of course, to go to the corporate coffee drive-through and then trek out to a suburban nail place where the day time clientele skewed a little older than Nacho Papi's fan base. But she missed her old hangouts. Was she really going to spend the rest of her life avoiding them, she asked herself, because of the slight possibility that some jerk might call her a name or give her a dirty look?

She parked the car and strode in bravely, silently daring anyone to say anything. The barista, a young man she'd never seen before, greeted her like any other customer. A couple of the patrons turned their heads and glanced at her as she passed, but that was it. No snickers or whispers. It was almost anti-climactic.

Half an hour later, Sandy sat at the corner table with a

chocolate almond iced latte, checking her e-mail and feeling like her old self. She opened an e-mail from an editor at the *Los Angeles Chronicle*, knowing that it was most likely a freelance opportunity. She'd received countless offers and calls for submissions from other organizations since Nacho Papi had begun, but was forced to turn them all down because of her contract's non-compete clause. She was already mentally composing a polite declination when she opened the e-mail.

Dear Ms. Saavedra:

I wrote to you a while back about doing a feature on what happened between you and your ex-boyfriend online.

However, after reading more of your work, I've decided that the LA Chronicle has an opportunity I think you'd be perfect for. Would you please call me?

It was signed Jim Mayer, Online Features Editor, and gave his office number and cell. Overcome by curiosity, Sandy called his cell.

"Jim Mayer."

"Hi, Jim. This is Sandy Saavedra, from Nacho Papi's Web Site. I just got your e-mail."

"Sandy!" His voice was genial, warm. "I'm glad you called. Are you someplace where you can talk?"

"Yes," she said. He must have meant somewhere other than the Nacho Papi offices. Now she really was intrigued.

"Good. Well, as I was saying in the e-mail, we're looking for an online writer for our new culture blog. It's a full-time position. Philippe recommended you, and I've been looking at your work and think you'd be perfect for this job. It's similar to what you do for Nacho Papi, but a little less snarky. And for a much wider audience, I imagine. I hope."

Sandy felt a shiver of excitement travel through her. She was being offered a job by a major LA newspaper! "I'm very flattered, Jim, but unfortunately, I have a non-compete with Nacho Papi that precludes me from accepting other assignments."

"I understand that. This is more than an assignment, though. It's a full-time position. We would be paying you to spend all your time writing for us."

Sandy caught her breath. He was asking her to leave Nacho Papi. A real newspaper editor was trying to steal her away! "Would I have to relocate to Los Angeles?"

"It would be easiest, yes. Would you be willing to move?"

"Maybe." Sandy knew better than to give a definite answer either way. "How soon are you looking to fill the position?"

"The blog launches in August, so you have some time to think it over. I hope you will. And that you'll send me a résumé and some formal clips, to show my manager in the meantime."

Sandy agreed to do so and hung up, already feeling her elation subside. Unless they were going to pay her way more than a standard staff writer's salary, there was no way she could afford to move to Los Angeles. She knew this from secondhand experience because her friend Veronica had tried it a few years ago and failed miserably.

Granted, Veronica had moved into an expensive loft in Hollywood with a flaky boyfriend and not into one of the cheaper areas. But still. Sandy was just cementing her reputation at her current job. It'd be foolish to leave now.

72

So my question is, what do you do when you feel like you can't share anything, good or bad, with anyone anymore?"

"M'ija, you forgot to turn on your camera." Tío Jaime's smile poked gentle fun at her. They were on his porch. His foot was stretched in front of him in its new blue temporary cast. Cano lay next to it as if he were its guardian. Except that, for the moment, he was snoring.

"I know. I just thought I'd try out some of your advice that's so popular with the kids these days." Sandy teased back. "Now that I have your signature, I might as well take advantage of it, right?"

He chuckled. But suddenly Sandy didn't feel like laughing.

In fact, she had an idea. She stood and moved her chair so that it was next to Tío Jaime's. Glancing down at herself to make sure she was presentable—no sugar-free banana bread crumbs on her T-shirt—she turned on the camera and took her place next to the Chupacabra.

"So, I'm thinking today's 'Ask the Chupacabra' will be special," she said. "This time, it's all about me." She turned to the camera and added, "Your hostess, Sandy S., in case you don't recognize me in a T-shirt and jeans, without all my makeup."

Tío Jaime smiled, his eyes twinkling like a rustic Santa Claus's under his straw hat. "What do you need advice for, m'ija? You're doing real good, aren't you?"

"No. That's the thing—I'm doing real bad." Sandy shook her head. Leaning back in the patio chair, she crossed one leg over the other, startling Cano awake. "I haven't been a very good person lately."

"What do you mean?" the Chupacabra asked.

Sandy considered her next words for a moment. This was strange, being the one answering the questions. "When I first started writing for Nacho Papi, I was an unknown writer. A hard worker, a nice person. It was important to me to go out and find out the truth about things, and to tell true stories to other people."

The Chupacabra and his dog said nothing. They simply sat and listened. So Sandy went on. "Now I write bad things about people for money. I don't search for anything. I look at a picture of someone and make up a bunch of new ways to say they're ugly or stupid. I point out that they're hypocrites." She laughed a little at that. "And, worse than that, I started thinking about people that way in real life, too. My friends. My family."

Sandy turned to face the camera. She knew, in the back of her mind, that this probably wouldn't make it to air. Angelica wouldn't let it; it wasn't "Hate-O-Rama" enough. But she was going to say it anyway. Even if no one ever saw it, it needed to be said. "A long time ago, I started this stupid blog—an online diary—called My Modern TragiComedy. It was supposed to be anonymous, but it wasn't, really. How could it be? It was on the Internet. I used to say all kinds of things, really personal things, in that blog. It was like, I didn't want to say those things to the people involved, but I wanted to say them to *someone*. I felt like, maybe if I said them to the world, the words would somehow get through to my boyfriend, my parents, whoever, and make them understand. But without me having to be the one to say it to their faces. You know what I mean?"

Tío Jaime didn't nod or say anything. He knew, probably, that she wasn't talking to him anymore. And she knew that the people she *was* talking to probably *would* be nodding, at this point.

"So of course my boyfriend and my mom eventually found out what I'd written about them. They found out, and so did everyone else. So I ended up having to deal with the issues anyway, but in a much worse situation than if I'd just talked to them privately to begin with. And now I feel like an idiot and a horrible person, and I don't know why I did something so stupid."

"Did you throw away the blog so no one else could see it?" The way Tío Jaime said the word made it obvious that he didn't say it often.

Sandy would've smiled if she hadn't been so focused on the unfunny aspects of the situation. "No, I never threw it away. I did delete the personal things about Daniel and my mom, but I haven't deleted the whole thing."

"Why not?" he asked.

"I don't know." Sandy sat quietly for a moment and thought about it. "I guess...well, because some people still like it. Some people seem to get some good out of it, despite the fact that I said a few hurtful things."

"Hmm." That was all he said.

"I mean, it wasn't *all* bad. I did try to write a *few* things that were meaningful at least."

There was a long pause while they sat together in silence, in thought. Then the Chupacabra recommenced his role as interviewer. "So what advice do you need? What did you want to ask?"

Sandy did laugh then. "Nothing, I guess. I already know what to do." Again, she faced the camera. "Daniel, I'm sorry. We weren't right for each other, so we broke up, and that should've been enough. I shouldn't have made fun of you online, whether or not I thought you'd ever see it. I'm sorry." She took a breath. "Mom, I'm sorry to you, too. We've already talked it out, but I still want to apologize here, so everyone who read what I said about you can see this, too. And, for the record, you're an awesome mom. I never said it online, but now I will: You've worked hard to keep things normal since Dad left, and you're always there when I need you. I know that and appreciate it. Now everyone else knows, too."

She glanced at Tío Jaime and saw him smiling at her encouragingly.

She needed to apologize to Veronica and Jane, too, but remembered that she'd never said their names online. So she wouldn't do it now either. "I'm also sorry to any of my friends I hurt. You guys know who you are, and I'll be calling you personally after this."

And what the hell? Sandy thought. While she was at it: "I also want to apologize to Lucia San Lucas, for making fun of her plus-size Latina vampire novel on the Nacho Papi site. Lucia, I read your whole novel in the bookstore, in one sitting. I couldn't stop reading it. Then I felt embarrassed, afterward, thinking about what other people would say if they'd caught me with a romance novel. But I'll be honest now: You wrote the best plus-sized Latina vampire story I've ever read, and you deserve your success. And, um..." Was it starting to be overkill now? Sandy wondered. Well, what did it matter at this point? "Amber Chavez, I'm sorry I called you haggard and talked so much about your body. I know you're trying really hard to be a serious actress, and…uh…I'm glad you're out there, showing girls what they can do."

Sandy heaved a great sigh. She felt simultaneously sobered and lightened, like she had after her first confession. She laughed again, then told Tío Jaime, "You'd make a good priest, you know that? Father Chupacabra."

He smiled. "It's not me. It's you. I'm just sitting here."

"No, you're doing more than that." She realized then what would make her feel even lighter. "This whole time, you've been listening to our problems—mine and the ones sent in by Nacho Papi readers—and you've given us your time and your insight, and you've asked nothing in return. And I misled you. Not only did I record these segments, but we sold T-shirts with your picture, and we put you on TV without your permission. And, for that, I'm sorry."

"Thank you," he said quietly. "I appreciate that. And I forgive you."

After all that confessing, Sandy suddenly felt overwhelmed. Moisture gathered in her eyes and she laughed to cover it, then wiped her cheek surreptitiously. "Chupacabra, what did we do to deserve you?"

"Nothing, probably," he said. Then he turned to face the camera directly himself, for the first time in all their interviews. "All of you people watching this need to stop listening to me. You need to quit surfing on the Nets and get back to work. Then, when you get off work, you need to drive to your parents' houses and your grandparents' houses and listen to them instead."

He turned back to Sandy. "That's it. That's the last thing I'm gonna say here. This is my last interview." His voice was gruff, but Sandy saw the twinkle still firmly in his eye.

"Okay. Thank you, then, Chupacabra. It was nice knowing you, and we wish you the best." She stood up then, and put out her hand. Cano's ears lifted. Slowly, Tío Jaime stood to shake her hand. After a few shakes, Sandy let go and reached over to hug him. "Thanks," she whispered into his ear.

After that, she turned off the camera.

73

READER COMMENTS ON **ADIOS, CHUPACABRA**

That was so cheesy and lame. What the hell is this now, the
Hallmark Card site?
Monstro

Oh my God! That totally made me cry!!!
Fresa Princessa

Wait, so there's no more Ask the Chupacabra? What the? Why?
What'd *we* do?
Jenny Loves Versace

Can't say I won't miss him, but I understand why it has to be
done. Bravo, you two.
Boston Mike

This site has totally jumped the shark now. I'm never reading it
again.
James Bondo

Shut up, Monstro. Sandy, I'm glad you're not taking your blog down.
La FiliPiña

This doesn't make sense. If Sandy's not gonna talk trash about people anymore, then how's she gonna keep working for Nacho Papi?
Diondre

It's all staged. None of this is real. They're only doing it for the page views, don't you people get it?
Taco Belle

Hey, Sandy S, if you're leaving, can I have your job?
Mensa

Sandy S, please don't leave! We can't lose you and the Chupacabra at the same time!
Wholio

She's not leaving. Look at all the comments she got here. Wonder how much money she's making on this post, alone?
James Bondo

Hey, James Bondo, I thought you weren't gonna read Nacho Papi anymore.
Rene Loves Amber Chavez

Somebody please send me the link to Sandy's personal blog. I can't find it!
Monkey Girl

The part where Sandy S almost starts to cry? That part made me cry. Sandy, I hope you don't leave us. But, if you have to, I wish you the best.
LB

74

On the second blazing hot Saturday morning in July, Sandy sat in her garage apartment and tried not to stress over the impending evening's events. It was the day of their big charity date, and all Sandy knew was that she was committed to dinner and a show with George, a woman misguided enough to bid on a date with George, and a reader who called himself Harvey Birdman.

Angelica claimed that all the auction winners had been fully screened to weed out stalkers or ax murderers. But knowing Angelica as well as she did by now, Sandy wouldn't put it past her to let one ax murderer through, just for kicks and higher ratings.

Of course, Nacho Papi readers had been buzzing about the auctions all week, saying that whoever won the date with Sandy should be prepared to have his "performance" dissected on her personal Web site.

Nonetheless, Sandy's bid amount had climbed steadily all week and was now second only to La Sirena's. She didn't want to think about what kind of man would pay so much to go out with a woman he only knew from the small screen, but at the same time this man's bid was paying a large portion of Tío Jaime's outstanding bills. And that, Sandy reminded herself as she packed up to go to the office, made it worth spending the evening with him, however creepy he might turn out to be. They'd be on camera all night, after all.

She arrived at the office at eleven and was immediately whisked away with Lori and La Sirena into a van manned by interns and cameramen. They were scheduled for salon appointments and final dress fittings with various sponsors, while George, Philippe, and Francisco were spending the day in their own van, visiting a swanky men's salon and Tony's Formalwear.

It was a double-shot mocha kind of day, Sandy already knew. Maybe even a triple.

At 6 p.m. all the staffers reconvened at the studio to meet their dates. Flashy white Hummer limos were already lined up outside in preparation for their big evening, making Sandy and Lori wince at the thought of all those environment-hurting emissions. But the limos were free, so Angelica wasn't complaining.

One by one, the auction winners were escorted into the "evening set," which was a room with a fake window that showed a fake Austin skyline by night. First was Francisco's date, who'd gotten him for the lowest price of any of the staffers. Angelica announced the girl's real name, then the fact that she was a longtime reader by the screen name of Geeky Chica. Sandy recognized her as one of Francisco's constant commenters. She couldn't have been more than nineteen years old, Sandy and Lori decided in whispered conversation while watching the taping. Geeky Chica had glasses and braces. Sandy wondered if she'd saved up her after-school job money for the auction, or if maybe her mother had footed the bill. Francisco, looking almost dapper in his suede jacket and blue jeans, gallantly escorted her to their limo. A cameraman clambered in behind them. They were on the way to a private event at the new Museum of Computer Science.

Next came Lori's date, a tall young woman in dread-locks and a tight-fitting tuxedo. Obviously having planned ahead, she handed Lori a giant tiger-lily corsage that matched her leopard-print dress. The two of them giggled like maniacs all the way to their limo, which was taking them to a tattoo parlor for matching hers-and-hers designs.

Philippe's date was a serious Nordic-looking man Sandy seemed to recognize. She'd seen him, she real-ized upon further scrutiny, standing in the background of pictures of Philippe at various events in LA and New York. They looked like two male models in their match-ing tuxedos.

"That's his boyfriend. He cheated." George had sidled up to her and was whispering in her ear.

La Sirena stood a few steps away in a very low-cut black dress, eagerly awaiting her own date. Angelica, still play-ing emcee, introduced him as John Doeman. He turned out to be yet another familiar face, this time an older man.

"That's Ronnie David. He's a TV producer from New York. We met him at Jacob's last thing. Jeez!" George hissed. He couldn't seem to curb his commentary, and Sandy wondered if he was as nervous as she was. She tugged discreetly at her magenta strapless gown and tried not to panic.

Angelica announced Sandy's date, Harvey Birdman. Next to Sandy, George chuckled. "That's a superhero's name."

Mr. Harvey Birdman came around the corner in a well-cut suit and a big smile.

"Richard!" Sandy gasped quietly. It was Tío Jaime's nephew. But how? *Why?* she wondered.

They shook hands and air-hugged for the camera, then moved aside to wait for George's date.

"What are you doing here?" Sandy whispered to him, unable to contain herself.

"Helping you. After you talked about paying my uncle's bills, I went to the Web site to make sure you didn't exploit him in the process. Then when I saw what you were really doing, I felt guilty." He turned to face her and continued in a low voice, "This is my family's responsibility, Sandy. You shouldn't have to do this for Tío Jaime. So now I'm paying for it myself."

"Oh, thanks," Sandy said, with as much sarcasm as she could convey in a whisper. He made it sound like he was paying a fine, or getting a root canal.

"What? This guy's your cousin?" George whispered on her other side. "What the—?"

Before he could finish that thought, Angelica was calling his date's name, Marisa Florentino. An older, well-rounded woman in a tight sequined tunic walked out. Between teeth tightly gritted into a smile, George whispered one last remark. "Great. The others get people they've been banging forever, you get your cousin a free meal, and I'm stuck with Cougar Lady here. Freaking great!"

Sandy watched George exchange pleasantries with the woman, who immediately gave him a bear hug and began chattering away in a raspy voice. She almost felt sorry for George. Almost, but not quite.

DINNER ENDED UP being more fun than Sandy had expected. They were forced to sit at a table for four in a private room at an outrageously expensive French restaurant. The cameramen never stopped filming, so Sandy couldn't talk to Richard about Tío Jaime. She couldn't even use his real name; he insisted that she call him Harvey. He also insisted on ordering for her, starting with the escargot, which provided ample opportunity for close-ups and reaction shots, and ending with a dramatic flaming brandy dessert. Sandy had no intention of eating snails, no matter how much they were going for. But she couldn't help but laugh at Richard as he not only ate them, but told obviously made-up stories about hunting bigger snails in the rainforest with a completely straight face. She asked him what kind of law he practiced. He told her he was currently representing the estate of a whole ranch of dead minks in a suit against Saks Fifth Avenue.

He had more of a sense of humor than she'd expected from the few exchanges they'd had in the past. At least, she reflected as she sipped the Beaujolais he'd ordered, he knew how to pick good wine.

Meanwhile, George's date competed for camera time by trying to matchmake George with her cousin's daughter. George had politely declined at first, but then, upon seeing the young woman's picture, he was persuaded. Marisa ordered two bottles of sherry and read tipsy George's palm over dessert. Sandy couldn't tell if she really wanted to set George up with her younger relative or if she was faking George out while attempting to seduce him.

During the limo ride to their next destination, Richard turned to George and asked, "So you're the guy who interviewed Sandy's ex-boyfriend for a competing Web site, right?"

"Uh. Right," said George.

"So tell me, George, what kind of man does something like that?" Richard sat and looked steadily at the other man, waiting for an answer. But there was none forthcoming.

"Um. Hey, it's a job, you know." George turned to Marisa and changed the subject. Sandy heard the whizzing sound from the camera in the next seat as its operator zoomed in for her reaction. She couldn't help but give a quick grin for the record.

After dinner they went to a symphonic performance at the Bass Concert Hall. The cameramen followed them to their seats and then, with ushers as escorts, went to shoot a little footage of the orchestra tuning up in the orchestra pit.

"This isn't really the kind of thing the Nacho Papi audience goes for, is it?" Richard asked her.

Sandy shrugged. "I guess they're thinking it will be if George and I write rave reviews of it later. We probably won't even stay for the whole thing."

She was right. Fifteen minutes into the performance an intern appeared and guided them back to the limo, which was now magically stocked with champagne. "Drink up," the intern encouraged them, probably according to Angelica's orders, Sandy knew. She took a sip from her plastic glass and decided she'd have to pretend to be tipsy, later, in order to please her boss.

Their next stop was a tango bar, of all things, in a quiet corner downtown. They were welcomed in by the owner himself, who made a big show of walking them to their candlelit table, which was already set with glasses of Argentinean red. He offered to lead Sandy to the floor and show her the steps.

"Ooh, show me!" cried George's date, stepping between Sandy and the man. And so the owner led her to the floor. Marisa was obviously an accomplished dancer, and she dipped and spun with more ease than Sandy would have expected.

"Great," said George into his wineglass. He took a seat

on one of the bar stools in the far corner and slumped against the wall.

"Want to dance?" Richard asked.

"I don't know if I can." Sandy eyed the half-dozen couples on the crowded little floor. Apart from Marisa, they all looked like movie extras, moving in perfect rhythm to the twangy Latin beat. "I've never tangoed before."

"Neither have I. How bad could it be, though?"

Before she could refuse outright, Richard led her out to the floor, where they almost immediately stepped on each other's feet and crashed into the couple nearest them. Sandy almost collapsed in nervous giggles, but Richard held her close and managed to lead her in a step that approximated what everyone else was doing and kept them safe in their own little space.

They were out of the hearing of the cameras now, even though the ever-present red lights focused on them from two corners of the bar. Now, Sandy thought, was the time for a serious conversation.

But Richard spoke first. "You know, you look really different without your glasses. Much less severe."

"Oh, really?" Her reply was immediate. "Maybe I should have left them on, then."

He laughed. "Maybe. It'd make it easier to be angrier with you."

She looked up at him in exasperation. "*Are* you still angry, though? Why? I never said anything bad about your uncle. Whatever else I may have done, you can't accuse me of that."

His look became thoughtful. "No, I'm not angry about that anymore. I'm not even sure I ever was. I guess I was just upset because you made me feel guilty. There I was, trying to visit my uncle as much as time allowed, and then you come along and change his whole life without me knowing anything about it. I had to figure out who you were and what exactly you were doing, and then I had to go home and explain it to my mother, who never reads the Internet, and who was in a complete panic that I was letting some strange woman take advantage of her older brother."

"Well," said Sandy, "when you put it that way, I guess I can see why you were a little upset."

He laughed. "Yeah. A little."

"But you realize now that I'm not evil, right?"

"I suppose so." He made a skeptical face and it was Sandy's turn to laugh.

"*I've* been feeling super guilty," she said, "because I had no idea he was diabetic, and I was drinking that sugary lemonade with him and buying him cookies the whole time. And then, his foot..."

"Don't worry about that. That's not your fault. My uncle, as I'm sure you've noticed, is a stubborn man. If he wanted to follow his doctor's orders, he would have done it with or without your encouragement. And obviously he didn't want to follow them."

The song ended and Sandy and Richard let the other dancers move past them, in silent agreement to stay on the dance floor and continue their conversation out of camera range. The next song started and they picked up their slow, turning shuffle again. The other remaining dancers gave them plenty of room, obviously aware by now that they were being taped.

"So," Sandy said, "you read that whole thing with George and my ex-boyfriend."

Richard nodded. "I did."

"And you're still pretty sure I'm not some evil man-hating witch?"

He chuckled. "Well, I can see that you're a good writer. And it's pretty obvious that your ex and George had issues with that. You know what people say—crabs in a bucket."

"Right. They try to pull you down." Remembering Tío Jaime's expression about envy made her smile.

"And I saw the last interview you did with my uncle, where you apologized to everyone on earth. I have to say, that took serious guts."

Sandy smiled and looked away. She didn't want praise for setting things right.

"Just to be sure, though," Richard continued, "I did take extra precaution tonight, with the pseudonym and the stories about my work. That way, if you *do* decide to write about me on your blog..."

Sandy laughed. "Well, that's assuming a lot, isn't it? I meet a lot of people on this job. You might not end up being one of the memorable ones."

"Ouch!" he said. "You *are* evil, after all. So, hey, did you ever do the Web search on my name? Because—"

"Sandy!" called their intern guide, standing near one of the cameramen's shoulder. "Beso!"

She looked over Richard's shoulder at him, frowning and shaking her head.

"Yeah, beso!" chimed the cameraman. Then the other one joined in. "Beso! Beso!"

"Sorry. These guys can be really immature," Sandy told Richard, who was watching in bemusement.

"Do you mind? We can put on a good show for your boss," he said.

She shrugged. *Why not?* Richard bent and dipped her then, low to the ground so that she was no longer facing the cameras. Then, with a wicked smile, he gave her an air kiss that must have looked very real to everyone observing. Then he lifted her up again and she felt all her blood rush back into place.

"Good one," she told him. "Angelica will love that."

Maybe, she thought, she should be more careful. She didn't want to get into another situation where people were gossiping about her personal life, did she?

Oh, who cares? She couldn't control the gossiping, she realized on second thought while starting the third dance. There was no use trying to do anything but live her life.

"What were you going to say?" she asked Richard. "About me searching for your name online?"

"Hmm? Oh. Just that you wouldn't find anything," he said. "Because I went home that night and deleted all the bad stuff."

Sandy couldn't help but laugh. "Too bad I didn't meet you before all this crazy stuff happened, then, so you could have given me that advice."

He smiled in return. "Yeah, it is too bad, isn't it?"

75

Time: Saturday, July 15, 10:56 AM
To: SandyS@nachopapiswebsite.com
From: Daniel.Thomas@112.utexas.edu
Subject: Coda

Sandy,

I think enough time has passed now for each of us to reflect on what's happened and how it's affected us. I see that you've reinstated a working relationship with George Cantu and seem to have recovered well from the fallout from his article.

I, for one, can admit that I regret participating in that article. For what it's worth, I was led to believe that it would be a profile of me and my work, and not solely a piece about the two of us. My quotes were taken out of context. I was probably just as surprised and embarrassed as you to read the final work.

I'm sure you've already admitted, to yourself, at least, your part in all this.

Despite everything, I've been able to continue working and am performing a reading of my thesis at the Fat Man this weekend, as per the link below. It's open to the public. However, I hope that any mention you make of it on your Web site refrains from too personal a tone.

Sincerely,
Daniel

76

Sandy deleted her ex-boyfriend's e-mail with a snort. He was completely ridiculous. She couldn't remember now what she'd ever seen in him in the first place.

It was the Saturday after the busiest week of her term at Nacho Papi so far. After the Big Date episode, they taped segments of every staff member delivering his or her auction donations to the charities of their choice. Sandy's visit to the Chupacabra was aired on the show, then posted on the site. Readers clicked in record numbers to see Sandy knocking on the door of the Chupacabra's house, only to find that no one lived there anymore. She'd used Aunt Linda's house as the setting. At the end she'd zoomed in on a goodbye note she'd written and tacked to the door ahead of time. It said *Gone to greener pastures.*

Reading the comments online now, Sandy saw that the readers' reactions were mixed. Of course. Several had come up with elaborate conspiracy theories about the whole thing being fake to begin with.

She closed down all her files and browser windows, then physically closed her laptop and left Calypso's corner table.

"Bye, Sandy! See you next time!" the barista called as she left.

A leisurely hour later she pulled into Tío Jaime's drive. As always, he was waiting on the porch for her with Cano at his side. His cast had finally been removed and he wore a sturdy new pair of tennis shoes.

Sandy accepted his offer of lemonade, following him into the kitchen to see the telltale pile of yellow sugar-substitute packets.

"I have bad news for you," he told her once they were settled on his porch, enjoying the ever-present cool breeze. His tone belied his words, though, and she suspected she already knew what he was going to tell her. "I'm moving to California, after all. I'm going to live with my little sister in East LA."

"Are you?"

"Yes. It's not because of the bills. The money you gave me was more than enough to cover them—"

"The money you *earned*," Sandy corrected.

"—and I don't know how I'm ever going to pay you back for that."

Sandy shook her head just the way he would have, and he went on.

"But, the truth is, m'ija, I am getting older. You probably can't tell, but my memory isn't what it used to be. I've been forgetting little things here and there, and it's starting to make me nervous."

Sandy didn't confirm or deny. She just let him talk.

"And, as much as I like visiting with you and my neighbors around here, I have to admit that it's been pretty lonely since your Aunt Linda died."

Sandy reached over and put her hand on the old man's shoulder. It was the first time she'd heard him speak directly about his relationship with her great-aunt, and she knew it must have been difficult for him.

"The thing is," he continued, "it'd probably be nice to go stay with my sister for a while. I'd get to see my nephews and nieces more, and a couple of my cousins. I'm gonna miss this old place. And you. But..."

"I understand," Sandy said. "I'll miss you, too." They sat in silence for a while. "When are you going?" she finally asked.

"In a couple of weeks. Richard's flying down to help me settle things, and then we'll take my truck and drive all the way back. Cano doesn't want to fly." He smiled down at the old dog, who lifted his head as if he got the joke.

"What'll happen to the ranch? Your goats?"

"They'll still be here. I'm going to rent the house to someone who's willing to babysit the goats and keep them safe from the real chupacabras. In fact, Richard's been talking to your aunt Ruby, and she's going to rent out Linda's house, too."

Sandy tried to imagine the two houses inhabited by strangers. There'd be no more long drives to the country for her, then. No more place to go when she wanted to get away from everything. The thought made her sadder than she would have expected. But she didn't want to make Tío Jaime's decision any more difficult for him, so she smiled and said, "Well, everything's settled, then. I'm glad you're going to be with the rest of your family. Maybe I can visit you sometime. Sometimes they send me to LA, you know."

"Or maybe you could get a job in LA," he replied. "Don't they have Web sites in California, too?"

Sandy smiled. It was as if he'd read her mind before she could even formulate the thought. But all she said was, "Maybe. We'll see what happens."

"So." Tío Jaime sat back and regarded Sandy through narrowed eyes. "What's this I hear about you and my nephew going on a date?"

Sandy laughed aloud. "Is that what he called it?"

"He said you had dinner together. But that's all he said, and I had to drag that much out of him."

"Well, then I'm not going to say any more than that, either. I don't kiss and tell," Sandy said, savoring the tingly feeling of keeping something secret. "Anymore."

77

A few days after that, Sandy stood in her boss's office waiting for Angelica to remove a pile of photographs from the nearest visitor's chair and set them on her desk. Sandy took the purple seat. Angelica closed the office door and took her own chair.

With a throat-clearing cough and no other excuse to put it off, Sandy began. "Angelica, I don't know how to say this. But...um..."

"You're quitting," the older woman said, completing Sandy's declaration with her signature professional smile in place.

"I'm quitting, yes. How'd you know?"

"Sandy, please. I've known since you did that swan-song interview with your Chupacabra friend. Actually, I knew when I hired you that you wouldn't last the year here. You're just not the type. You're too full of integrity and idealism. Talent. All those other things." Seeing Sandy's surprised face, she added, "That said, you've done very well. Better than I expected."

"Thank you." Sandy didn't know what to say now. It'd been said for her. "Well, I should tell you that I'm glad I met you. You taught me a lot, Angelica, and I'll always be grateful for that."

Smile firmly in place, Angelica shook her head. "Oh, stop. You don't need to do that. So tell me, where are you going?"

"To the *LA Chronicle*."

"With Jim Mayer?"

"Yes."

"That's great. You're going to love Jim. He's wonderful. I need to call him and tell him he owes me dinner for stealing one of my writers away."

Sandy was surprised at how well Angelica was taking the news. It almost hurt her feelings, a little, that her boss wasn't more upset. "I'll stick around for at least two weeks," she offered. "As long as you need me, in order to train my replacement."

"Actually, Sandy, you don't have to stay more than a week if you don't want to. And you can work from home if you like. I haven't had a chance to make the announcement yet, but we're already hiring two new writers, and they should be enough to take your place for the moment. We might be able to hire one more now, in fact."

"Wow," Sandy said. "I guess you weren't kidding about knowing I was going to quit."

"Well..." At this Angelica's mask fell, and she leaned forward. "I'll tell you this in confidence, knowing that Lori or one of the others will probably tell you anyway. Jacob Levy is moving us to a new salary structure again. One that pays a little less than the current model. So, if anything, you quitting now saves me from having to advise you to get another day job." She smiled wanly.

Sandy felt relieved to see the real Angelica again, one last time. "Thanks for telling me the bad news and making me feel better."

Angelica chuckled. "Then I'll tell you the rest of the bad news, too. Before you go, you need to do a conference call with Legal so they can go over the terms of your contract that still bind you for a year after its termination. There are a couple of things we'll ask you not to write about, basically, under threat of lawsuit. But nothing too binding. It shouldn't affect your job with Jim. Much."

Sandy narrowed her eyes. "Note to self: Hire a lawyer to look at the next contract."

"That sounds like good advice." Angelica stood and walked around to the other side of her desk. Sandy stood to receive her boss's hard little hug. "I want you to call me if there's anything I can do for you, okay?"

Sandy nodded. "I will."

"And, if you wanted to do something for me, as a parting gift…" Her boss smiled suggestively.

Sandy had no idea what Angelica could need from her, but she said, "Sure. Name it."

"In your last few posts, if you could drop a couple of hints that you're leaving because of some kind of personal drama—maybe something like a fight with George, or a new man in your life—that would really help us with the page views. I'd forward you a bonus check."

Sandy laughed. But she knew Angelica wasn't kidding. "I don't think so. I've retired from spilling my guts online. But I'm sure if you ask George he'll be more than happy to make something up."

"Ooh." The distant, scheming look instantly filled Angelica's eyes. "That's a really good idea."

And, with that, Sandy left Angelica Villanueva O'Sullivan's office for the last time.

78

Post on Nacho Papi's Web Site, Friday, July 21

Nacho Papi's News about Nacho Papi News
by Lori

Hola, everybody! Bad news first: Sandy S. and La Sirena are leaving us. ☹ Sandy has taken a job with a real live newspaper, the Los Angeles Chronicle, and is moving to California. Sandy, don't forget us when you're gone, girl! Volver, volver, volver!

And La Sirena is leaving us for the East Coast to be the new hostess of *Hyper Hydraulic*. La Sirena, it was good knowing you! I tell you—keep watching Nacho Papi for the stars of tomorrow, peeps!

And now, the good news: Nacho Papi is holding auditions for four new staff members! Send your clips and your tapes to Angelica Villanueva O'Sullivan at the address below.

The other good news: None of this bad news is changing our plans to put on Nacho Papi's First Annual Singles' Mixer, right here in Austin, Texas, with me as your hostess with the mostest! So stay tuned for more deets on that and the other Nacho Papi Singles' events coming to cities near you.

READER COMMENTS ON **NACHO PAPI'S NEWS**

So La Sirena goes on a site-sponsored date with a competing producer, and then he steals her away? Smooth move, Big A. Not!
Gen Ex

Sandy's leaving? Sucks!
Luisa

I bet Sandy ran off with the guy she went on the date with, too.
Darth Waiter

Darth: Gross. That was her cousin. He's Chupacabra's nephew, and the Chupacabra is Sandy's dad.
Manny

Manny: No, Sandy is Chupacabra's niece, and that guy is his lawyer. He scored them a package deal in LA. My mom's a nurse at the hospital where Chupacabra had his operation.
Big Wheel

You're all full of it. Sandy and George have been dating all along. They did all this stuff for publicity, and now Sandy's going to LA to write a book about it.
Payasa

79

Time: Monday, July 24, 11:39 AM
To: sandy@misstctx.com
From: vforverguenza@razamail.net
Subject: Hey woman!!

I'm glad we made up and that you aren't mad at me anymore about all that stuff that happened.......
because I can't wait to stay at your place in Los Angeles!!!
And yeah, I know it's really in Santa Ana and not right there in LA. But still!! California hook-up in the house!!!

Love,
V

Time: Wednesday, July 26, 1:03 PM
To: sandy@misstctx.com
From: philippe@nachopapiswebsite.com
Subject: hey sexy

Just wanted to write and say that you're lucky you left when you did. Angelica just gave us new contracts. Not only are we getting paid less, but?

We're going to start hosting **singles events** in multiple cities throughout the year. Attendance mandatory.

Can you imagine anything so completely horrid?

Love,
Philippe

Time: Friday, July 28, 10:22 PM
To: sandy@misstctx.com
From: papichulo@nachopapiswebsite.com
Subject: hey Sandy

It's me George. How's it going? Have you gone to LA yet?

Listen. I have to tell you that it sucks not having you and Sirena here. Lori and the new chick are cool, but I miss having someone to argue with like Angelica used to make us do. Remember?

I was thinking. Do you want to give me an interview about your ex-boyfriend? Sort of a revenge piece, in response to the one he did about you? I'd give you a cut of my page-view bonus.

Let me know okay?

George
aka Papi Chulo

Time: Monday, August 7, 8:24 AM
To: sandy@misstctx.com
From: marco.saavedra@tcminc.com
Subject: Hi, from your dad

Dear Sandy,

Thanks for your note. Sorry I didn't get to see you before you left town. But I'll be in LA on business in a couple of weeks. Maybe we can have lunch?

I know I haven't said it lately, but I'm proud of you and all the things you're doing. Especially the way you pulled through after all the crap that happened to you earlier this year. Even though I've been busy in my own little world, I hope you know that I'm always here if you need me. I love you.

Love,
Dad

My Modern TragiComedy
Tuesday, August 8
Here's a little story, a pattern in my life.

It was a sunny March afternoon, my first day as a staff writer for Nacho Papi's Web Site. I was nervous, and unaware that my life was about to completely change. . . .

Sandy leaned back on the living room sofa and looked out the window at the sun emerging through the Santa Ana haze. She'd gotten into the habit of waking up early and working in the living room while Megan, who was her landlady and roommate and her friend Jane's cousin, slept late. But right now Megan was out of town. In the kitchen behind her Sandy's sole housewarming gift, an espresso machine from her mother, gurgled and hissed.

She read her father's e-mail a second time, then closed it. She'd write back and agree to have lunch with him, but not yet. Right now she had a lot of work to do. There was her daily quota for the *LA Chronicle*, of course. She had a deadline for a Buzz News article, as well. Then, of course, there was the never-ending technical writing that made it possible to afford her portion of the rent.

Then there was her own Web site to update, with links to her latest articles. She'd written only one blog entry since moving out here, and her readers were clamoring to hear more of the story.

She decided to work until one and then drop by her aunt Ruby's for lunch and a little photo-album viewing. After that, she had plans to join Tío Jaime and Nephew

Richard at the zoo. After that, she was dropping by UCLA's creative writing department. Just to take a look.

But first, to work.

Sandy opened her word-processing program and shuffled through her files. There were so many now that she would have to come up with a new system for organizing them. In a folder called LatinoNow she found an old article she wanted to use as a reference for something new. Just seeing her old byline, Dominga Saavedra, made her smile, a little sadly. She had been so young back then. It was only a year ago, but she'd had so much to learn.

In the same folder she found another document that brought back bittersweet memories: a draft of the novel she'd been pretending to write, way back when she was dating Daniel and fantasizing about being a poet's muse. She barely remembered, now, what it had been about. She opened it to find out.

Chapter One

Dominique Salazar closed her laptop on the latest article she'd been writing as her mother's voice rang in her ears like an unanswered phone echoing in an empty room. *"When are you going to get married, Dominique? When?"*

Dominique didn't have time to get married. She was busy working on the news series that was destined to win the Pulitzer Prize. At least that's what she was hoping.

"Hey, babe. Do you want to go get a beer with my friends?"

Dominique sighed. That was her boyfriend, David. David was tall, dark, and very handsome. The only problem was, he didn't understand her need to write serious news.

Sandy had to laugh, at her own words and at the girl she used to be.

And then she had an idea.

She closed that file and opened a brand-new one. After staring at the empty page for a few minutes, Sandy began to type. As fast as her fingers could spell it out an outline for a new book appeared.

She was going to write a book about her great-aunt, Linda, from her upbringing in the Rio Grande Valley to her struggle to become an independent woman, to her realization of the love of a lifetime.

After all, it was a fascinating story, and she had all the resources she needed to write it.

The sun rose higher and shone brighter as Sandy typed away. She was too busy to notice, but, somewhere in the distance, a chupacabra howled with joy.

ABOUT THE CHUPACABRA

Chupacabra means, literally, "goat sucker" in Spanish. It's a mythical animal that attacks livestock, particularly goats, and drains them of blood. They're supposed to be four-legged mammals the size of large dogs or small bears, with spines on their backs.

I say it's mythical, but there are people who swear on the Bible they've seen them, in Texas and in Puerto Rico, and as recently as the other day.

I don't want to call anyone a liar, but I've never seen one. I have seen, right in the middle of Houston, a goat hanging in the doorway of my cousin's suegro's garage, skinned and drained in preparation for the making of menudo. But I guess that's not exactly the same thing.

My family was more into La Llorona, the ghost-woman who cries for her children in the night. My cousin's friend's cousin actually saw her, outside the cemetery late one night.

My brother swears he saw a Lechuza—an owl of the demonic persuasion—inside the same cemetery, on a completely different occasion, with minimal liquor involved.

I never see any of that stuff. But I listen to the stories, and I avoid cemeteries at night.

ACKNOWLEDGMENTS

Thanks to Jenny Bent for her perseverance, and to Selina McLemore for her patience and continued mental telepathy. Thanks to Linda Duggins for being an untiring warrior at my side. Thanks to Karen Thompson for making me look smarter.

Thanks to my bosses and co-workers at VALIC for providing a good place to work, and for not only being tolerant of my other career but supporting it.

Thanks to all my peeps on Twitter for not unfollowing me when I babbled like a maniac late at night while trying to finish this book.

Thanks to all my readers for reading my stuff and making the work worth it.

Thanks to Ashley for listening.

Thanks to Dat, who was my fiancé when I started this book and will probably be my husband by the time you read it, for feeding me while I wrote.

Thanks to Jacob, Austin, and Luke for all their hard work in our band, Led Zepeda, the video-game performances of which kept me joyous and balanced this past year.

READING GROUP GUIDE

1. Sandy gives various reasons—to her friends, to her fans, to herself—for keeping a blog online. What do you think her real reasons are?

2. What do you think of the practice of keeping a "journal" online for everyone to see? Do you have a blog? If so, are there limits on what you'll discuss in your blog, or on what you think others should discuss in theirs? Did Sandy make mistakes with what she chose to say in hers?

3. Do you enjoy celebrity gossip? Does it ever go too far? Is it wrong to criticize celebrities' personal lives? Or is that the price they pay for wanting to be famous?

4. What is a celebrity? Do you have to be a movie star or pop star? Are authors and journalists celebrities? What about bloggers? Sandy gossiped about celebrities for her living. Was it okay for her readers to begin gossiping about her? Why or why not?

5. Among Sandy and her co-workers, did you see differing levels in what they were willing to do for fame? Do you notice that among journalists or entertainment writers in real life?

6. What do you think about Sandy's relationship with Daniel? What happens when two people in a relationship have similar ambitions? Can it work out?

7. Sandy is obviously affected by her parents' divorce even though it takes place when she is an adult. How did it affect her?

8. What do you think of Sandy's boss, Angelica? Angelica says Sandy reminds her of a younger version of herself. Is Angelica a good role model for Sandy?

9. What is Sandy's relationship to Tío Jaime? Is it realistic for someone her age to befriend someone his age? Do you think their friendship was genuine? On what was it based?

10. Tío Jaime talks about "crabs in a bucket," meaning people who drag each other down instead of helping each other achieve success. Do you know that expression? Do you have any crabs in your bucket? Why do people do that, anyway?

11. What does Sandy's mother want for her in life? What does Sandy think her mother wants? With which one do you sympathize?

12. Tío Jaime says he doesn't want to be famous and talks about "false idols." What does he mean? Sandy doesn't understand him. Why not?

13. Have you ever been embarrassed by someone exposing personal details of your life to public scrutiny? How did you handle it? Did Sandy handle it well?

14. Do you want to be famous? Why or why not?

15. How does Sandy see herself at the beginning of the book? At the middle? At the end?

GUÍA DE LECTOR

1. Sandy da varias razones—a sus amigos, a sus fans, a sí misma—por mantener un blog en línea. ¿Qué cree usted son sus razones verdaderas?

2. ¿Qué piensa usted de la práctica de mantener un "diario" en línea que todo el mundo pueda leer? ¿Tiene usted un blog? ¿Si es así, hay límites en lo que usted discutirá, o en qué otros deben discutir en el suyo? ¿Se equivocó Sandy con lo que eligió decir en el suyo?

3. ¿Le gusta a usted al chisme de la celebridad? ¿Cree usted que a veces el chisme es demasiado? ¿Es injusto criticar las vidas personales de las celebridades? ¿O es el precio que ellos pagan por su fama?

4. ¿Qué es una celebridad? ¿Tiene que ser una estrella del cine o una estrella del pop? ¿Son celebridades los autores y los periodistas? ¿Y los bloggers? Sandy chismeó sobre las celebridades para ganar la vida. ¿Fue aceptable para que sus lectores comenzaron a chismear sobre ella? ¿Por qué o por qué no?

5. ¿Entre Sandy y sus compañeros de trabajo, hay diferencias entre lo que estaban dispuestos hacer para la fama? ¿Nota usted una diferencia entre periodistas y escritores de diversión en la vida real?

6. ¿Qué piensa usted de la relación de Sandy y Daniel? ¿Qué sucede cuando las dos personas en una relación tienen ambiciones similares? ¿Puede resolverse?

7. Sandy fue obviamente afectada por el divorcio de sus padres, aunque ocurrió cuando ella era adulta. ¿Cómo la afectó?

8. ¿Qué piensa usted de la jefa de Sandy, Angélica? Angélica dice que Sandy le recordó de una versión joven de sí misma. ¿Es Angélica un buen modelo para Sandy?

9. ¿Cuál es la relación de Sandy y Tío Jaime? ¿Es realista que alguien de la edad de Sandy pueda ser amiga con alguien mucho más mayor como Tío Jaime? ¿Piensa usted que esta amistad fue auténtica? ¿En qué fue basada?

10. Tío Jaime usa la expresión "cangrejos en un cubo" para describir a la gente que arrastra a otros abajo en vez de ayudarlos alcanza éxito. ¿Conoce usted esa expresión? ¿Tiene usted cangrejos en su cubo? ¿Por qué lo hacen?

11. ¿Qué desea la madre de Sandy para su hija? ¿Qué piensa Sandy que su madre desea? ¿Con cuál uno se compadece usted?

12. Tío Jaime dice que él no desea ser famoso y habla de "ídolos falsos." ¿Qué significa él? Sandy no lo comprende. ¿Por qué no?

13. ¿Se ha avergonzado usted cuando alguien expuso los detalles personales de su vida al escrutinio público?

¿Cómo lo dirigió? ¿Cree usted que Sandy lo dirigió bien?

14. ¿Desea usted ser famoso? ¿Por qué o por qué no?

15. ¿Cómo se ve Sandy al principio del libro? ¿Al medio? ¿Y al fin?

ABOUT THE AUTHOR

This is my second novel but my fifth book. Before this I wrote:

- *Houston, We Have a Problema* (novel)
- *Sunflowers* (kids' book)
- *Growing Up with Tamales* (other kids' book—that one won an award)
- *To the Last Man I Slept With and All the Jerks Just Like Him* (edgy small-press short prose collection)

Actually, I've written way more than that, but those are the books I've actually sold. Besides that, I did a lot of writing for various Web sites, back in the day. And, you know, I could tell you about all the rejected manuscripts and the poetry chapbooks and such, but let's leave a little for our next meeting, all right?

I was born in balmy inner-city Houston in 1971 and spent a couple of years at the University of Texas at Austin. After that I had a few kids, then after that I started up with the book selling.

When I'm not writing books for you and hoping you're enjoying them, I'm hanging out with my kids or my cats or my fiancé, who will probably be my husband by the time you read this. I also like to read books by other people, and sometimes I make necklaces or play video games.

If you ever get curious and want to find out more about my life, or see if/when I'm coming to your town, feel free to visit GwendolynZepeda.com, which is the latest incarnation of the Web site I've been writing since 1997.

Cheers.

IF YOU ENJOYED *LONE STAR LEGEND*, THEN YOU'RE SURE TO LIKE THESE AS WELL—

Now available from Grand Central Publishing:

"This book is a delightful feast for the reader."

—Susan Wiggs, *New York Times* bestselling author of *Just Breathe*

A secret journal threatens to destroy a young woman as she uncovers the truth about her deceased mother's past in this stunning debut novel.

In this hilarious first book of the Crafty Chica series, a group of unlikely allies teams up to compete in the world's biggest craft competition, and discovers that fostering a friendship is truly an art.